ENIGMA

Kim Idynne

ISBN: 978-1-7350798-1-3

for Danny

1: Strange Weather

Many people know about the girl who fell into a hole at an Arizona monument, who disappeared into the enormous underground maze and became lost—but few besides Dominic knew that she ended up in the stars, and for a long time no one suspected that her adventure had anything to do with the weather.

The dust of Wupatki had settled that morning, clumping heavily along the earth as the air thickened with moisture. The wind had died down, and the animals seemed to be at rest, perhaps waiting for the southwestern rains to move in and chase away the heaviness in the air.

Dominic walked the trail that led through the archaeological site. Some distance behind him, a tall, fair-haired man had stopped to photograph the landscape. He caught up to Dominic in a few long strides. "It's so gloomy today," Chad said, shoving his sunglasses up so that they rested on top of his head. "We should have come yesterday instead. All these browns and reds look better in sunlight. Actually, I should think of this as an opportunity; *everyone* takes pictures of Wupatki in the sunlight, but how many take the pictures *I'm* going to take?"

Dominic barely heard the rest of Chad's speech about photo credits and mass-market photography. He gazed over the pale stretch of land dotted with green shrubs, thinking of his previous excursions to the site. Since moving to the city, his life had become a frenzy of demands; his time was consumed with college classes and working long hours to pay the rent for his tiny apartment. Though he enjoyed life in Flagstaff, Dominic often sought an escape from the noise of the city. Wupatki had become his favorite place of retreat.

Nearly a millennium ago, Sunset Crater had covered this land with volcanic ash that moistened the soil. People moved into the fertile lands, building pueblos, kivas, and courts. Eventually they moved on, and for several hundred years the sandstone dwellings had been left to crumble. Ruins of ancient pueblos graced the area with streaks of earthy color, their surfaces textured with smooth pits and crevices that played tricks on the eye— but what most intrigued Dominic was the area that could not be seen: a vast network of underground tunnels, cutting through layers of prehistoric bedrock formed from the skeletons of sea creatures. Most of those tunnels were too small for a human being to pass through, and their inaccessibility made them all the more mysterious.

Dominic approached the ancient ball court, admiring the red-hued sandstone walls mottled with shades of gray. He had hoped to find it empty—but though it was early in the day, several people milled around. Children ran back and forth, shrieking with delight.

Chad's face twisted with displeasure. "Too many brats," he muttered. "Let's keep going."

Beyond the court was a strange hole in the ground, leading deep beneath the surface of the earth. The park managers had fixed a metal grate over the hole and built a square platform around it. Chad and Dominic had taken a few silly, obligatory photographs of themselves standing over the hole with their shirts and hair billowing; this was because of the great wind that came blowing through the hole. Dominic always took a few moments to lean over the blowhole with his eyes closed, letting the air cool his face and whip his hair around his head. For a moment, with that strange wind blowing all around him, he could imagine that he was flying.

A lone figure stood at the stone platform: a young girl, maybe ten years old, with two dark braids hanging down the back of her red vest. Chad spoke up as he approached: "What's it doing today?"

The girl turned and scrutinized him, and gave Dominic the same once-over. Chad stepped up beside her and put a hand over the hole. "Wow . . . it's really going," he said. "Feel that, Dominic."

Dominic extended his hand to feel the rush of air, and quickly withdrew it. The air wasn't blowing out today. It was drawing the air in so fast that Dominic felt it pulling at his hand. For a moment, he was grateful for the metal bars that kept the hole from sucking him in.

He tipped his head back to look at the sky. "It must be the weather that's causing it. We're supposed to have strange weather today." He looked at the girl. "Do you know if it's supposed to storm?"

Something about the question seemed to catch her off guard. She stared at Dominic for some time, and then looked at the ground. "We might have storms coming from the southwest, but it isn't supposed to happen until later."

Chad grinned at her. "Why don't you climb up here? Let's see if it sucks you in. It's so strong today, I bet the grate will break if you stand on it."

"Climb up yourself," she replied.

"I wonder if the other holes are gated off," Dominic mused. "I think they're all connected to the same system. If they're all sucking this hard, I wouldn't want to walk over one of them by accident."

The girl's eyes lit with sudden interest. "There are other holes?"

"Sure. They're not by the trail, though, and they're off-limits."

She glanced out across the landscape, and then reached a hand tentatively toward the wind tunnel. "Where do you think the air goes?" she asked.

"It goes into the earth's lungs," Chad replied with a smirk. "That's the earth breathing. It takes a huge breath at night. Pretty soon, it'll stop and hold it in for a while, and spend the rest of the day blowing it all out. It takes a full day and night for just one breath because the earth is so huge."

She looked at the patronizing grin on his face. "What a crock," she replied.

Dominic chuckled.

Chad shrugged. "All right, fine, if you're not interested in the natural wonders of the earth . . . ."

"It doesn't always blow out during the day," she cut in. "It can keep blowing inward when a high pressure weather system moves through. I read about it at the visitor center."

"The air goes into the earth cracks," Dominic said. "There's a huge system of natural tunnels underneath us. They were created by earthquakes."

"But, where does the air *go*?" Hannah asked. "If it goes in, it must be coming out somewhere."

"Not necessarily," Chad replied. "When you breathe, the air doesn't come out another hole. It stays in your lungs and comes back out the same way."

"Yeah, but that's because your lungs expand. Where does the air go, if the earth isn't expanding to make room for it?"

Chad rolled his eyes. "I don't know. Go ask a scientist. I didn't come here to give geological lectures to twelve-year-olds." He laughed at her and turned away.

"I'm eleven," she replied, and started back toward the court.

Chad laughed again as the girl departed. "Kids are

brats," he said, and then he imitated her in a shrill voice: "Where does the air go?"

Dominic and Chad returned to the trail and walked the grounds for some time, photographing petroglyphs and the reddish hues of sandstone against the desert backdrop. The air seemed increasingly thick. Dominic had never felt such weather at Wupatki. It was typically warm and dry, light and windy—but today the air crawled with a strange, cool moisture. It clung to his skin and made him shudder.

At Lomaki pueblo, Chad stopped near some of the ancient stone carvings. He knelt and balanced the camera on his knee. "It's amazing how similar these glyphs are," he said, "not just in the Americas, but all over the world."

Nearby, somebody shouted. Chad turned his head for a moment and muttered: "Parents yelling at one of their brats." He adjusted the lens and snapped the shutter closed. "You can find these spiral glyphs anywhere," he continued, moving aside to take the photo from another angle. He used the hem of his shirt to wipe a raindrop from the lens. "When I was traveling around the Mediterranean . . . ." Chad trailed off. He squinted his eyes, looking past Dominic and frowning. "What's going on out there?"

Some distance away from the trail, a group of people had crowded together. One of them yelled—and then another, just a brief shout, as if they were calling someone's name. A figure left the group and ran toward the visitor's center.

"Are they supposed to be out there?" Chad asked.

"I doubt it."

Chad put the camera away. "Come on, let's take a look."

The group was crowded around another blowhole in the earth. This one was unshielded. A man and woman knelt beside it, gripping the edges with their fingers, staring down with intense anxiety. The air was still being sucked inward. It pulled at their hair and flapped their sleeves.

"Hannah!" the man cried. "Hannah!" He shone a small flashlight into the hole, angling the beam this way and that.

Chad reached the circle of onlookers. "What happened?"

"A girl fell into the hole," someone said.

Dominic felt a pang of alarm, remembering the girl he'd been talking to only an hour earlier. "A girl? How old?"

"Eleven," the woman choked. She looked up with a feverish face and frightened eyes. "She's our foster daughter. She wandered out here by herself. We were calling for her to come back, and we saw her disappear into the ground."

The crowd murmured its sympathy in hushed tones.

"Was it the girl with the braids?" Chad asked. "And a red vest?"

The woman nodded tearfully.

After a few moments, Chad elbowed Dominic. He leaned over and, very quietly, whispered: "At least now she'll know where the air goes."

"Hannah!" the man cried again, frantically.

An old woman stood near the hole, covering her mouth and staring into the void. Suddenly she turned to the crowd. "Someone should climb down and make sure she's all right."

Dominic made a small sound of disbelief. *Climb down?* He thought about how stupid it would be for any of them to try climbing down a tiny hole that led deep into the earth, without any equipment, without any skill.

"There are ledges inside the hole that someone can climb down," the woman insisted. "You can see the bottom if you shine the light into it. It isn't that far. Isn't there anyone who's small enough to fit inside?"

Again, Dominic didn't take her words seriously. But several moments later he realized that everyone had turned to stare at him.

Dominic was twenty-one years old, and just over four feet tall. He was, by far, the shortest of all the adults—shorter even than many of the kids who were gathered nearby, certainly shorter than Hannah. But he wasn't *small*, not in the way that Hannah was small. He wasn't skinny. Surely people wouldn't expect him to attempt such a stupid thing.

Chad grinned. He shook Dominic by the shoulder. "*You're* small. Why don't you try it?"

"Me?" Dominic looked from face to face, waited for someone to protest on his behalf. Everyone seemed to be waiting for him to answer. "Why don't we wait for help to arrive? If we panic and send someone else in, we're just going to end up with another person who needs to be rescued."

"But the girl is down there all alone," the woman persisted. "We can't see her at the bottom. She might be trying to find a way out. She could get lost down there."

"Yeah," Chad agreed. "With all that air rushing around, she won't be able to get hold of her senses."

Dominic gave him a scathing look. He stepped to the edge of the hole and looked into it cautiously. He could hear the air being drawn forcefully into the earth. "I won't fit in there," he said.

"The girl fit," the woman replied. "You're no bigger than she is."

"*You're* small. Why don't *you* climb down?" Dominic asked.

"*Me?* I'm old. I have osteoporosis."

"I won't fit. I'm too fat."

"Hannah!" the foster mother cried. She leaned over the

hole. It sucked the tears from her face, pulled them deep into the void. "*Hannah*, can you hear us? Someone's going to come and help you. Just stay where you are and wait."

Silence followed. After a time, the old woman shook her head. "Poor girl," she said softly.

Chad pointed to the ground. "Dom, you could fit easily. Look, there are practically steps for you to use. Just go down a little ways, and see if you can see her."

"Shut up," Dominic replied.

"Just a little ways."

"I can't. I'm too fat."

Chad poked at him. "You're not fat. You're just chicken."

"I won't fit into the hole," Dominic said, "and my legs are too short for the steps, and the air is being sucked in too fast, and it's starting to rain. It'll be slippery."

"Coward."

The old woman was pleading again, her eyes full of worry. "Please, just try going down a little. You can come back up if it's too hard."

Now the foster father was screaming: "*Hannah! Hannah!*"

Dominic glanced toward the visitor center. No one was coming yet. He looked back into the hole and sighed.

"Just try a couple steps," the old woman prodded him.

"Fine . . . fine. I'll see what I can do. Move out of the way."

Dominic stared into the opening and tried to plan his way down. The air pulled at his foot as he took a first careful step. He stomped against the limestone rock, testing it before trusting it with his full weight. Chad grabbed his arm for support, holding him until he had eased well into the hole. "Give me your flashlight," Dominic demanded. Chad handed him a tiny flashlight, still grinning, and Dominic slipped it into his pocket.

The foster mother squeezed Dominic's other hand and thanked him tearfully. For a moment, as Dominic looked into her eyes, his irritation vanished. He thought of the girl lying injured below, alone and frightened.

"That's it. You fit just fine," the old woman murmured. "See, you were meant to be here. Bless you, young man. You'll find that girl."

The woman's words didn't give Dominic any comfort. They just made him feel pressured. "Do me a favor," he replied, "and stop talking."

"Let's stay quiet, in case she calls out," the foster father said.

The wind sucked at Dominic's clothes so much that he worried about losing his pants. After a minute he made it all the way into the hole, so that he was completely below the ground. He could feel the wind beating against his legs and around the top of his head; it whipped in his hair, lashed at his shoulders. The passage narrowed as it descended, so that Dominic's body was squeezed inside of it, nearly blocking the air flow. He shivered as the cool breezes struggled to rush past him into the chasm below.

It was true that there were little ledges onto which he could step. He couldn't see them anymore because his body was in the way. He felt around with his foot, tapping against the rocks, moving as carefully as possible. The raindrops came faster now, thick and wet on his face, and the stone felt slick beneath his feet. After a while he seemed to have reached the final ledge. He turned and dipped his foot but couldn't feel anything beneath it.

The old woman was trying to give him encouragement. "Just a little farther, just go down and see if you can see anything." Her voice sounded faint and far away. "You'll be all right."

But she was wrong, and Dominic was right. It was

stupid, really, to climb into such unstable and unknown terrain, without the proper equipment. Just as he opened his mouth to say that he couldn't go any farther, the rocky platform broke beneath his feet, and the wind sucked him into the underground labyrinth.

Rock walls scraped his arms as he tried to hang on. Then he was falling through empty space, feeling nothing but panic. His feet hit the ground unexpectedly and sent him tumbling forward onto the limestone rock.

Dominic groaned. For a moment he lay face down, slowly moving his limbs. He heaved himself up and rubbed his knees. The space around him was small and close. Clumps of loose soil were scattered about, some turning to mud in the pooling rain. Remembering the girl, Dominic looked around, but she was nowhere to be seen. He rocked back onto his heels and tried looking upward. The wet wind tore at his face. His eyes stung so much that he decided to crawl off to the side, in the hopes of avoiding the wind tunnel.

The edges of the small cavern were a little more comfortable. Dominic sat gazing up at the shaft of daylight. He cupped his hands around his mouth and yelled: "CAN YOU HEAR ME? I'M AT THE BOTTOM."

In the dimly lit space he could make out some jutting ledges in the battered limestone. Dominic studied his surroundings for some time, his mind clouded by anger and fear. "Stupid lady," he muttered, and imitated her in a high-pitched voice: "*Someone* needs to climb down, but not *me*. *I* have osteoporosis." He cursed under his breath as he ran his hands along the rock. There was no way to get back up. He could only climb up a foot or two, and the hole leading to the surface was unreachable.

A sharp, stinging sensation made him pull his hand away. He gasped in pain, his eyes riveted on the spot where his hand had been. A small figure moved among the shadows. When it emerged into the light, Dominic felt a surge of alarm.

A scorpion stood there on the ledge. It paused, and Dominic studied it intently, trying to convince himself not to panic. It didn't look like the dangerous bark scorpion. In fact, it didn't look like any scorpion he'd ever seen. It was large and white, gleaming strangely in the darkness. It stayed still for so long that Dominic began to wonder if he was imagining it—until it turned and scuttled into the shadows.

Again, Dominic tipped his head back and shouted. "CAN YOU HEAR ME? I CAN'T SEE THE GIRL, AND THERE ARE SCORPIONS DOWN HERE."

But there was no response except the whistling wind and the pattering of water against the stone floor. Dominic took another look around the cavern, and for the first time he got a good glimpse of the eerie, fascinating underworld into which he'd fallen. The wind was being sucked into a series of dark, narrow tunnels that cracked through the limestone all around him. Dust and soil were drawn down into the spaces, glinting as they passed from light into unknown darkness. Raindrops burst and sparkled as they were hurled by the current. Most of the tunnels were much too small even for a child to fit through, but one of the largest passages was lit up, and Dominic focused on that one. *That's probably where she went*, he thought. *She probably thought she could climb back up to the light.*

It didn't seem like such a bad idea. Even if he couldn't find a way back up, he might at least find the girl. Dominic knelt at the edge of the tunnel and tried to peer inside. The tunnel veered sharply just ahead of him; he couldn't see the end of it. But he decided to crawl into it anyway, at least to see if it was traversable. If he couldn't find Hannah, he could always back up and return to the cavern.

As he crawled, he muttered: "Here I come, scorpions. If there are any scorpions in here, kindly move out of the way. . . ."

The passage continued to slope downward through difficult twists and turns. After a short venture, Dominic could see that the light was pouring down through countless cracks in the bedrock. He felt certain that Hannah had come this way. There really was nowhere else she could have gone.

And then he heard it: a soft whimper. The sound of weeping.

Dominic crawled farther, though he knew he was retreating far from the blowhole. He pulled himself through the tight passage until he saw a flash of red ahead of him. He crawled out into another small chamber—and there was Hannah, curled up against the rock wall, illuminated by tiny slits of light.

"Hannah?" he asked.

Hannah looked up. She immediately stopped crying. "Hi," she said quietly.

"Hi. I'm Dominic. Do you remember me?"

She nodded. "You came down here to get me?"

"Yes. We can't get back up, though—not yet. We'll have to go back to the hole and wait for someone to pull us up."

"I got lost." Hannah wiped her tear-streaked face. She hugged her arms tightly to her chest. "I couldn't find the place where I fell in."

"It's right back there," Dominic said consolingly, moving toward her. His own anger, his own fear were forgotten. Instinctively he focused on soothing the fears of the girl in front of him. She was scraped up, her face and fingers crusted with tiny streaks of blood. Water leaked through the small spaces above, trickling down the walls and spattering on the floor, soaking her jeans. "That fall must have hurt. Any big cuts? Anything broken?"

She paused. "No."

"All right. We'll have to crawl back to the hole and wait for someone to help us out. They'll probably throw something down to us, a rope or something, to pull us back up. I know it's kind of scary, but you're not alone, and not lost anymore—so there's really nothing to be afraid of."

"That's not why I was upset," Hannah said, a little defensively.

"No? What is it, then?"

"Carmina and Andy . . . they'll get mad at me."

"Are they your stepparents?"

"My foster parents," she corrected him.

"That's what I meant. They're not mad at you. They're afraid you're hurt. When you get out of here, they'll be so happy, they won't care about how you got down here."

"They'll be mad," Hannah insisted. "They're already disappointed because I quit summer camp."

"Trust me: they'll be relieved. I saw them up there, and they just want to know you're all right."

Hannah lowered her eyes.

"Did you try to climb down on purpose?" Dominic asked.

"No! I didn't even know about the hole. There was a scorpion coming toward me, and I was backing away from it, and all of a sudden the ground fell apart. I tried to stop myself from falling, but I couldn't hang on."

Dominic shuddered at the mention of the scorpion. "All right. Let's get going." He gestured to her arms; she was still holding one of them tight against her chest, covering it protectively. "Is your arm hurt?"

She nodded and withdrew her hand.

Dominic felt a moment of shock as he saw the round, swollen area on Hannah's forearm. "Did you get stung?"

"Yeah. A scorpion stung me."

He paused. "Before you fell, or after?"

"After. There was another one, down here."

"A white one?"

She nodded. "Do you know what kind it is?"

"No, but try not to worry about it. I got stung, too."
Dominic showed her the back of his hand. It had only a
slight swelling, a light pink circle around a tiny puncture
wound, but it throbbed with pain. "Have you been stung
by a scorpion before?"

"No."

"I have," he said. "It's going to hurt, and it might make
you feel a little strange, but it's nothing serious. The pain
will go away eventually. Does it hurt yet?"

"It hurts a lot, and I feel funny."

Dominic felt pangs of alarm, but he forced himself to
look calm. "Are you allergic to bee stings?"

"No."

"It might be the scorpion venom making you feel
funny, but like I said, it's nothing serious." He turned
and studied the tunnel behind him. He looked at the rain
pooling on the floor and tried to reassure himself that the
caverns and tunnels wouldn't fill up with water. "Let's
get back to the hole. Can you crawl after me?"

Hannah frowned. "You mean . . . back the way you just
came?"

"Yeah."

She looked at him uncertainly.

"It's all right. It goes straight to the hole," he assured
her.

"Okay." Hannah moved to the tunnel, dropping to her
hands and knees.

Dominic crawled ahead of her. He went carefully,
scanning the shadows for movement, placing his hands
only in the lit areas. Navigating the tunnel was hard. The
rock had become wet and slippery; some of the shadows

turned out to be wide cracks in the limestone; the passage twisted and jutted awkwardly against his body, and when he'd gone only a couple yards, he found himself face to face with a split in the passageway.

He stopped and stared. He hadn't noticed any other tunnels branching off from this one; he wasn't sure which one he'd come through. They both seemed equally dark. And there was no wind. The underworld had become eerily quiet.

And there was another problem. Dominic was having trouble breathing. It was probably the scorpion venom kicking in. He remembered the last time he'd been stung, the feelings of suffocation, the palpitating of his heart. Or maybe it was the closeness of the walls, the lack of oxygen. Dominic felt his heart racing, heard his breath coming fast and heavy. He couldn't think straight. He simply knew that if he chose the wrong tunnel, the two of them might become trapped, or hopelessly lost.

"Are you lost?" Hannah asked behind him.

"No," he replied, and moved into the left-hand tunnel. He decided that it seemed a bit wider.

But more crawling brought him to a dead end. The tunnel became so twisted, so tight, that Dominic got stuck.

"Hannah, I need you to back up." He heard the frantic note in his own voice. "It's a dead end. Just keep backing up all the way to the chamber."

He heard her sliding away behind him.

Dominic tried to free his shoulders from the vise of the rock walls, but it was too hard to move his arms. His knees slid uselessly against the floor.

"Hannah!" he called again. "Hang on—I need some help. I'm stuck. I need you to pull on me, and see if you can get me loose."

For a moment he heard nothing. He worried that she was gone, that he was alone in the underground labyrinth.

Then Hannah was wrapping her fingers around his ankle. "Ready?" she asked.

"Yeah."

She pulled hard, stretching out his leg and yanking him free of the tunnel.

"Thanks," he said breathlessly, trying to regain his composure. His body shook. He was sweating now, hot and winded, and wanted only to get out of that tight, suffocating space.

Slowly, the two of them worked their way backward. They returned to the fork in the passage, and Dominic started down the other route.

But that, too, led to a fork. Each passage seemed to lead into darkness. Again Dominic chose the left-hand tunnel, and again it led to a dead end.

"Let's go back," Hannah suggested. "I tried this tunnel already, and I couldn't find my way out."

"All right," Dominic agreed.

They crawled backward again, all the way to the small cavern where he'd found Hannah, the cracked-open room with its blessed streaks of daylight. Dominic slid down against the damp wall and breathed deeply. Sweat ran down the sides of his face.

"Okay," he sighed. "I've had enough crawling through tunnels for a while." The rain and the leaking water had stopped. Dominic stared up at the ceiling, listening—but all he heard was the sound of ragged breathing, Hannah's and his own.

Dominic cupped his hands around his mouth. "HELLO! CAN ANYONE HEAR ME?"

"I tried that, too," Hannah said.

"HELLO!" he shouted again. He glanced around the chamber, studying the other openings. There were two other passages that looked large enough to crawl through, not far from the chamber floor. "Did we pick the wrong tunnel? Maybe I got mixed up . . . ."

Hannah gave him a glum look. "That's what I thought, too, but I saw you come in through that one."

For a few minutes they waited in silence. Dominic thought it was a good idea to keep yelling, but felt so winded he could scarcely draw a breath. He sat with his eyes closed and his head tipped back against the rock until he felt calmer. At length it occurred to him to check on Hannah.

She knelt across from him, studying one of the limestone walls. Dominic noted with relief that she didn't seem to be suffering. She appeared calm, focused.

"We'll have to just sit here and hope someone finds us," he told her. "If we keep trying to find our way back, we might wander farther away from the hole."

Hannah didn't respond.

"Are you all right?" he asked.

"There's something in here," she replied, her eyes still fixed on the jagged rock.

Dominic tensed. "A scorpion?"

"No," she said. "It's an enigma."

2: Scorpius

Dominic stared at the wall in disbelief. Someone had scratched a number of glyphs and English words into the rock. He took out Chad's flashlight and shone it on the wall to get a better look, and realized with amazement that the words made up a strange poem:

Your options are less than four;
it's high time you found the door
leading unto the healing antidote
of Kush where the white scorpion smote.

One of them shall not tell,
but another will guide you well
to the healer who balances life and death
and stops the poison from stealing your breath.

"It says we're going to die," Hannah said in a trembling voice.

"What? No, it doesn't. It's just a poem. It's a poem that somebody . . . carved into the rock . . . somehow." Dominic tried to make sense of the words and glyphs. "One of the researchers must have done it as a joke. It's not an Anasazi carving. They didn't speak English."

"I know that." Hannah gazed at the words, mystified. "It's an enigma. I'm sure of it. 'Two of them shall not tell' . . . it sounds like a word clue. Or . . . . ." She stepped toward one of the passageways. "I think it's saying that we have to go through one of these tunnels."

"We're not going anywhere."

She beckoned him. "Come and look."

Dominic sighed and followed her. Hannah took the flashlight from his trembling hand and shone the beam on the wall above the tunnel. "See?"

A single glyph had been etched into the wall: the figure of a person holding two long, vertical poles, one on each side of its body.

"There are other ones, above the other passages. There's one above the tunnel we just came out of." Hannah shone the light over the opposite tunnel, revealing the figure of a scorpion. Over a third passage she revealed another figure, half animal, half human, holding an archer's bow.

Dominic felt a strange sense of relief. The glyphs, at least, would keep Hannah occupied while they waited for help. He ran his fingertip over a shell-like pattern in the stone. "Looks like there's plenty to explore in this cave. See these ripples and shell imprints? This rock was formed hundreds of millions of years ago, at the bottom of the sea. It's actually made from the skeletons of sea creatures. If you look around, I bet you can find all kinds of ancient imprints."

Hannah wasn't interested. "Someone carved the same symbols over here, above the poem. They could be astrological symbols. Scorpio, and Sagittarius . . . but I don't know the other one."

Dominic studied the carvings with interest. *Someone must have been stuck down here for a long time.* He felt his breath quickening again. Surely, if someone had disappeared here, he would have heard about it in the news. And there were no human remains lying around. *They could have crawled away. They could have crawled into one of these other tunnels and died.*

He shook himself. "Cool," he muttered, and lowered himself to the ground. He took a deep breath and tried to relax. "That means someone else has been down here, and probably got out again."

"See, it says that our options are less than four," Hannah mused, ignoring him, "and we have to find a door leading to the antidote. There are three tunnels here. That's less than four—"

"We're not going anywhere," Dominic repeated. "These tunnels go on for miles. If we start crawling around in them, no one will ever find us. We'll get lost."

"We're already lost."

"We can't be that far from the hole." Dominic peered upward, into the light-bearing cracks. "HELLO! WE'RE DOWN HERE!!"

"Ow." Hannah covered her ears. "Warn me when you're gonna do that."

"Sorry." Dominic nodded at the writing. "What's an enigma?"

"It's a word game, like a riddle."

"How do you play it?"

"The letters for the answer are hidden somewhere in the poem. You have to figure out where they are. The poem gives you clues."

"All right, then, why don't you see if you can solve it? That will give you something to do while we wait." He leaned his head back and closed his eyes. Silence descended over the chamber.

"Maybe it isn't an enigma," Hannah said at last. "Maybe it's just a riddle. It says that we have to find a healer to treat the poison." She pointed at one of the etchings. "This is the Sagittarius constellation. Sagittarius is a half-horse . . . a centaur, like Chiron. Have you heard of Chiron?"

"No."

"He could heal anyone, except himself. I can't find his name in the poem . . . and I can't find Sagittarius, either . . . so I think that maybe this is just a riddle, because it sounds like it's talking about Chiron."

"Keep trying. You'll figure it out," Dominic encouraged her.

She slumped to the ground, her back against the rock wall. Hannah was silent for a minute. Then she said: "Dominic, it's hard to breathe. I'm afraid I'm going to die."

"You won't. Even if a bark scorpion had stung you, you wouldn't die."

"It wasn't a bark scorpion! You said you don't know what kind of scorpion stung us!"

"Fine, but the bark scorpion is the most venomous," he said calmly. "So it follows that whichever scorpion stung us is less harmful than a bark scorpion."

She began to stand. "I'm just going to see what's down that tunnel."

"Hannah, sit down. We can't go anywhere. It would be a stupid thing to do. I already did one stupid thing, and that's how I ended up stuck down here. I'm not going to do anything else that's stupid. Okay? Just sit here, and wait, and listen, and don't panic."

Hannah drew her knees up to her chest and sat silently.

Dominic didn't confess it, but he was finding it difficult to sit still. His heart pounded wildly in his chest; he began to feel an almost irresistible urge to move, a racing anxiety in his whole body. His brain felt like it was expanding against his skull. *It's the poison. I just have to wait it out the best I can.*

But his breath seemed less and less useful. He wasn't getting enough oxygen. *It's the lack of air. We're going to suffocate.*

He opened his eyes to check on Hannah—but she was gone.

Frantically, Dominic looked around the chamber. "You've got to be kidding me," he muttered, and called out: "*Hannah! Hannah!*"

The flashlight had been abandoned at the entrance to the Sagittarius tunnel. Remembering what she'd said about the centaur, Dominic peered into it. "Hannah!" he called again.

Now what? He was sure she'd gone down the tunnel. He couldn't leave her alone. He would have to crawl after her—and this time he would check carefully for any interconnected tunnels, so that he wouldn't get lost again.

Dominic pocketed the flashlight and crawled into the small passageway. Anger flared up in him. His head hurt so much that he could barely think. He was dizzy, breathless, and his senses seemed warped and distant. *I am going to die in here. Stupid kid. Stupid old lady . . . .*

"Hannah!" he yelled.

The tunnel, it turned out, was not so difficult to get through. It was tight, but short and fairly straight. Dominic's illness was the biggest challenge. He probably would have gone back if not for the light up ahead. It got brighter as he approached, and he began to think that Hannah had found a route to the surface. He struggled onward, arms trembling—and collapsed to the ground. Moaning and gasping, he forced himself to continue.

The tunnel inclined sharply. Dominic found himself climbing straight upward, his toes and fingertips clinging to rock ledges. By the time he made it out of the tunnel, he was so out of his senses that he could barely see. His vision had blurred. His clothes were soaked with water and sweat, and his throat was dry and raw. But he knew he had found Hannah. He could hear her voice. She was talking calmly, as if in conversation.

As his hands touched the ground, Dominic stopped in surprise. He felt grass beneath his fingers. "Ahh . . . we made it," he groaned in relief, pushing himself out of the hole. "I need an ambulance. Quickly, please."

But his vision started to clear, and he realized that they probably hadn't made it, after all.

Hannah stood at the edge of a grassy field surrounded by a dense thicket and high rock walls. The sky was filled with a haze of clouds, subduing the tones of a landscape colored in blues, greens, and golds; the grass was a rich shade of blue-green, the thicket a sleek and glistening blue-black. And directly ahead of Dominic was the most bewildering sight of all: a rock wall carved in the guise of a giant yellow scorpion. Its surface had been detailed with all of the scorpion's features, and here and there it was marked with white spirals.

"Dominic, look at what I found!" Hannah pointed to a stone outcropping.

He watched as she danced excitedly from foot to foot. She seemed cartoonish, unreal. Her movements gave Dominic a rushing bout of motion sickness.

"I'm hallucinating." He rolled helplessly onto the ground. He closed his eyes and laid limp and silent.

"Dominic!" Hannah called again. She ran to him, leaning over and shaking his shoulder. "Get up!"

"We've been poisoned," he groaned. Dominic was quickly succumbing to a sense of doom, certain he'd been stung by a breed of underground scorpion that had never been studied. He had no idea what the poison would do to him. It might be frying his brain. He was probably in the hallucinatory throes of death. "Hannah, if you can hear me, don't move. Just sit here and wait it out. I'm not opening my eyes until I stop hallucinating."

"I figured out one of the enigmas," Hannah insisted.

"No, you didn't. It's a delusion." Dominic rubbed his eyes and groaned. "What a dumb way to die. Here I've been moaning over my spoiled plans for the day, and . . . if I had known I was going to die, I would have cleaned up a few things. I would have thrown my diary in the garbage. How many twenty-one-year-olds still keep diaries?"

"Dominic!"

"My sister will read the whole thing, for sure. She'll read it every night and cry."

"Let me show you something," Hannah prodded him. "It will make you feel better."

"No, Hannah, don't move," he moaned. "Don't believe anything you see. Just sit next to me until help arrives."

3: Sagittarius

Hannah didn't heed Dominic's advice.

Near the edge of the blackthorn thicket was a yellow rock outcropping, about the same height as Hannah, with a flat, smooth face. Two enigmas had been scratched neatly into the stone. Hannah was certain she'd already solved the first one. The second wasn't like any enigma she'd seen, but she thought she knew how to figure it out:

Hearths often hesitate;
corpses ionize.
All beginnings will define
the target and the prize.

"All beginnings," Hannah murmured. She stared at the words as though mesmerized. "*All* beginnings . . . ." She sat down in front of the stone, whispering to herself as she sounded out various words. "Hear, heart . . . of, oft . . . of he . . hesco . . . of heco, hecion . . . corpion . . . scorpion!"

After some time she quietly stood and gazed at the giant scorpion rock. Her eyes roved over the strange spiral glyphs, settling finally on the largest spiral below the head.

"Heart of the scorpion," she whispered. "All beginnings will define the target . . . ."

Absently, she turned toward Dominic.

The sight of him filled her with sympathy. Every once

in a while, he would sit up; he would look all around and make strange faces, widening his eyes and then narrowing them, as if that would somehow improve his perception. Then, still seeing the strange surroundings, he would lie back down and remain motionless.

Presently he sat up again. He put a hand over his mouth and leaned forward. "I think I'm going to puke," he said as Hannah approached.

Hannah held out a hand to him. "Stand up," she suggested. "You feel better if you move around. I feel sick, too, but it's not as bad when I'm moving."

"I can't walk. My brain is melting."

Hannah looked into his pallid, blotchy face and tried to sound encouraging. "Just try it. If you just sit in your misery, you'll get stuck in it." Again, she offered her hand. "That's what my dad always used to tell me."

He looked up at her. His eyes were dull and bloodshot. After a moment he uncovered his mouth and took Hannah's hand.

She helped him to his feet and pulled him gently in the direction of the stone panel. "I found something really neat," she told him in a confiding tone. "When you see what it is, you'll feel better. I know how to find the cure for the scorpion sting."

He came to a halt. "You're hallucinating."

"Just take one look. It's not going to hurt you."

He walked beside her silently. Then, as they neared the stone, he muttered: "No, probably not. It can't hurt me because I'm dead. I'm in limbo."

"Look." Hannah pointed to the first enigma:

Craft that by which the arrows flew;
rehearse until thine aim is true.
Secure thus from the giving tree, and
wobble not what you set free.

"It's an acrostical enigma for sure," she said. "I already solved it, and I solved the second one too."

Dominic looked at the stone expressionlessly.

Hannah explained: "The letters of the answer are hidden somewhere in the poem. The poem sometimes tells you which letters to look at. This one tells you to find them at the beginnings. See?" She pointed at the final passage, reading aloud: "'Beginnings, reversed.' The letters are found at the beginning of each line; that means it's a kind of acrostic. Except the letters are reversed, so you have to spell them backwards." With her finger, Hannah traced a line below the first three letters, going backward from *a* to *C*.

"A, R, C," she said. Then she traced letters below the second line, from *h* to *r*. "H, E, R. And then S; and then B, O, W. When you put the fragments together, it says, 'archers bow.' And I know it's the right answer because the poem *talks* about an archer's bow. Do you see it?"

Dominic's eyes remained flat and dull, but he said, "I suppose I see it. So what?"

"You have to read the second enigma, too. 'Hearths often hesitate; corpses ionize. All beginnings will define the target and the prize.' *All* the beginnings have part of the answer—every word has a part of it. The first word is heart; and then you use O-F-T and H-E to make 'of the.' If you put all the letters together it says 'Heart of the scorpion.'"

Dominic paused. "Okay."

"The heart of the scorpion is there." Hannah pointed at the giant scorpion figure in the distance. "See all those spirals? It's the Scorpius constellation, and the spirals are the stars. The big spiral on the scorpion's chest is Antares—that's the brightest star, and it's at the heart of the scorpion. So, the enigmas are saying that we have to use an archer's bow to hit the target—and the target is the Antares star."

"I'm going to lie down." Dominic dropped to the ground in front of the stone, lying flat on his back and closing his eyes.

"You're going to feel sick," Hannah warned him.

"I don't think it can get much worse."

She muttered: "When is that ever true?" Hannah gazed at the sole tree that rose from the center of the grassy field. She hesitated, looked from the tree to Dominic, and added: "I'll do it myself."

Hannah set out across the field. It was true that she still felt sick; her arm throbbed and stung, her heart raced and her breath came too quickly, and every once in a while she shivered with a strange chill. She made herself feel a little better by pretending that this was how she was *supposed* to feel. It seemed pointless to worry about it, since there was nothing she could do about it for the time being—and this strange, wonderful world distracted her from the pain. The surroundings helped her forget her troubles, and moving around in them made her feel better. And she was proud of herself for having solved the enigmas—especially the first one, because it had been the most difficult.

At the tree, she stopped and looked into the low branches. It wasn't a large tree. The trunk was thin, and the branches were wiry with very few leaves. It looked like a sickly thing.

She reached up and took a bare, thick branch in her grasp. "Sorry about this," she said to the tree, pulling hard and snapping the branch.

The stick she ended up with was more than two feet long. It felt dry, but it was sturdy and didn't crack when she bent it. After giving it a thorough examination, Hannah leaned it against the tree and began running her hands over the trunk.

"Dominic!" She looked over her shoulder. "Do you have a pocket knife?"

He didn't answer.

Hannah's fingers roamed over the bark until she found a rough spot—a little knob, dry and crusty, that was breaking away from the tree. She pushed her fingertips behind it, prying it loose. Beneath the hard exterior was a finer, lighter-colored layer of bark. This was the part that Hannah needed. She peeled away chunks of the meatier bark and began to strip away its soft inner fibers. When she had collected those, she peeled long strips from the exposed part of the tree.

When she thought she'd collected enough, Hannah sat with her back resting against the trunk. She pulled apart the strips of bark into thin fibers and weaved them together. She braided them in three sections, adding more fibers when her supply started to thin out, until she had a long, thin rope. Then she tied one end of the bunch of fibers onto the broken branch.

"Dominic!" she called again.

He sat up, making that strange face. His eyes bugged out one moment, and in the next he was squinting at her.

"Dominic, come and see what I made!" Hannah entreated him. "It's an archer's bow." She finished tying the other end of the rope to the branch. Then she stood, pulling lightly against the rope with her finger, testing it. "I need you to help me make some arrows. Then we can shoot Antares and see what happens."

Dominic flopped back onto the ground.

"Fine," Hannah muttered impatiently. She frowned, staring up into the tree. She couldn't see any thin, straight branches from where she stood—nothing that would make a good arrow. And the tree didn't look particularly safe to climb. It was too thin, its branches too weak-looking. But Hannah didn't know what else to do. She grabbed hold of the thickest branch and began to heave herself upward.

The tree shook under her weight. The upper branches swayed wildly back and forth. As Hannah hung there, suspended on the branch, she heard a great rustling. Small branches were snapping loose from their bearings, falling to the ground around her.

Hannah lowered herself back to the ground in amazement. The sticks that were scattered around weren't just branches; they were arrow-straight. What had looked like leaves were actually feathers, three on one end of each stick—two bright green feathers and one brown.

"I found arrows!" she shouted, but Dominic ignored her.

She picked one of them up and studied the tip. "It doesn't have a point," she mumbled, frowning. "How am I supposed to . . . ." She glanced up at the scorpion rock, at the big white spiral that marked Antares. "I suppose it doesn't matter." Hannah picked up a handful of arrows and raced to the edge of the thicket.

"Come on, Dominic, I'm doing all the work myself!" she shouted as she ran past him. Hannah sprinted to the edge of the thicket. Very near its border was the tunnel through which she and Dominic had come, and Hannah took care not to stumble into it—but as she passed, she slowed to a stop, staring into the hole with a sense of awe.

The hole had begun to suck air inward. It pulled at the edges of the grass and sent bits of soil hurtling into its abyss. But the motion wasn't what surprised Hannah the most. The hole was impossibly dark—so dark that Hannah couldn't even see an inch inside of it, not even the slightest fragment of rock. If it wasn't for the movement of the air, Hannah would have thought that the hole was a solid black circle. She moved away from it and focused on the task ahead.

The thicket was dense and steely blue-black, with strange little thorn-topped vines that curled out toward the field. It stretched across the ground ahead, blocking Hannah and putting a good distance between her and Antares. She moved as close to the thicket as possible. She leaned forward, inspecting its thorns to see how sharp they were—but she quickly stepped back. The bush appeared to be moving. Its little vine-like protrusions glinted in the subdued light as they uncurled and moved their sharp, thorn-like points closer to Hannah's legs.

"Scorpion bushes!" she cried.

That got Dominic moving. He sat up, looking back at the thicket with alarm. "What? Scorpions in the bushes?"

"They're *scorpion bushes*. Come and look."

The bushes grew appendages that looked exactly like scorpion tails. For a moment Hannah had been fearful, thinking that the bushes were full of scorpions, but she quickly realized that she was seeing part of the plant. The tail-like protrusions were everywhere, so numerous that Hannah couldn't possibly guess how many there were. She could only suppose that they were poisonous.

"Watch out for the hole," Hannah said as Dominic walked toward her.

"Isn't that the tunnel we came out of?"

"Yeah."

"Are you sure? It doesn't look like a tunnel." Dominic knelt beside the opening and slowly reached out his hand. "It just looks like a black hole."

Hannah grabbed his arm before he could place it into the passageway. "Don't," she said, feeling inexplicably fearful. She beckoned Dominic toward the thicket. "Come and look at the bushes." She pointed a finger, careful to keep it a good distance from the odd-looking thorns. "See, they look like scorpion tails."

Dominic approached and leaned forward, cautiously eyeing the bush. "I'll be . . . ." He made a sound of disbelief. "A scorpion poison that makes you hallucinate about scorpions."

"Look. I made a bow, and I found arrows, too." Hannah showed him one of the arrows with its trio of feathers. "I didn't put the feathers on, either. They just came like that. They fell out of the tree. That's because we're supposed to use them to shoot Antares. See, if you walk all over on the grass, you can see that there are stones placed around, and they all have spirals on them. That's because we're standing in the Sagittarius constellation. All the spirals represent stars. Sagittarius' arrow star is pointing that way, toward the scorpion rock—and that's what we're supposed to do, too. If we hit the heart of the scorpion, I bet we'll figure out how to heal the poison, and then we won't feel sick anymore."

"What's this? Did you just make this?" Dominic reached for the bow, and Hannah let him hold it. He studied the woven rope.

"Yes," she said.

The sudden excitement seemed to have helped him. His cheeks were a bit flushed now, instead of pale and sickly. His eyes were bright with attention. "You made it from the tree? Where'd you get the rope?

"I made it from the soft bark—the part that's on the inside. I braided it together for a rope."

"And it works? Don't you have to use something more elastic?"

"No, you do it like this. I made one before and it worked fine." Hannah dropped all the arrows but one, eager to demonstrate. She took the bow in her left hand and turned it carefully, drawing the arrow across and taking aim at the great spiral.

"Nice job," Dominic said. "Did you learn that at

summer camp?"

She lowered the bow. "No, in a wilderness class. We didn't learn that kind of stuff at camp. All we did was cook food and make crafts. Well, maybe they did other things, but . . . ."

"But you quit."

"I had to. None of the other girls liked me, and the camp leaders got mad at me."

"How come?"

"The camp leaders use these silly fake names during camp, like Gumby and Strawberry, and they don't tell us their real names until the last day of camp—but I found one of the camp programs with all their names on it. The camp leaders made me promise not to tell anyone; but some of the tenth-grade girls started being really nice to me, and they said they'd let me hang out with them if I told them how I knew the real names. So I showed them the program, and they ratted on me."

"Uh-huh," Dominic said. "Is that all?"

"All the camp leaders were rude to me after that, and one of them gave me a speech about how she was disappointed that I broke my promise. I told her that the older girls tricked me, and that I didn't have any friends at camp, and I said I wanted to call my foster parents so I could go home. All the camp leaders stopped being mean to me and tried to get me to stay, but I didn't want to."

"Well . . . that all sounds very dramatic."

Hannah's eyes narrowed. "Don't get sarcastic with me."

"I'm not trying to sound sarcastic."

"I know you're not trying to *sound* sarcastic," she muttered. She raised the bow and took aim at the giant scorpion.

Her first arrow flopped through the air and into the thicket. Hannah stared after it worriedly. "What happens if we run out of arrows?"

Dominic shrugged. "I don't know. I suppose we keep hallucinating until the poison wears off. Or until we die."

"Quit talking about dying! I had to do everything myself because you're busy waiting to die."

Dominic sighed. "Please don't talk in that shrill voice."

"What?"

"*Don't be sarcastic,*" he imitated in a high voice. "*Quit talking about dying.*"

"Stop imitating me."

"*Stop imitating me!*" he squeaked. "Stop whining, and I'll stop mimicking."

Hannah picked up another arrow, turning pointedly away from him. "You shouldn't have come looking for me," she said, and in a low voice she added: "Jerkwad." She aimed and released the bow string—and abruptly dropped the bow to the ground. "Ow," she said, staring down at her left hand.

"What's the matter?" Dominic asked.

"One of the feathers cut my hand."

"Let's see."

Hannah had a gash across the lower part of her thumb. Dominic leaned in to look at it, but Hannah hid it from his view, holding it on the other side of her body. "Stop touching me," she said.

He rolled his eyes. "I didn't touch you."

Hannah selected another arrow. She aimed carefully, trying with all her might to relax and focus, but the arrow arced slowly through the air and into the bushes.

"It's too far," she complained, suddenly overwhelmed by frustration. "I'm never going to be able to hit it."

"Wait a minute," Dominic said, holding up a hand. "I'll ask you again: Please don't whine in that tone of voice. I can't stand the sound of kids whining."

Hannah looked at him in disbelief. "Does the sound of

grown-ups whining bother you?" she asked, picking up another arrow. "You've been whining the whole time we've been here because you think you're dead." She studied her wounded hand, frowning at the blood that congealed there.

"Here," Dominic said. "Why don't you take a break, and let me try it. What are we aiming for?"

"The biggest spiral, at the scorpion's heart."

He loaded the bow and aimed. The arrow slid from his grasp. He tried in vain to hold it in place.

"You have to turn the bow so that the arrow rests on top of it," Hannah said.

He did as she said. A moment later, the arrow sailed lopsided into the thicket.

"You have to pull harder than that," Hannah told him.

Dominic picked up another arrow. He pulled it slowly across the bow, straining against the rope.

"Not *that* hard!" Hannah said. "You'll break it, and then I'll have to make another one all over again."

"I just asked you not to talk in that tone," Dominic replied irritably. "I already have a splitting headache. Do me a favor and shut up for a minute."

He aimed again, but suddenly lowered the bow. "Listen."

Faint scuttling sounded within the bushes.

"Do you hear that? It's coming from the place where my arrow fell."

Hannah listened nervously. "It's just the bushes. They move."

"Yes, but doesn't it sound like it's getting closer? I can hear it over there, too, where your arrows landed." Dominic paled again. "It had better not be more scorpions."

Hannah listened nervously. "They can't come closer. They're plants."

Dominic paused. "Well, whatever they are, I'm pretty

sure they're not happy about being shot with an arrow."
He aimed again.

A moment later he cried out in pain. The arrow
somersaulted across the grass in front of him; the bow
fell to the ground. "Son of a . . . ."

Hannah stared at his hand, wide-eyed. Dominic, too,
had gotten cut by one of the feathers—worse than
Hannah. Pieces of green fluff had lodged in his hand.

"Is it bad?" Hannah stepped toward him. "And don't
yell at me for asking."

"I'm not going to yell."

Blood was already dripping from his thumb. The back
of his hand was swollen and red from the scorpion sting.
Hannah felt herself softening; she stared at the wounds
with a sense of remorse. "Do you have anything to wrap
it with?"

"No."

She began to remove the red vest she was wearing.

"Forget it, I'm not using your shirt as a wrap,"
Dominic said.

"It isn't for you. It's for me." Hannah wrapped the vest
around her left hand. "I'll try shooting like this. It might
get in the way, but at least I won't get cut again."

She pointed the bow and arrow high into the air. Out of
the corner of her eye, she could see Dominic trying to
pick bits of feather out of his thumb.

Suddenly he backed away from the thicket. "They're
coming. Hurry, Hannah."

A small, black tail moved across the grass toward
Dominic, dragging itself by tiny legs. Hannah couldn't
see a head, but the stinger was visible from where she
stood, curved and glistening.

She raised the bow. The next arrow went farther, but it
struck to the left of Antares. Hannah looked at the
makeshift bow in frustration. It had seemed to make so
much sense at first; the poem had directed her, the

arrows had been there. But how could she reach the far-off target with such a crude instrument?

"You do it," Dominic called to her. "I'll try to lure the scorpions this way, because, see, they are *all* following me . . . okay, there are a lot of them. Hurry up, Hannah! Why are you just standing there?"

"This isn't—" Hannah cut herself off. She was about to yell, to protest the unfairness of the situation, but she looked at Dominic and stopped. He was slumped and stumbling, his eyes red and dull. For the first time Hannah noticed the scratches along the side of his face and the bruises on his arms. His left hand was streaked with blood. He looked so pathetic, so pale and sickly and miserable—and now he was being trailed by a pack of mutant scorpions.

"I'm sorry I called you a jerkwad," she replied as she lifted the bow. "I'm glad you came to help me. I don't like talking about camp; it puts me in a bad mood."

"This is really not the time," he replied. "Just shoot, please."

A movement at the edge of the bushes caught her attention. She drew in her breath and stepped back. *More scorpions!* Her grip slipped; the arrow arced lazily into the thicket, shaking loose a number of scorpion tails. Hannah watched as they writhed on the ground.

She gathered the arrows and backed up again, even farther from the target. Every step seemed to create an impossible distance—but Hannah still had three arrows left. She would try her best until there were none, and if they failed, she would try something else.

"They're backing me into the other bushes," Dominic shouted. "I have to come back towards you."

Hannah aimed again. The arrow sailed high and straight. She watched as it slowed, as it began to arc downward, and she held her breath.

The arrow hit directly in the center of the Antares

spiral. It bounced off the rock and fell to the ground.

Hannah was so surprised that she couldn't react. Dominic approached behind her, breathless from sprinting away from the scorpions. "You got it," he said, and then jumped back. "Hannah, look out."

"I know, I see them."

"That was it, wasn't it?" Dominic looked around the clearing. "Okay, well, nothing's happening, but that was an interesting interval in my throes-of-death hallucination." He made a sound of disbelief. "Let's move, before they surround us."

But something *was* happening. The rock was groaning, scraping, shifting; it cracked like thunder, and the breast stone dipped forward with a great noise.

"Run," Hannah said, and grabbed Dominic's arm.

"Wait! This way—around the scorpions."

Together they made top speed toward the tree. They cowered behind it as if for protection, grasping its narrow trunk as the giant boulders fell heavily from their places. The stones dropped across the thicket, snapping and crushing. Clouds of debris flew into the air as the Antares stone hurled through the bushes and across the grass. The terrible sounds hurt Hannah's ears, but she was too frightened to cover them. She grabbed Dominic, ready to make a run for it, but the stone sped past them and tumbled onward. It rolled all the way to the opposite side of the thicket; it tore through the bush and smashed against the high rock walls, cracking them and splitting them apart, opening a great doorway. Just beyond the doors it came to a halt.

The Antares stone had obliterated the poisonous bushes, smashing the scuttling trails of scorpions and creating a wide path. Hannah could see that behind it, the gap was filled with light, as though the sun was shining on the other side of the rock wall.

Silence descended over the land. Hannah and Dominic

stared for some time at the crushed path and the opening beyond; then Hannah danced from foot to foot, exclaiming, "I told you so!"

"Okay," Dominic said, "I'll . . . ." He trailed off uncertainly.

"I bet the cure for the poison is over there." Hannah pointed to the gap. She quickly unwrapped her hand and slid the vest back on.

Dominic was silent. Hannah peered at him. "Do you still think you're dead?" she asked.

"Definitely," he replied.

"But how can you still think things if you're dead?"

"I think that I'm dead, and I'm in limbo."

"What's limbo? I thought that was a game."

He smiled. "The one where you go under a pole? No, it's not that kind of limbo. It's a kind of delusion . . . no, it's a dimension. It's a dimension you pass through after you die, until your soul figures out where it's supposed to go. Or something like that. It's just an idea. I didn't believe in it, but now . . . I don't know."

"Fine, then. Walk through limbo with me. Let's see where it goes."

Dominic gave her a strange look—one of mystified fascination. He said: "I don't know if you're really talking or if I'm just imagining you."

"You're not imagining anything. We're in an underground world! And I bet that there are other people living here, and they're the ones who wrote the enigmas. And anyway, even if we are imagining things, there's nothing we can do about it right now anyway—so why does it matter?"

He shrugged and gazed through the opening of the split rock. "I don't know. All right, let's see what's over there."

"First you have to promise you won't yell at me. If I sound like I'm whining, just tell me nicely. And you can't tell me to shut up."

"I'll see what I can do."

"You have to promise!" she insisted.

"Sorry, I don't make promises. But I'll shake on it." Dominic extended his right hand. He gripped Hannah's hand firmly and shook it.

"Shaking on something is the same as promising," she said. "And you have a boring handshake. Do it like this." She opened his hand and slapped it across the front and back, then wiggled her fingers into his.

"Wait, it's not finished yet," she said as he pulled away.

"I don't do fancy handshakes," he replied. "Come on, let's go before something else happens."

They started away; but as they approached the path, Hannah said, "Wait." She glanced back at the tree. It now had a long, oozing strip along one side, where Hannah had torn away the bark. Jogging back to the tree, she set the bow against the trunk. Then she stood back and gazed up into the skinny branches.

Dominic walked up behind her. "Do you have anything to offer?" he asked. "We shouldn't take things for granted in a place like this; we should give something as thanks. I don't suppose you have any water."

"No."

He searched his pockets. "I don't have anything useful. Do you know any songs?"

Hannah gave him a puzzled look. "Songs, for what?"

"Never mind." Dominic stood with his hands behind his back, gazing up at the tree. He closed his eyes and began to sing—a lilting, soothing melody that Hannah didn't recognize—but he stopped after a few seconds. "I forgot it," he said.

"What song is it?"

"It's . . . a thankyou song my grandma used to sing, but I can't remember the words. Do you have something to sing?"

"Me? No."

"No? No camp songs from summer camp?"

Hannah frowned at the tree. "I don't think it cares if we sing to it. I'll feel stupid, singing camp songs to a tree."

"Fair enough. Let's . . . ." He paused, then turned and gazed at the wide pathway. "Do you hear that?"

Scuttling, like soft whispers, sounded at the edges of the path.

Dominic turned back to Hannah. "Okay. Let's run."

4: Capricorn

The Antares stone rested in an expanse of rock and sand. Beyond it was the sea. The rock walls on this side led far into the distance, but they looked nothing like the smooth, yellowish stone surfaces that surrounded the Sagittarius chamber. These were rough and gray, sloping and jutting like any cliffs Hannah would expect to see in nature. She lifted her face, searching for the sun—but though the sky was clear and bright, she couldn't see where the light was coming from.

"What were you singing?" Hannah asked as they walked. "I mean, even if you can't remember the words, what was the song *about*?"

"My grandma sang it in Hopi, but I don't know the language. In English it goes something like, 'I have nothing to offer but my voice, in a song of peace and thanks. Though I have nothing more to give, I have everything I need. I received care and help, and when there was none to be found, I learned compassion and strength. Even when the world looks dark, I have everything I need.'"

"That's nice."

Dominic chuckled, and Hannah narrowed her eyes at him.

"Are you laughing at me?" she demanded.

"No. I'm just remembering things. Don't be so paranoid."

As Hannah and Dominic ventured out onto the beach, they passed beside the Antares stone. Hannah stopped and pointed. "Look. There's writing on it."

The stone was positioned so that the writing happened to be near Dominic's eye level. Another poem was scratched into the rock, and above it was an ornate, colorful drawing of an animal—half donkey and half fish, with a donkey's head and forelegs, and a fish's tail and fins. The tail swirled in a spiral shape amidst other brightly colored spirals.

The poem read:

Wait upon the rocky cape
and gaze into a sea of riches;
in the shifting patterns, vast and ornate,
lives a guide who helps to grant your wishes.
Three first threes in the tails sets you on the right track
and thanks you for remembering to give something
back.

"It knows what you did," Hannah said, awed.

"What?"

"It's thanking us for remembering to give something back . . . I think." Hannah moved her finger along the sentences, whispering to herself. "Three first threes in the tails . . . three *first* threes." She stopped and looked at Dominic. "See if you can solve it."

"Me? I don't know anything about enigmas."

"But I told you how to solve them."

"I don't remember. And I don't know anything about constellations, or mythology, or anything like that, so you're on your own."

"But this one is easy," Hannah insisted. "What if something happens, and we get separated? You might have to solve them on your own."

"I won't bother."

Hannah rolled her eyes. "At least tell me where to find the letters. It says 'three first threes in the tails,' so where would we look?"

He shrugged. "At three first threes in the tails. I don't know."

Hannah gave him a scathing look.

"All right." Dominic studied the poem. "The words that have three letters?"

She stared at him in disbelief. "You didn't listen to anything I said." She pointed at the last word in the first line. "You have to look at the first three letters at the tail ends of the first three lines. I know the answer already; it's 'Capricorn.' See? C-A-P, R-I-C, O-R-N. And I know it's right because there's a picture of the Capricorn sign above the poem—an animal, a donkey or something, with a fish tail. I bet Capricorn is next to Sagittarius in the zodiac, on the other side of Scorpio." Hannah turned and looked out at the sea, frowning. "Except . . . I don't know what we're supposed to do. Do you see something that looks like a rocky cape?"

Dominic pointed to the rocky bar of land that jutted out into the sea. "The cape is right there."

"Where?"

He looked amused. "You don't know what a cape is?"

"Yes I do, it's like a cloak."

"Not this kind of cape. A cape is a piece of land that stretches out into the water."

"Oh." Hannah's eyes lit up with anticipation. "Let's go out there and see what happens."

"See, I'm useful after all," said Dominic as he trailed along behind her.

"I never said you weren't."

Hannah walked all the way to the edge of the cape, looking expectantly to the sea as it sent sprays of water misting over her. She waited a minute, then another— and then Dominic gently pulled her back, saying, "Come on. You'll get soaked."

They retreated a few feet, and Dominic lowered

himself to the ground. His face was becoming pale again, taking on a strange grayish hue. He leaned forward, covering his face, while Hannah gazed at him with concern.

"Are you feeling worse?" she asked, rather timidly.

"Yes."

"So am I. I think it's standing still that does it."

"I don't think I can sit here," Dominic groaned. He uncovered his face and tipped his head back, shutting his eyes tight. "The sound of the waves is giving me motion sickness. Every time I close my eyes, I can see waves crashing through and ripping everything to shreds. They're ripping my life apart."

"Then keep your eyes open."

"That doesn't help." He dipped his head. "I hate this place. I know I'm dead. My parents will be devastated when they find out. My sister—"

Hannah was about to chastise him for whining, but a flash of light on the water caught her attention.

"Look!" Hannah shook him and pointed eagerly toward the waves. "Something's coming." A large, silvery object was barreling through the water, occasionally flipping just above the surface, its body glinting in the light. As it came closer Hannah caught glimpses of a fan-like tail.

"It's the Capricorn!" she cried. "Or it's a big fish. I can't tell yet."

Dominic stood up. Together they watched and waited, and as the thing reached the cape, they stepped back nervously.

The creature flipped in the water, jerking and writhing as if in the throes of terrible pain. Hannah worried for a moment that it was hurt—but then she saw two long, curved horns ascending from the waves, followed quickly by the head and neck of a goat.

The animal that came toward them no longer had any

resemblance to a creature of the sea. It appeared to be a perfectly normal goat—though a colorful one, with mingling shades of tan, brown, and black that shone in the light, and white streaks around its head and belly. Hannah wrung her hands as it approached. This was the first animal they'd encountered since their arrival in this strange world. During their brief venture, they had not even come across the smallest insect.

The goat made for an intimidating specimen. It was large and strong, sure of step as it made its way onto the rocky shore, with dangerous-looking horns and intelligent eyes. But Hannah felt herself calming as she locked gazes with the animal. It looked back at her with a soft, assured gentleness.

The goat took a few slow steps closer to them. "If you're ready," it said, "I'll help grant your wishes. Both of you are eager to find a cure for your illness, and to get back home." The goat had a rich, calming voice.

Hannah's heart pounded—whether from illness or fear, she wasn't sure. She glanced at Dominic, but he was staring at the animal as if mesmerized. "Well . . . yes . . . we want to get back to Wupatki," she said slowly. "My foster parents are looking for me there, and I don't think we can go back the way we came. It turned into a black hole."

"You've been stung by Scorpius. The antidote to the venom will allow you to return home, and you can find it by walking the zodiac road. You'll have to travel across the water, to the Aquarius island, and continue from there. I'll take you across. You can ride on my back."

"Is there another way?" Dominic asked faintly.

The goat stepped forward again, until it stood within inches of Dominic. It looked steadily into his eyes. Hannah could feel Dominic tensing; his fingers clenched her arm.

"You have a very *nice* singing voice, Dominic," it said.

"Thank you for remembering to give something back. Most people don't remember."

"How do you know his name?" Hannah asked.

"There's no such thing as time in this dimension—no before and after," the goat replied gently. "So in a sense, I know you because we've already met."

The response made Hannah suspicious. "That's not true," she said. "We were standing back there before, reading the stone, and we came down here afterward."

"From your perspectives, perhaps. Not from mine."

It didn't make sense to Hannah, but she glanced at Dominic and decided it didn't matter much. He looked like he needed to keep moving. "How are you going to take us across the water?"

The goat retreated, splashing through the salty waves. When it was half-submerged, it stopped and called back to them: "Climb on."

Hannah pulled Dominic's arm. "Come on," she whispered.

He hesitated, staring at the creature in the water. The goat seemed to be bucking its rear legs, writhing strangely beneath the waves.

"Come on, it's like a game," Hannah prodded him. "It'll be fun." She dragged Dominic into the water, and they clutched each other more tightly, trying to prop each other up as the waves crashed against their shins.

When Hannah touched the goat's body, she realized that most of it had undergone a drastic transformation. Its sides were rough and covered with gray-green scales, and the rear legs had morphed into a long, finned tail. Hannah and Dominic exchanged quiet glances; then they helped each other onto the animal's back. When they were seated, the goat's forelegs seemed to vanish beneath it, and it swam gracefully into the sea.

Hannah enjoyed the feeling of cool water splashing up between her fingers, the currents caressing her legs. The water was calmer as they retreated from the shore. It was also remarkably clear. She could see patterns along the sandy bottom, but no fish anywhere, and no plants. For a "sea full of riches," it seemed rather bare.

"How come you can turn into a fish?" Hannah asked.

"I must be able to transform; that's all."

Hannah frowned. *That's not a real explanation*, she thought.

"I can turn into other animals as well. I can even turn into a human." The goat turned its head, looking sidelong at Hannah. She watched as the face shortened and morphed into the face of a woman—a plain, human woman, but with the neck of a goat. Hannah leaned back in surprise, bumping into Dominic.

"Careful, Hannah," he grumbled.

The head rapidly returned to its former guise. "I have to transform so that I can survive in all environments," it explained. "I'm meant to learn from all environments, and to teach in all of them. If I have to live on land, I become an animal that lives on land. If I have to survive in the sea, I become an animal that thrives in the sea."

"But how do you do it?"

"The same way as other beings. You, too, are capable of transformation."

"You mean . . . I could turn into a fish?" Hannah asked.

The goat-fish laughed. "Not in your dimension. A human being has limits for a reason, and it also has potential for a reason. Both allow for great learning."

"But why can you do it here? What's different about this place?"

"Time and memory. I'll give you an example. Do you know the story about Enkidu?"

"No."

"He was a man who was born in the forest and raised among animals. He knew how to live as a part of the woods. None of the townspeople who passed through would have even known that a human being lived there, but Enkidu gave himself away by trying to scare off the loggers and hunters. He created such a problem that the townspeople devised a plan. They sent a woman into the forest to befriend him, and she persuaded Enkidu to come and live in the town. Enkidu went, and eventually he became friends with the king. King Gilgamesh invited Enkidu to live with him in the great palace. Enkidu ate fine foods and indulged in all the riches that the king provided, until the ways of the townspeople became normal to him. When Enkidu's thinking was like that of the townspeople, King Gilgamesh took him on a quest into the great cedar forest. The forests were being cut down by the townspeople, and the wood was being sold to foreign traders, so quite a lot of trees were being cut down; the forests were depleted much faster than they could replenish themselves.

"But the townspeople faced an obstacle. A mysterious being lived in the forest. It prevented the loggers from going to the thickest, richest parts of the woods. The people called this being 'the spirit of the forest.' The king thought Enkidu might have some insight into conquering this being. Enkidu helped him track it down, and Gilgamesh cut off the being's head. Then they cut down the greatest, oldest cedar, and they floated it down the river back to Gilgamesh's kingdom. The loggers returned to the forest to take the rest of the trees; but when they arrived, they discovered that the entire wood had died. Without its spirit, the forest had become a stinking wasteland, full of animal corpses and flies. Enkidu, who had been raised by the wood, also became sick of spirit and died.

"Watching Enkidu's slow, sad death made Gilgamesh frightened of his own mortality. He tried to find a way to beat death, but his quest only made him ever more weak and frightened—and then he died."

Hannah waited, listening to the sound of water rushing around them. "Is that the end?" she asked.

"That's the story, yes."

"But what about the forest?"

"It died."

"Didn't it grow back?"

"It became a barren plain."

Hannah thought about that for some time. Behind her, Dominic was silent. She only knew he was there because his hands were gripping her waist.

The goat-fish continued: "If Enkidu had remembered and understood his life in the forest, he would never have helped Gilgamesh slay the forest spirit. But as time passed for him, and as he became wrapped up in his way of life in the town, he lost his ability to identify with the forest. It's harder for us to exploit and destroy those things we can identify with.

"Let me tell you another story. The townspeople that King Gilgamesh ruled over eventually had to leave their land and move closer to the ocean. As the years passed, they took even more resources from the earth and gave nothing back. They ended up with landfills full of waste. Eventually they ran out of room to store the waste, so they dumped their trash and toxins into the ocean and watched it vanish. The animals choked on the waste and became poisoned. Eventually, all the fishing enterprises suffered because the fish population was dying out, and the ones that were left were diseased—but instead of taking better care of the oceans, the people decided to eat poisonous fish."

"That's dumb," Hannah said.

"But that's how you live now. Your people have forgotten that they, too, lived in the sea and breathed its waters."

"What do you mean?" Hannah asked. "You mean

people came from fish?"

"I mean that you, Hannah, live in the salt water of your body, and breathed the salt water of your mother's womb. When you weep, you weep salt water tears. When you toil, you release salt water through your pores. As time passes, and people grow, they forget their lives in the waters; they forget that they *still* live in those waters. I don't forget. In this dimension, there is no such thing as time, so there is no such thing as action and consequence. They are one and the same to me."

"What do you mean?" Hannah asked again.

"Just what I said."

Hannah thought for a moment. "But, time is passing," she said. "A few minutes ago, we were on the land."

"It seems that way. The illusions of time is created for beings like you, who learn from action and consequence."

Hannah mulled that over for a while.

The goat-fish asked: "What about you, Hannah? Do you have a story to tell? I've told two, and I'd like to hear yours."

"Um . . . I can't think of one. Well, here's one; it's a story I read at the library."

Hannah told the tale of The New Mother, in which a cruel young girl tricked two smaller girls into behaving so badly that their mother went away, leaving them a new mother with glass eyes and a wooden tail. Then she told the story of Otesánek, a ravenous wooden child that devoured anything it could, including people—until it ate an old woman's prized cabbage patch, angering her so much that she split Otesánek's stomach open with a garden hoe.

"Fantastic!" the goat-fish remarked. "Dominic, do you have a story?"

"I'm getting sea sick," he replied weakly. "I might have to throw up."

"You won't," the goat-fish assured him. "But I'll tell a story about someone who did. Have you heard of Ketos, the eater of lies? She was a little girl who lived in a harsh little city. One day Ketos was blamed for breaking a store window, even though some other children had done it. Then she was blamed for stealing a child's bicycle. No one listened to her when she tried to defend herself. Because she was accused so many times, people continued to use her as a scapegoat. Ketos became so frustrated that she stopped talking. Her parents yelled at her; they made up stories about a great monster that ate little children who wouldn't talk. Ketos knew they were lying, but she quietly swallowed the lie. Other kids said she couldn't talk because she had become stupid. That was a lie, but Ketos didn't argue. She swallowed that lie, too. Time passed in this way, and Ketos got bigger and bigger. Eventually, Ketos was so swollen from the lies that she reached her breaking point. She opened her mouth and, all at once, she began to vomit all those lies back into the world. They flowed all through the town and stuck to the people who'd created them. But when they came out of Ketos, they came out as truth, and people could finally see them for what they were."

Again Hannah was silent, anticipating more, but the goat-fish didn't continue. "That's the end?"

"That's the story."

"But, did the people apologize for lying?"

"Perhaps; perhaps not. The more important thing is that Ketos recognized those lies for what they were. When we live with such things until we can't tolerate them any longer, they start to come out. Sometimes we're so angry or hurt that the lies come out as more lies. But if we're wise, they come out as truth, because they've had time to transform inside of us. They can come out like refined gold."

The goat-fish approached the island. It slowed as they

came close to the sand, and Hannah felt its body shifting. The scales melted into its rubbery flesh; its skin became soft beneath her fingers, and a moment later she felt the hardness of bone as two shoulders appeared. Her fingertips were pricked by coarse fur. She and Dominic struggled to stay on the creature's back as it mutated into its goat form.

"Climb off now," the goat instructed them.

Hannah pushed herself into the water and hurried onto land. She was soaked nearly from the chest up. Dominic fared no better. He sputtered through the waves, looking with anxious curiosity at the layout of the island. It was sandy and bare, except for some beige-colored rock outcroppings in the center. One in particular was large and circular, closely surrounded by the other slabs of rock.

The goat stopped at the edge of the water and nodded at the structure. "The next gate is within those walls," it said. "I would wish you luck, but my wishes won't change your fate."

"Is that good or bad?" Hannah asked.

"Neither."

Hannah gazed at the sandy-colored walls, wondering what lied inside. "Thanks for taking us across."

"You're both welcome."

Hannah nudged Dominic. He stood slouched and dripping, gazing into the sea as if mesmerized.

She turned back to the goat. "He feels sick," she said apologetically, "and he thinks he's dead."

The goat fixed its stare on Dominic, and he finally met its eyes. "I assure you that you're not dead. And neither is this girl." It spoke those last words with emphasis, and added: "Never stop helping this girl until she gets home."

With that, the animal began to turn away.

"Wait," Hannah said. "If there's no time here, does that

mean you know everything that's going to happen?"

"If I speak as though something hasn't happened yet, it's only for your benefit," the goat replied. It turned its head, looking sternly toward the jutting stones. "Remember the stories I told you, Hannah. Don't forget them. Your adversary is already here, and he's watching you."

Hannah looked over her shoulder, studying her surroundings, but she didn't see anything unusual.

"Who's watching?" she asked, but the goat was already turning back into a fish, flipping in the frothing water. It heaved into the waves and vanished.

5: Aquarius

A doorway into the central stone chamber became
visible as Hannah approached. It was somewhat hidden
behind one of the tall stone slabs, and upon entering the
room, Hannah saw that there were three other doorways,
likewise hidden from outside view. But those entrances
weren't what caught her immediate attention. The inner
chamber was lined all over with stone shelves, and on
each one sat a large vessel—and some of those vessels
were so ornately decorated as to take Hannah's breath
away. There were tall bronze jugs painted with intricate
arrangements of figures and patterns, and glazed vessels
carved with symbols, and others of brilliant gold, and all
kinds of different jugs and pitchers that made the simple
room blaze with color. Spaced equally between each
doorway were four water spouts, placed high in the inner
chamber, which seemed to draw water up through the
thick walls. The water spilled onto the stone floor and
drained into a crack along the edge of the wall. Each
spout was formed in the shape of an animal's head, and
all were different: they were the heads of a ram, a bird, a
horse, and a dragon.

A large glazed basin took up the middle of the
chamber. It was more than large enough for two people
to sit in comfortably. Hannah thought at first that it must
be a bath tub, but she quickly realized that it was full of
sizeable holes. The vessels that sat on the shelves, too,
were full of so many holes as to render them useless.

A section of one wall had no shelving. Instead it bore a

sort of plaque, engraved with a pair of poems:

Forty-nine have tried and failed
where other vessels might prevail;
be they clay or purest gold,
none but the true cup shall hold.
When the basin is fulfilled,
avian stars are duly thrilled;
for what is a cup unless it has life,
and what be your journey without any strife?

Keepers of the mystery
toss about within the sea;
victorious becomes that youth
sprung forth in beauty and in truth.

"Dominic!" she called.

He didn't answer. Hannah ran to the beach and found him still standing at the shore, staring out at the vast sea. "Dominic . . . what are you doing?"

"Have you ever been in the ocean?"

"Yeah, a few minutes ago."

"I used to go to the ocean every summer, in New Hampshire. I'd stay in the water all day, with my sister, and at night I could still feel the salt water in my skin, and I could still feel the motion of the waves, and it felt like Mother Nature was rocking me to sleep. The trees did that, too . . . there was a skinny one in my yard, with low branches that I could climb, and the wind would blow and rock it back and forth. And you know . . . I don't believe that we're not dead. I'm standing here thinking about how beautiful our planet is, how unique and incredible it is in the universe, and I'll probably never see it again. No ocean, no rivers, no forests . . . ."

Hannah danced from foot to foot impatiently.

"And maybe no colors or music or friendship, or

anything I've experienced there," he continued. "I'll never have the experience of looking into a pair of human eyes and seeing the emotion there. I'll never see . . . a girl with braids and a red vest, dancing on the beach."

"I found the enigmas," Hannah replied.

He let out a slow, weary sigh. "Fine. All right. Let's solve the enigmas."

Back at the plaque, Hannah frowned as she looked from one poem to the other. She tried to sound out words from different groups of letters. "This is hard," she complained. "It doesn't even tell you where to find the letters."

"Maybe that's not how you solve it," Dominic suggested, trying to wring salt water from his shirt. "How's your scorpion sting?"

"It's fine," she replied absently. "Maybe this is just a riddle. It sounds like it's talking about the Danaids."

"What's that?"

"There's a Greek myth about fifty sisters who had to marry their cousins," Hannah replied. "Their father told them to kill their husbands on their wedding night, and they all did it, except one. The husband who survived killed the women's father, and the other forty-nine sisters had to spend the rest of their lives trying to fill a tub that was full of holes."

"I see. You read some heavy stuff, for . . . how old are you?"

"Eleven."

"For an eleven-year-old. Wooden babies that eat people, wooden mothers who come to terrorize bad children . . . ."

"It says 'when the basin is fulfilled,'" Hannah continued. She glanced around the room. "How many jugs are there?"

"Let's count."

Carefully, they counted every jug. Each of them, no matter how richly ornamented or well crafted, was riddled with holes. Hannah counted forty-nine, and Dominic counted the same.

"How can there only be forty-nine?" Hannah asked in consternation. "It says 'forty-nine have tried and failed.' Shouldn't there be a fiftieth jug—one that doesn't have holes?"

"Maybe it's hidden," Dominic suggested.

So they embarked on a careful search of the chamber. They inspected the base of the giant basin, in case anything was hidden beneath it; they inspected the stone floor for any loose panels. But the search turned up nothing new.

Hannah read the poem again. "A cup that has life . . . let's look for a cup that has a symbol of life on it."

"I really don't know what to look for," Dominic replied. "Some of them have so many symbols . . . ." He frowned, picking up a small clay jug engraved with the image of a winged horse. He read the accompanying inscription out loud: "'Pegasos.' Is that like Pegasus, the horse from *Clash of the Titans*?"

Hannah went to his side and peered at the image. "Yeah, it's the same. 'Pegasos' is probably closer to the Greek spelling. It's just a different transliteration."

Dominic raised his eyebrows. "A different what?"

"Transliteration. 'Pegasus' is probably the Latin spelling. A lot of the Greek constellation names have two spellings, because one is based on the Greek alphabet and the other one is a Latin transliteration. Vowels that sound like 'o' in the Greek alphabet sometimes get replaced with a 'u' in Latin."

Dominic looked dumbfounded. "You're really into this stuff. You read a lot about constellations and mythology?"

"I do now. We're still on school break, so I can read

whatever I want." Hannah watched as Dominic turned the cup in his hand. On the opposite side was another image: a strange fish-like creature with a giant mouth and a long, bulky tail. "That might be Cetus," Hannah said.

"Might be what?"

"SEE-tuss," Hannah pronounced carefully. "The sea monster. Pegasus and Cetus are both in the part of the stars that's called 'the sea.' Pegasus is supposed to have sprung from the sea, and . . . actually, I think they're both by Aquarius. All the constellations in that part have something to do with water." She looked around the room contemplatively. "But . . . I don't know a lot of these symbols. Let's try all of the jugs, just to see if one of them works."

They tested the jugs one by one. They tried the bare, unpainted jugs; they tried the jeweled metal jugs; they tried the jugs that had strange symbols etched into them. Hannah tried to block the holes with her fingers, but she couldn't stop the water from flowing out. The holes were too numerous and too large. She even took off her wet socks and tried to stuff the holes with them, but the socks just slid out onto the floor.

"This is stupid," Hannah said. "None of them will work. What else can we use?" She went back to the rock slab, reading through the poem again. "The true cup," she murmured, and shook her head. "But there isn't any other cup."

"Maybe we should take a look outside," Dominic suggested.

"But there's nothing out there—and the Capricorn told us to come here."

"Oh, yes. The wise Capricorn," Dominic said dryly.

Hannah narrowed her eyes. "Are you being sarcastic?"

"Oh, not at all. That was some great storytelling. I especially liked the one about the girl who swallowed all the flies."

"What?"

"The girl who kept swallowing flies, and got bigger and bigger until she vomited flies all over the whole town."

"She swallowed *lies*, not flies! Why would she swallow flies?"

"I don't know why she swallowed a fly; perhaps she'll die," Dominic sang. "I was sitting in the back. I couldn't hear as well as you could, but it all sounded very preachy."

"The story was about a girl who swallowed other people's *lies*. They stayed inside of her and she changed them into truth . . . or something."

Dominic was studying an inscription on one of the brass cups, turning it slowly in his hand. Suddenly he stopped; his gaze wandered. "You know, that gives me an idea," he mused. "Maybe the cup isn't something that was already here. It might be something we brought with us."

"Like what? I didn't bring anything that can hold water."

"I thought that, too, but we *did* bring something. We're both alive, and if we *swallow* water, for instance . . . ." He trailed off, raising his eyebrows suggestively.

"It stays inside of you," Hannah finished. "For a while, anyway. Let's try it."

"Hold on. If we're going to try that, why don't you let me do it first? Just in case the water isn't—"

"No, me first!" Hannah cried—and before Dominic could interfere, she thrust her face beneath the nearest spout, swallowing several mouthfuls of water.

"Now you've done it." He sighed as Hannah crawled over the rim of the glazed tub. "Hannah . . . ."

"Don't lecture me yet! Wait and see what happens."

"Don't tell me when to lecture you. You should use

more caution in this place; I don't think it's all meant to
be fun and games. The goat-thing was giving us all kinds
of warnings, and it said there's an adversary watching
you."

Hannah looked at him sheepishly from inside the tub.
"I don't know what that means."

"Really? You can read Greek and Latin, but you don't
know 'adversary'?"

"I can't actually *read* those languages. I only know a
few transliterations."

"An adversary is a foe. An opponent."

She regarded him blankly.

"An enemy," he clarified.

Hannah's eyes widened. Her face blanched. Dominic
thought she might be overreacting to the idea of having
an enemy, and was about to reassure her—but Hannah
put a hand over her stomach and said, "Dominic . . . I
feel funny."

He peered at her over the rim of the large cup. "Funny,
how?"

"Don't drink the water, it's bad!" Her eyes filled with
fright. "It's doing something to me!"

"All right, just try to relax. Stick your finger down
your throat and see if you can throw up."

But Hannah was frozen with fear. From somewhere
above came the sounds of rhythmic pulsing—faint at
first, but quickly gaining volume. At first it sounded like
some kind of computerized signal; then it sounded like a
helicopter. But the thing that approached from the sky
wasn't any kind of machine. It was a great, beastly bird,
with many-colored wings that beat the air with seeming
viciousness. Its eyes burned with white-hot light.
Hannah saw the giant talons stretching toward her, and
she screamed: "Dominic!"

The bird descended into the chamber, letting out a
horrific squawk. It slid its talons over Hannah's

shoulders and beneath her armpits, clutching her in its steely grasp. Dominic lurched forward, trying to grab at Hannah's legs—but the bird was fast, and created such a great wind that Dominic and Hannah could hardly keep their eyes open.

And then she was in the air, rising above the chamber so quickly that Dominic vanished from sight. She thought she saw him a few moments later, running out of the chamber and across the sand. He shrank into a tiny dot, and then the island itself was barely visible, and it disappeared. Hannah saw nothing but the vast ocean rolling out endlessly beneath her.

Her mouth felt strange and dry. The sound of the bird's wings was unbearable. It seemed to beat at the very tissues of her brain. Her stomach heaved, and she thought she might vomit—but the impulse was quickly forgotten, wiped away by surprise and fear. The giant bird had dropped her. Hannah sailed downward, arms and legs thrashing helplessly at the air. She slammed into the cold water.

Hannah's flesh stung from the impact. She plunged so deeply, and was so disoriented by the fall, that she couldn't tell which way was up. She tumbled futilely in the belly of the ocean. She swam one way, and saw nothing but water; in a panic, she swam another way, and saw more of the same. The whole world seemed to have turned to water.

I'm going to die, Hannah thought in despair. *This isn't fair. How come I could solve the other enigmas, and now I'm just going to die?*

She swam hard, holding her breath though her lungs begged for air. She tried to pinch her lips and nose shut with her hands. But at last she couldn't help it; she sucked in a breath. Her lungs burned. She thrashed beneath the waves, consumed by panic. Vomit and water spewed painfully from her mouth. She felt as if every cell in her body was being punched by a violent fist.

But the aching and burning subsided. Hannah thought at first that she must have died, and that her spirit was still hovering there in the ocean. But she could still feel her body. She was alive, and breathing. She was breathing *water*.

Hannah tried to swim, to move her arms. But her arms—it was as if someone had lopped them off! She tried to turn her head to look at them, but it was as though she no longer had a neck. And her legs—not legs anymore! She curved her body and swam in a circle, trying hard to get a look at her legs, and instead she saw a sleek, greenish-gray tail.

Hannah tried to scream in protest, to release a sound of grief and rage—but no sound came out. *I'm a fish! I'm a giant fish!* She flapped her tail, swirling madly in the water.

She tried to calm herself by remembering the Capricorn. The Capricorn, too, could shape-shift into a fish when it went into the ocean. Surely, if Hannah made her way to land, she could turn back into a human.

But how to find land? Hannah thought about the Aquarius poem and tried to think of any clues she might have missed, but she couldn't make any more sense of it. She tried to dredge up some sort of fish intuition, hoping to get a sense of direction, or at least of land somewhere nearby. Yet she was simply lost. And so she swam aimlessly into the deep.

6: Pisces

Dominic watched the great bird until it vanished. Then, without pausing to think, he raced back into the chamber and stuck his mouth below the ram fountain. He swallowed a few mouthfuls of water and heaved himself into the large glazed tub.

He was still crawling over the edge when he felt a creeping sense of alarm. The still-throbbing scorpion sting, the restless pounding of his heart—those symptoms were forgotten as Dominic was overcome by an intense strangeness. He belly churned. His body seemed to buzz with some new, foreign signal. *I'm changing!* Dominic thought, and for some reason he felt certain that he was going to change into some kind of other creature—much like the Capricorn had changed from goat to fish.

He reeled with panic. He wished he hadn't swallowed the water. Whatever was happening to him, it was too much for him to endure.

But it was too late. The giant, noisy bird had returned. Its burning eyes fixed on him; its gleaming talons reached for his shoulders. Dominic hunched his body into a ball, but the creature grabbed him by the waist of his pants and lifted off into the air.

Dominic tried in vain to clutch the bird's feathery leg. He was being raised high above the ground—but the change in his body was more terrifying than the heights. An unpleasant buzzing sound filled his ears. Closing his eyes, Dominic gagged and retched, tried to eject the strange water from his body. It was no use. He felt as if he was suffocating. The air burned his lungs, and he could get no relief from it. His arms and legs seemed to turn to liquid. He was in such a terrible state that he didn't even realize the bird had dropped him.

Dominic was a fish by the time he hit the water.

At last he could breathe. His panic slowly began to subside. The buzzing faded to blessed silence. Dominic felt so much better that when he realized he'd become a fish, he was not quite as upset as one might imagine.

Not at first, anyway. But after his breathing was steady and he felt somewhat relaxed, he started to become aware of the great watery emptiness around him. He became aware of the fact that he had lost his own body—and that he couldn't swim very well in his new, unfamiliar, scaly gray-green body.

Dread overtook him. How could he be a fish? Where was his own body? Where were his arms and legs? He couldn't be a fish. He wanted his own body back—not this strange fish body! He had to get out of it!

If there had been any other fish looking on, they surely would have been puzzled by Dominic's bizarre antics. He thrashed in a frenzy, darting this way and that, flailing his fins. It was only when Dominic exhausted himself that he finally ceased the strange behavior. He lingered there, dazed, and was trying to regain his senses when he noticed another fish in the distance.

This other fish was about the same size as him, and the same color. It was female—he could sense it somehow, and he sensed even more than that. The fish was Hannah. Dominic was sure of it. How he could have recognized her in such a form, he didn't know, but she seemed to recognize him too, and began to swim in his direction.

It was then that Dominic saw a dark shadow moving amongst the depths. The outline of a great creature was approaching. In his sudden alarm, Dominic tried to call out to Hannah—but he was a fish. He didn't know how to alert Hannah of any possible danger. He hadn't even gotten the hang of swimming. The monstrous figure emerged from shadow, and Dominic could see the details of its giant head: a large mouth, wide enough to swallow a hundred fishes in one gulp; a glaring red eye that burned through the dim light; a bloated, elongated body covered in barnacles, and all kinds of sucker fishes scattered haphazardly over its scarred and mottled flesh. Dominic saw the mouth opening, watched the creature cutting fast through the water toward Hannah. She swam directly across its path.

Dominic reeled with alarm. But he was a fish! A helpless, bumbling creature who didn't know the first thing about being a fish. He swam toward Hannah, as if to protect her, but what could he do? The great mouth opened, and in a second the creature glided past him, and Dominic bumped uselessly against its long body. He saw some of the sucker fish looking back at him lazily. He, too, tried to grip the monster, but in this he was again helpless. Another few seconds and he was left far behind, searching the vast ocean for signs of Hannah.

It was her! It was! Had the creature swallowed her? Had Dominic gone to such lengths to find her, only to lose her again? And what now—how to chase after her, in such an awkward, unfamiliar form, and with no hints or enigmas to solve?

He swam onward, trying to follow the creature, but all seemed in vain. Its currents quickly vanished, and once again Dominic faced the bare loneliness of the deep.

Hannah had never known such darkness. It seemed almost to have a material feel to it. She tried to swim within the belly of the sea monster, but felt strangely smothered by the movement. She couldn't feel the flap of her tail, couldn't sense the currents around it. Was she still a fish? Or had she, too, become a dark nothingness?

Time passed without any change. Hannah could not swim—not that she was aware of—and could see nothing, hear nothing, feel nothing. She was alone and helpless with only her thoughts to occupy her. How long would it last? Where was the next enigma? Had she failed, and become hopelessly trapped?

I've been eaten by the sea monster Cetus, she thought fearfully. Cetus, the ravenous water-creature who swallowed unfortunate human beings, represented everything that humanity feared in the deep unknown. Hannah could think of no way to escape it. She didn't have the slightest clue.

Hours crept by while Hannah waited in tormented helplessness. The stifling darkness was maddening. Hannah even tried to close her eyes against it—but were they already closed? At first she couldn't tell the difference, but after some time she began to imagine that she could see fuzzy, muted colors before her. *Hallucinations*, she thought bitterly, and her thoughts fixed on Dominic. She had seen him out in the ocean, in the form of another fish—and recognized him instantly, as if through some extraordinary bond. He, too, had known her. Hannah had not the smallest doubt of that. She could detect his thoughts, and had even sensed a state of panic in him just before she saw the monster coming. By then it was too late. The creature's mouth had been too large, its speed too fast.

And then everything was darkness, and Hannah had no way of knowing Dominic's fate. Had the monster swallowed him, too? Or was he still wandering that vast, empty ocean?

It happened that the ocean was not entirely unpopulated. First, of course, Dominic had come across

the monster and its many tag-alongs. Eventually, as he
drew into the warmer waters, he saw smatterings of
scraggly plants and tiny fish. Abruptly the underwater
world exploded with life.

Countless figures moved within the sea. Dominic was
awed by the multitude of strange faces that looked back
at him. In his midst were creatures with round, flat arms
that moved wave-like through the waters, soaring
through the currents much as birds flew through currents
of air. Giant turtles flapped their long flipper-like legs
while fish ate the algae from their shells. All kinds of
creatures moved along the ocean's bottom—and
everything was alive, from the smallest plant to the
strangest animal. Dominic had never seen such a lively
city. Its buildings and grasses were all sentient; they
responded to his movements as he passed by, curling
away or leaning close. When he looked up, he was
astonished to see a giant school of fish moving overhead.
There were hundreds of them, at least—perhaps
thousands—floating past in a giant living cloud. Ahead
was a stretch of coral in varying forms, blazing with
color in the intensifying light. The water felt
increasingly warm, and the daylight became more
illuminating; Dominic sensed that he was getting closer
to land and didn't particularly care.

The trial had become an adventure. Dominic's
discomfort was displaced by a sense of awe. He had
never expected that the sea could contain such wondrous
beauty, could be so fully inhabited as this. He poked his
face curiously into various plants, sometimes realizing
with a shock that the plant was actually an animal, or
that it hid fascinating life forms within its furls. The ease
of the underwater community was occasionally
interrupted; the life forms sometimes preyed on one
another, after all, and Dominic felt relieved to be such a
large fish that he could escape the mouths of others.

But a more dangerous predator sent even the larger fish scurrying. All at once, Dominic saw the others racing past him in alarm—and he didn't have to use any kind of fish intuition to know what had frightened them. He saw quite clearly, in the illuminated water, the figure of an oncoming shark, its mouth opened to reveal rows of gleaming triangular teeth.

Suddenly Dominic's fish body seemed less clumsy. He swam alongside the others with speedy precision, driven by pure instinct. The shark was coming up behind him. It seemed so unreal all of a sudden, so bizarre and so unfair. He could not die this way.

I'm not even a fish! he thought desperately.

He tried to save himself through the full memory his existence as a man. He had crawled into this strange world as a man. He had . . . he had come here with a girl.

Hannah! How could he have forgotten her? He was supposed to be looking for Hannah, and instead he'd forgotten himself—too busy indulging in being a fish!

Dominic shot into the shallow waters alongside the other, smaller fishes. Even when he thought that the water wasn't deep enough for the shark to follow, he still sensed that fatal mouth full of razor-sharp teeth following close behind. Dominic swam until the air touched his dorsal fin and his belly scraped the sand, and even then he struggled onward, driven by a desperate urge for survival that he no longer understood. Even when he beached himself on the sand and flopped madly into the harsh air, he knew he must go on—*because I am a man, and not a fish!* The air tormented his lungs. Sand stuck to his eyes, obscuring his vision. He writhed and flopped madly.

And it happened again: the loud buzzing in his ears, the unbearable pain. Such a strange and terrible process that Dominic cried out—and when he did, he heard his own voice.

Slowly he began to feel sensation in his arms and legs. He blinked the sand from his watering eyes. When he could see again, he found himself lying on his back and looking up at the sky, and he lifted his arms in hopeful anticipation.

"Ah," he breathed, staring with immense relief at his own hands.

The transformation had so exhausted him that he could only lie there in the sand, letting his arms flop down by his sides.

Dominic turned his head so that he looked out over the sea. He watched the waves crashing against the shore. How different everything looked from here—especially now that he was a man again! His adventures in the deep waters now seemed distant and alien, nothing more than a vivid dream.

He tried to make sense of all that had happened. Thinking over his journey, some of the Capricorn's words came back to him: *They've forgotten that they, too, once lived in the sea and breathed its waters. . . .*

Was Hannah still swimming in those waters? Had she met some terrible fate in the belly of the monster? Or had she, too, washed up onto shore, and become human again?

Tired as he was, Dominic knew that he had to look for her. He heaved himself onto his feet and searched the horizon. Inland, he saw nothing but a flat expanse of sand and dirt—and then, in the distance, two objects that looked like small houses.

Houses, probably with people living in them, he reasoned. Perhaps someone had seen Hannah. Perhaps she had even taken shelter there.

Dominic wrung out his shirt. He hitched up his soaked jeans to keep them from sinking toward his knees; and, holding his waistband and willing himself onward, Dominic staggered away from the sea.

Vague forms began to take shape in the darkness.
Every time Hannah thought she saw color springing
from some place or another, she riveted her gaze on that
spot, hoping to see something that would lead her back
to safety. As the indistinct smears became more vivid,
she began to recognize the blurred figures of her camp
leaders, and of the other girls.

Hannah looked away from the specters. She didn't
want to think about camp. But now that she had so little
to occupy her attention, she couldn't help remembering
how miserable it had been.

First there was the fire duty mix-up. All the girls
wanted to be on fire duty because it was easy and fun.
The camp leaders always picked their favorite girls for
it. Hannah was surprised when she saw that she had been
chosen—but when she was finished with the work, the
camp leaders scolded her for not doing her own chores.
She hadn't been chosen for fire duty after all. She had
simply read the chart wrong, and robbed another girl of
her rightful task. The other girls accused Hannah of
trying to "sneak" the best chores for herself.

Nothing that Hannah did turned out right. The gumbo
that the girls cooked for lunch gave her indigestion.
After eating her lunch alone, she tried to talk to one of
the nicer girls—but when she opened her mouth to say
"hello," a great big belch came out instead.

And then there was Mona. Hannah could see her there
in the darkness, staring back at her with a ghostly smile.
Mona was small and loud, and always said mean things
to Hannah. When the girls gathered around the bonfire to
sing, Hannah had never hesitated to sing along with
everyone else—but Mona put a stop to that.

On Thursday evening they'd been singing together as
usual. Hannah intentionally stood behind Mona, hoping
that Mona wouldn't see her. But Karla, Mona's friend,

noticed her and whispered in Mona's ear. Then they both
turned to Hannah and smirked.

After a few minutes Mona turned around again, her
face pinched up with disgust. She made a show of
putting her hands over her ears. "Don't sing so loud right
in my ears," she said to Hannah—loudly, so that the girls
around them could hear. "Your voice sounds like a
banshee."

At the word "banshee," Karla's smile got so wide that
her missing teeth showed, and she covered her mouth
with both hands. The other girls looked uncomfortable
and kept singing.

After that, Hannah was afraid to sing out loud. If the
camp leaders noticed that she wasn't singing, they would
make all kinds of gestures at her, and mouth the word:
Sing! So Hannah moved her lips and pretended to sing
along.

At dinner, Hannah had to serve food to the other girls.
When she dropped a spoonful of macaroni onto Mona's
plate, Mona looked down at Hannah's hand with disgust.
"Look at Hannah's hands!" she exclaimed. "Her fingers
are all fat and rubbery. They don't even look real."

Gwen, the nice girl, was working beside Hannah. She
turned and looked down at Hannah's hand—but Hannah
quickly withdrew it, hiding it behind the casserole pan.

"They look fine," Gwen replied calmly.

"You can't even see her knuckles," Mona retorted.
"Her fingers just look like sausages with fingernails at
the ends."

Karla stuck her plate out in front of Hannah. Again,
Hannah had to expose her hand. Karla recoiled with
exaggerated disgust at the sight of it.

Gwen frowned at Mona and didn't say anything. When
Mona and Karla were gone, she continued to be polite.
She was always nice—even after Hannah had belched in
her face.

But when Hannah was leaving the kitchen, she ran into Mona and Karla again. Mona smirked at her and said: "Gwen is just being nice to you because she feels sorry for you. Is that the only way you can make friends?"

Hannah could still see the image of Mona there in the darkness, becoming bolder and more detailed. It sneered mockingly; its eyes shone with ridicule. Hannah still couldn't close her eyes, and so she lifted her hands to cover them—and there they were! She could feel both of her hands now. She wasn't a fish anymore! She was a girl!

Her excitement was dampened by the Mona figure. It looked at those hands with such disgust that Hannah immediately hid them behind her back.

She tried to turn away. She was tired of thinking about camp. Thinking about it wouldn't change anything. But when Hannah turned, she saw more figures—more people staring at her.

The images of her schoolmates swirled to life. There were so many people there—kids, and then teachers, and people from town. The clearest figure was Annabelle Thompson. Hannah could see her tightly braided hair and nervous eyes, and could even make out the faded flower print on her pleated dress. Hannah had met Annabelle after she moved in with her first foster family; she'd had to change schools, and Annabelle was in two of her classes. She was quiet and timid, and always smiled at Hannah when she saw her. Hannah thought that they might become friends.

But she didn't think that for long. Even now, Hannah could see the cloudy images of other children turning to Annabelle and looking at her with disdain. One of the boys opened his mouth and silently spoke the word: *scrub.*

That's what the other kids called Annabelle. Her braided hair always looked greasy, and her clothes were worn and full of holes. The kids called her a "scrub" because she looked like she needed a good scrub with soap. They told all kinds of strange stories about Annabelle's house. They said that Annabelle's parents were too poor to pay their water bills, and that they pooped in jars because they couldn't afford to use the toilet, and that they had a room that was full of jars of poop.

Hannah was pleased that she had learned a new word. She, too, began making use of the term "scrub"—and there in the dark she could see her own form among the others, looking at Annabelle and mouthing the accusatory word: *Scrub.*

Hannah saw the clear, vivid sadness in Annabelle's eyes. She felt ashamed of herself. Watching her own image, she thought: *I am just as bad as everyone else.*

The other Hannah continued to move her mouth silently. Her face scrunched up with meanness. All the other apparitions were watching the other Hannah now—that cruel, belching, clumsy, stupid Hannah with a weird voice and ugly, rubbery hands. And there were still more figures, truly frightening ones that she remembered from her past.

Desperately, Hannah searched the ghostly faces for a kind one. Where was Gwen? Or Carmina, or Andy, or one of her nice teachers? Where was her father?

Hannah tried to focus on thoughts of her father. He was living in a nursing home a hundred and fifty miles away from her. Now that it was summer, Hannah could visit him sometimes. She could almost see him, here in the dark; he was sitting in his wheelchair, and one of the nursing home staff was helping him eat. Hannah would walk up to him and say "Hi, Daddy," and hold his hand if he was in a good mood.

Some of the kids at school said mean things about him. They sneered and laughed, saying that he'd been in an

accident because he was a drunk. It wasn't true—but
even if it had been, what a cruel thing to smile at! The
taunting words hurt Hannah so badly that she had to shut
her feelings down completely to keep from bursting into
tears. She would wait quietly, not looking at or speaking
to anyone, and when she was alone in her room she
would cry for a long time. She liked to fantasize about
the day when she would be old enough to drive. She
only had five years left. Then she could get into her car,
drive out where no one could see her, and cry as much as
she wanted. She could wail and sob until she was
exhausted, and then go back home with a pair of
sunglasses covering her swollen eyes. No one would
judge her then. No one would ask questions. They
wouldn't even know.

Another phantom was materializing before her. It
flashed muted colors and slowly took shape, coming
together in the form of Hannah's mother. She was
wearing a red blouse with little black flowers and a short
black skirt. Hannah remembered that outfit. She could
see her mother wearing it the night that two of her
friends had come over for dinner. The friends were
professional photographers. Hannah could almost see
them, too, like vague phantoms exchanging silent words
with her mother in an invisible dining room. She
remembered them clearly. They told her mother that
Hannah had a "unique" look, and that they wanted to do
a photo session with her. She could have a portfolio and
perhaps become a child model.

Hannah didn't want to model. When the photographers
were gone, she told her mother that she wouldn't pose
for the pictures. Her mother begged, but Hannah kept
refusing. Her mother was furious.

Whenever Hannah's mother was furious with her, she
had a certain thing that she did: she insisted that Hannah
needed to "run some errands" with her. Then, when they

were in the car, she would scream at Hannah and say all the things that she couldn't say when other people were listening.

Now, Hannah could see the apparition's lips moving. Though there was no sound, Hannah could read the furious words on the phantom mother's lips: *You will never get another chance like this. They didn't even say you were pretty; they said you were 'unique looking.' That's like saying that you're weird looking, and who else is going to give this kind of chance to a weird looking girl? Especially one who dresses the way you do? I try and try to teach you how to have a sense of dress, and you can't even take the trouble to comb your hair. Oh, you'd rather play softball and do gymnastics? I'm the one who pays for those things, and I'll tell you what: I'm not enrolling you in softball or gymnastics or any other sport, ever again. Not after this. I already told the people at work that my daughter is doing a photo shoot. What am I going to tell them now? They'll think I lied. They'll think I'm just trying to cover up the fact that I have a homely daughter. . . .*

Hannah felt a hollow spot working its way into her heart—a wide, empty abyss that she felt every time her mother said these things to her. She began to hear those harsh words clearly in her mind. The tirade went on, loud and uncensored, as if all the stress and frustration her mother had accumulated over the week was being unloaded onto her daughter. The hateful words tumbled into the abyss and vanished there; Hannah could pretend that they were gone, that they couldn't hurt her. She would sit, stone-faced, and show her mother that she wouldn't react to those heartless words. Usually, she could stay that way until nighttime. Then, when she was lying in bed and thinking about her troubles, the words would float up from the depths, and Hannah would bury her head under her blankets and cry.

But on this occasion she hadn't been able to hold back the tears. Her mother's debasement went on for so long that Hannah broke down. She sobbed openly, wiping at the flood of tears that spilled down her face. The errands were finished, and her mother finally had to drop her off at gymnastics class. She parked outside the school and admonished Hannah for crying. She asked: *What are people going to think when they see that you've been crying like a baby?* Hannah wiped her face and went into the school, but her teachers could see that she was crying. Tears kept rolling down her face, and when one of the gymnastics teachers took her into a private room and asked what had happened, Hannah burst into another fit of sobs that lasted the entire hour.

The teacher had been kind. What was her name? Hannah couldn't remember now, and it seemed strange that she could forget. The teacher had hugged Hannah and spoken comforting words. Through her grief Hannah tried to explain what had happened.

At the end of the hour, when Hannah's mother returned to pick her up, the teacher marched Hannah outside. She walked up to the car with an angry face. *Your daughter has been crying for the past hour*, she said, and then she yelled at Hannah's mother for all the things she'd said. How could any mother speak that way to an eight-year-old?

Hannah's mother was pale and quiet. Finally, she murmured, "She's exaggerating, and it's none of your business."

Hannah got in the car. Her mother yelled at her for speaking truthfully to the teacher. This is what Hannah continued to see: shouting, anger, disgust. Hannah was making her mother look bad. Hannah was an embarrassment. Mona and Karla re-appeared with taunting smiles: Hannah is a bad singer. She has a voice like a banshee. Hannah is a disappointment. She doesn't

have any rightful place in the world. It's no wonder that
Hannah was banished away to some strange world; her
own world doesn't want her. She doesn't belong there.
Even this strange new world doesn't want her—it has
already cast her out, into the same dark abyss where she
tried to banish all her sorrows! Those feelings had never
disappeared, but accumulated here in the pit—and
Hannah would vanish with them into nothing, swallowed
forever by the darkness. Hannah had fallen into the hole
in her own heart.

She buried her face in her lap and wrapped her arms
tightly around her head. She willed the apparitions to go
away. She felt sick and uncomfortable, and wished that
her body would vanish again—that her feelings would
vanish with it. *Why am I stuck here?* she wondered
despairingly. *I must have been here for days, and there's
no end, and no way out. I must be in hell. I must deserve
to be here.*

But what about the Capricorn? It claimed that there
was no past and future in its perspective, and it didn't
seem to have foreseen Hannah's demise. Surely, if it
had, it would have at least dropped a hint of warning.
And the poem on the chamber wall—had it spoken of
this ordeal? Had it mentioned Cetus, the great sea
monster?

Keepers of the mystery
toss about within the sea;
victorious becomes that youth
sprung forth in beauty and in truth.

Hannah pondered those words. They were a clue, to be
certain. How to spring forth in beauty and truth? She
considered that for some time, but didn't know what to
do. Her belly started to hurt from being crushed against
her legs. Hannah uncurled herself and looked up.

The Mona figure was sneering at her from the darkness. *The Capricorn isn't real, dummy! And even if it was, you wouldn't be able to understand anything it said!*

Hannah ducked her head again. Even with her eyes closed, she could still see the apparitions taunting her. She blocked them out by focusing on the poem.

And then she saw it: the answer to the enigma.

"Ketos," she whispered. She remembered the Capricorn's story: *Have you heard the story of Ketos, the eater of lies?*

In the Aquarius chamber, Hannah been talking to Dominic about transliterations. In the Latin spellings of Greek names, the 'o' sound was usually changed to 'u'—and though she hadn't mentioned it, she knew that the 'k' usually changed to 'c'. *Ketos* and *Cetus* were certainly different forms of the same name. In the poem, the words 'keepers' and 'toss' began with *ke* and *tos*. It wasn't a coincidence—it couldn't be! But, what to do with it? What else had the Capricorn said?

They made up stories about a great monster that ate little children who didn't talk. . . . Eventually, Ketos was so swollen from the lies that she reached her breaking point. She opened her mouth and, all at once, she began to vomit all those lies back into the world around her. And the lies came out as truth.

But how?

Hannah looked at the image of Mona, still standing phantom-like among the other apparitions. She remembered Mona's harsh words: *Your voice sounds like a banshee. . . .*

Lies, Hannah thought. Surely those were lies. There was nothing wrong with her voice, or with her hands. Something else was making Mona say those things.

Even though Mona wasn't in the same grade as Hannah, Hannah often saw her—in the hallways at school, at camp, in town. Mona's father owned a gift shop. He was a loud, red-faced man, talkative and sociable, but quick-tempered. Hannah remembered a time when she'd been in the gift shop and Mona had come in. When her father saw her, he took her into a back room and shouted at her. He yelled so loudly that everyone in the store heard what he said. He was upset because the school principal had called him; Mona kept forgetting to bring her gym clothes to school, and so she repeatedly had to sit out during gym class, and she was getting a poor grade. Mona's father asked her why she was so dumb that she couldn't do the simplest things. He told her he was sick of having to make excuses for her. The customers looked surprised, embarrassed, concerned—but no one said anything. When Mona came out of the room, her face was red and she had tears in her eyes. People ducked their heads and didn't look at her. Hannah hid behind a shelf so that Mona wouldn't know she was there. Mona left the store with her shoulders slumped and her head drooping.

Mona had a younger brother who was in Hannah's grade. He was bigger than his sister, and meaner. Every time he saw his sister in the hallway, he told her she was dumb and ugly, and called her "monkey face."

Fine, Hannah thought, *maybe she's mean because she gets picked on, but what about other people? Grown-ups have no excuse, and kids with nice parents don't have any excuse.* She frowned at the circle of faces that peered back at her from the dark. There were kids from school, laughing mockingly; grown-ups who looked down at her with scorn; people who only pretended to be nice when they wanted something; scary people who did horrible things. And Annabelle! She was still standing there with her worn clothes and sad eyes. Hannah focused on her with sympathy. She had told lies about Annabelle. She hadn't forgotten the things she'd said behind the girl's back.

"You're not a scrub, Annabelle," she said. "You're a girl, and I'm sorry that I ever used that word, and that I didn't stick up for you."

The words may have been genuine, but they didn't do anything to free Hannah. She was still trapped in the darkness, surrounded by phantoms.

The image of Mona sneered at her. Without a sound, it mouthed the words: *See, you're not smart enough to figure anything out. You don't even mean it. You're just saying nice things to help yourself, and you're showing everyone that your voice sounds like a banshee voice.*

Hannah's voice trembled as she spoke: "I don't sound like a banshee."

To prove it, she decided to sing. It took her a few moments to think of a song. She almost chose one that she'd learned at camp, but then she remembered Dominic's song. And she remembered all the stories she'd heard about the great sea monster. Andromeda was saved by Perseus, and Hesione by Heracles, before Cetus could swallow them—but no one was going to rescue Hannah. There was Odysseus' crew in *The Odyssey*, Professor Aronnax and his friends held prisoner inside the *Nautilus*. Pinocchio and Geppetto. Jonah and the whale. After Jonah had been swallowed up, he, too, had offered up a song of thanks.

Although Hannah didn't know the words, she sang anyway: "I have nothing to give, except my voice. When I can't find care and love . . . kindness is my choice. Even when the world looks dark, I have everything I need."

She sang slowly, trying to make the words clear and melodious. She imagined that her voice sounded rather pretty, here in the gentle darkness, without other noises to drown it out. It didn't sound like a banshee at all. She hummed and felt the vibration of her voice moving through her body.

The fuzzy apparitions sneered. Mona and Karla covered their ears in disgust. Hannah looked directly at them and sang the song again.

7: Aries

Tired and unsteady as Dominic was, he felt good about being able to walk on his own legs again. He wobbled his way inland, never stopping until he came to a wire fence covered with sharp metal barbs.

The fence itself wasn't what stopped him. He could have fit between the wires easily, without catching himself on the barbs. What stopped him was the sight of a large animal lying motionless on the ground. It was a ram, covered in curling golden-brown fleece, lying just inside the boundary.

Upon closer inspection Dominic saw that the animal was alive. As he stood over it, it moved its eye and locked gazes with him. The ram had a startlingly tired and gentle gaze, without the slightest trace of fear. Its large, curving horns were covered with ridges, and its shaggy golden wool was dirty and matted from rubbing against the ground. The wire was twisted around one of the ram's hind legs. Metal barbs pierced its flesh. Dominic could see that the animal had tried to struggle free, to no avail. Around the wire were raw, open wounds, crusted over with blood.

"Poor thing," Dominic muttered. He slowly reached out a hand. The ram looked at him with those soft eyes and didn't move.

"All right, buddy, I'm going to see if I can pull this loose," Dominic said, "so don't start kicking at me." He gripped both ends of the wire, placing his fingers carefully between the barbs, and pulled them toward one another. He made a little bit of slack, but it wasn't quite enough. Dominic pulled harder. The barbs began to dig into his flesh. His fingers bled, but he pulled and pulled until he could finally slide the wire out from around the leg.

"Ah, there." Dominic pushed the wire aside. He stood with his bleeding hands on his hips and looked the ram up and down. "What now? You think you can stand up?"

The animal just laid there, looking at him.

Dominic carefully separated the wires and stepped between them, so that he stood beside the ram. He leaned over and petted its head. The ram closed its eyes, rubbing its muzzle against Dominic's hand.

"I suppose I can go and get some help for you," Dominic mused, gazing at the farmhouse in the distance. He thought of Hannah, all alone and probably frightened, and muttered: "Since I can't do anything else of use."

The ram began to move its legs. It lifted its head from the dirt and scraped its hooves into the earth helplessly.

"Hang on," Dominic said, "Let's see if I can give you a hand." He walked around the ram and pushed his hands under its ribs. His fingers slid into the matted fleece, and he pulled with all his might, trying to heave the animal off the ground. Together they struggled. The ram managed to lift itself into a crouch, and Dominic turned his back, bracing himself against the goat's flank and pushing his feet into the ground.

When the animal finally stood, it looked rather majestic. Its serene eyes glowed, and it carried itself with an air of strength despite its wounds. Dominic leaned against it, panting from his efforts. The two of them took some time to regain their bearings; then the ram started across the field, with Dominic walking alongside.

Even as the ram hobbled and bled, Dominic found

himself unable to feel pity. Its wool, filthy as it was, shone brilliantly in the light. The horns curled gracefully around its dignified head. And those eyes! So full of sentiment, they looked almost human—perhaps more than human. Looking into them, Dominic was reminded of a greyhound he'd had as a child. She was a retired racing dog, of the same meek and grateful manner as this ram; she was always looking at Dominic with such love and trust in her eyes that it was sometimes a shock to look at her. Would a human being ever look at him in such a beautiful way? Certainly not. The gaze of humanity was far too complex, never pure and simple like the love of a dog.

Every once in a while the ram would turn its head aside, looking at Dominic with those soft eyes, gently nudging him with its muzzle. If Dominic stumbled, the ram stopped and leaned toward him a bit, as if to give him support. Dominic gratefully accepted the help. After a time he could hardly walk without supporting himself against the ram's ribs, and was fully leaning on the animal when the two of them arrived at the house. The second building looked like a barn, and in its doorway stood a figure that filled Dominic with awe.

Finally, he thought, *a human being!*

An old woman stood gaping at them. She was tall and lean, with grey hair piled wildly above her head, and her face seemed hard and leathery. Hanging loose over her body was a faded dress, and a fringed shawl was draped around the shoulders; and below the light, worn clothing was a pair of thick brown boots. The woman looked from one visitor to the other—Dominic stumbling along in his wet clothes, the ram limping on its crimson leg. Then she let out a low, dry chuckle. Her eyes brightened. "What a pair!" she exclaimed.

"This your ram?" Dominic replied weakly. "His leg got tangled . . . ."

"The fence, wasn't it? That fence is always a problem, but it keeps the scavengers out. And what about you, young man, what did *you* get tangled in?"

"The ocean." Dominic sank to the ground as he spoke, too exhausted to stand any longer.

"Ah, of course. I see how it is." The woman greeted the ram tenderly, petting it around the ears and along its muzzle. "You just stand here a minute," she told the ram gently, "and I'll tend to that leg, but let me put this other one at ease first." She gestured for Dominic to get up. "Come on, young man. Get inside the house. I'll find you some dry clothes and show you to a bed."

The little house and barn sat in solitude upon a flat patch of land, almost bare of bush or tree, with a cornfield rising some distance away. Near the house were scattered several garden patches and one lush apple tree, and beside the barn was a water well circled round with bricks, and a long wooden coop full of dozing chickens, and a small outhouse. The house itself looked neat and cozy. The walls were rough wood, hung with tins and knives and all kinds of tools. There was one small bedroom, barely bigger than the bed it contained, and an open linen closet; and in the main room was a large fireplace with a stone hearth. It was in the main room that the old woman set up a place for Dominic to sleep. In the corner was a straw mat. The woman bundled woolen blankets over it to make it soft, and another blanket for snuggling into.

When she was finished, she stood and looked Dominic up and down. "Hmm. I don't have any clothes small enough to fit you," she said, frowning, "but . . . let's see what I can throw together."

She disappeared into the little bedroom and returned with a white sheet. "I found this," she said. "It's a tablecloth, but it'll do until your clothes get dry. Just tie it around yourself."

Dominic took the cloth in his hands and stared at it.

"Don't you mind how you look in it," the woman added. "You'll soon be asleep anyway, and your clothes will likely be dry by the time you wake."

"Thanks," Dominic replied without enthusiasm.

"I'll go and tend to the animal. When you're dressed, just set your wet things on the porch, and I'll hang them for you." She walked briskly out the door.

Muttering, Dominic pulled off his wet clothes and tried to decide how to best use the tablecloth. He wrapped it around his body and tied two corners together over his shoulder, like a toga. Looking down at his ridiculous state of dress, he was glad that there wasn't a mirror in the room to bear his reflection—but he wasn't embarrassed for long. He tossed his wet clothes onto the porch and settled into the wool blankets, and within minutes he sank into a deep sleep.

Dominic woke some time later to the sounds of a crackling fire. Drowsily, he pushed himself upright. The old woman was bent over the flames, busying herself at some task. The firelight sent shadows dancing madly around the room. The sole window was uncovered, and through it Dominic saw that the daylight seemed to have faded. He had never seen a sun in this world. Did it rise and set here, and keep time, as it did in his own world?

"Is it . . . is it evening?" he asked thickly.

The old woman looked up, laughing at the sight of his sleepy demeanor. "It is. You've slept the day through. And how did you come to be here, young man? I suppose you was shipwrecked. Ay, it happens a lot 'round these parts—lots of shipwrecks and lost souls."

"I was a fish," he replied weakly.

The woman narrowed her eyes. "What's that? You were a-fishin'?"

"No . . . I turned into a fish."

She stared at him with bemusement. "Sure you did."

Pointing to the fire, she added: "There's a stew boiling. It'll be ready for eating soon. It will do you some good to get food in your stomach, and then we can talk."

The mention of food made Dominic realize how hungry he was. His belly ached with emptiness, and his mouth began to water so much that it hurt. "Sure," he replied, and rolled back into the blankets.

Then he remembered Hannah. He shot back into a sitting position. "There was a girl with me," he told the woman. "Have you seen her?"

"Haven't seen anyone but you," she replied shortly.

"She was out in the ocean . . . ."

"Well, she's likely to turn up in a few days. Most people do."

Dominic got to his feet with some difficulty. Re-tying the cloth over his shoulder, he walked across to the window and stared out toward the sea. The pale dirt seemed to stretch on and on into the horizon. He couldn't see where the plain ended and the sandy beach began, or even where the rolling waves touched the shore.

"Most people do?" he repeated uncertainly.

"Sure, in two or three days, I imagine."

"It's usual for people to wash up out of the ocean?"

"Sure."

"But not so usual for people to turn into fish?"

The woman gave him a queer look and didn't answer. She poked at the fire and sent bits of ash flying onto the hearth.

A metal rod stretched over the fireplace from side to side, bearing the weight of two charred cooking pots that hung by crescent handles. The smaller pot sat in the middle, its bottom licked by flames. Steam wafted from its rim and sent out a savory smell that filled the room. Dominic couldn't resist taking a closer look. The pot had a spout in one side for pouring, and as Dominic peered past it, he saw that the stew was bubbling wildly.

"Shouldn't be long now," the woman assured him. "Ah, you look a sight in that tablecloth! And to think of all the times I ate from the top of it!"

Dominic recoiled, suddenly embarrassed. The cloth was so comfortable, so soft and loose around his figure, that he had forgotten how ridiculous he must look.

"Why don't you rest a bit more?" the woman asked, waving him away. "You look like you could use it."

Dominic retreated to the straw mat with its heap of blankets. When the stew was finished, the old woman poured it into a large kettle. Then she filled the other pot with water and pushed it over the fire. Dominic felt that he should help her, but he was in such a cozy state of recovery that he could hardly stir from it. He watched as the woman set the kettle on the bare wooden table and laid out two sets of dishes. She let the stew cool in two ceramic bowls. Then there was sliced bread with butter, and two cups of fresh water—and at last the woman entreated Dominic to put his dry clothes on and come to dinner. Soon he was comfortably dressed in his own things, filling his belly with the flavorful stew and sweet buttered bread, enjoying the feelings of a satisfied mouth and belly.

The woman didn't seem to believe his story. When he talked of being snatched up by a giant bird, she narrowed her eyes as if to study him more acutely, and didn't say much in reply. She simply murmured: "Hm. Mighty peculiar."

"You live out here alone?" Dominic asked. "It seems a long way from anything."

"A long way from anything! Everything I need is gathered around me. But I suppose it seems lonely to someone who's used to being around people. I did have a man to keep me company—a very good one. Of course, he died."

The woman had finished her meal. She sprang from the table like an eager youth, taking two large, coiled objects from the fireplace mantle and studying them with satisfaction. "Ram horns make fine flutes," she said. "I guillotined the one you brought back and took the meat. He makes a fine stew, doesn't he?"

Dominic choked in mid-swallow, spraying a mouthful of stew across the table.

"What's the matter?" the old woman cackled.

"What? You did what?"

"Ah, I see. You got attached to him, did you?" She laughed again, seeming to enjoy the pained expression on Dominic's face.

"You killed my ram?" Dominic felt his eyes stinging with sudden tears. He remembered the ram's meek round eyes, its trust of him, the softness of its muzzle against his hand.

"Oh, he's *your* ram, is he?" She rose and tossed the horns into the boiling water, poking them about with the ladle. "And there's more to him than that. I dried the other cuts while you were asleep."

Dominic watched her with a growing sense of horror. "Are those his horns?" he asked, staring at the pot. Those horns, so beautifully sculpted and finely shaped— were those really the horns of his ram? How could the woman have butchered him to such an extent? Had Dominic really slept that long?

"Lovely, aren't they?" the woman replied. "They'll make a good sound, I'm sure."

Dominic pushed the bowl away. The mouth-watering scent of the stew now seemed repugnant.

The woman asked eyed the bowl as she returned to the table. "Lost your appetite?"

"Yes."

"Well, don't let it go to waste. Go out and feed it to the chickens."

Dominic recoiled at the thought of feeding that lovely ram to a bunch of chickens. On the other hand, he didn't want the food to go to waste—especially not out here, where there seemed to be so little food.

He trudged out to the coop and found several chickens running around freely. They pranced about his feet, snatching so greedily at him that he didn't dare lower his dish to the ground for fear of having his hands pecked. He flung the stew away instead, so that the chickens turned and ran after it. He couldn't watch them eat. Dominic lifted his eyes toward the barn—and there was the terrible instrument! A primitive-looking guillotine, its gleaming metal blade scrubbed clean and hoisted back to the top of the shaft. Beside the well was the butcher's block, also thoroughly washed. Dominic shuddered and hurried back to the house.

Now that he was fed and rested, the woman bade Dominic to make himself useful. He cleaned the kitchen and the dishes while the old woman tended to the horns. With a pair of tongs, she drew one of the horns from the boiling water and set it aside to cool.

"Now come over here," she said when Dominic had laid the dishes out to dry, "and I'll show you how to make a ram's flute."

She sat and worked on the horn with her thin, calloused hands. "See in there—that's the bone," she explained, showing Dominic the fibrous interior of the horn. "You have to get that out of the way." The old woman gripped the bone core with a pliers and pulled. Within seconds, a large fragment of the core broke loose, and the woman pulled it gently from the outer covering. Dominic watched in disturbed fascination as she poked various tools into and around the horn. She tested it to see how much hollow space was inside and drew little markings on the exterior. She stomped one of her thick boots over the horn and sawed it in half, along one of the markings;

then she took up a small mechanical device, a sort of hand-operated drill, and made holes where she'd measured out the spaces with her fingers. For several minutes she toiled, pushing and drilling into the hard material. Then she carved a mouthpiece into the closed end of the horn, where there was still a small layer of bone that needed to be poked through.

The old woman blew bits of debris from the instrument. With her fingertips she covered all the holes but one—and she blew, and sounded a clear, steady note from the horn.

"Pretty neat, isn't it?" she asked Dominic. "It needs some fine tuning. Now, you make the other one."

"Me?"

"No, you," she said, and laughed at her own joke.

She looked on, giving directions while Dominic crafted a flute from the second horn. His reluctance ebbed away. He did the work himself, sawing and pulling, measuring and marking, drilling and carving. Hours passed as he worked by the fire. The old woman was still rubbing and scraping, filing down the spaces around the finger holes. Every once in a while the two of them would play their flutes, testing the sound—and then they might scrape and carve a little bit more, until the music they made was rich and pleasant.

"What an amazing thing," the woman said at last, with a satisfied sigh. "Tough to work with, but what a sweet, soothing sound!" She stood and stretched. "Hard work wears me out. I'm off to bed. Goodnight, young man."

"Thanks, goodnight," Dominic said.

He started toward the straw mat—and thought again of Hannah. During the past few hours, he had practically forgotten her.

Dominic gathered up one of the wool blankets. He went to the rough wooden door and opened it, gazing out into the cold, starless night. *She'll freeze out there,* he thought, wrapping the blanket more tightly around him. He felt guilty for being so comfortable, so warm, so well fed. The effects of the scorpion venom seemed to have subsided. Aside from the fact that he was still in this strange world, Dominic felt normal again. In fact, he couldn't remember the last time he'd felt so good. The stresses of his life were, for the moment, far away and intangible. Hannah was his only worry now.

In spite of his thoughts, he slept easily.

The old woman had more chores for him in the morning. She had sheared most of the ram's body before killing it. A section of the hide had already been scraped on both sides, salted with sea salt, and nailed to the floor on one side of the porch. The hide was stiff and flat by the time she and Dominic pried the nails loose. The woman bade Dominic to soak it in the pot of water, and then to wring it, and then she set it down and showed him how to rub it with lard.

Hesitantly, Dominic asked: "Is it the ram's lard?"

"Oh, some of it, and some of his brains are in there too. It's lard and brains that does the job best."

Dominic felt his stomach heaving. He stood and covered his mouth.

"I'm sorry," he said after a moment, "but I'm not up for this."

She shrugged. "All right, then. Make yourself useful somewhere else."

He set himself to picking and scrubbing vegetables from the gardens. After lunch, he cleaned up the kitchen while the old woman walked the fields and checked on the animals. He drew water from the well and made another repair to the fence.

In the afternoon they cleaned the ram's wool to prepare it for spinning into yarn. Dominic worked late into the evening, handling the coarse fibers with occasional pangs of sorrow. *That beautiful animal! Those sweet, trusting eyes!* Together they picked through the wool and diligently combed it out, until the woman stood with a sigh and announced: "That's enough for today." She cooked up a stew with some bread, and once again Dominic ate the savory meal with gratitude, and once again he rolled onto the straw mat and slept like the dead.

Another morning came. The woman finished treating the fleecy sections of the hide and set them aside to make a pair of warm boots. Then she showed Dominic how to use the bare ram's hide to make the head for a frame drum.

"We'll be quite a duo when it's dry!" she cackled as they fastened the hide around the frame. "You on your flute, and me on the drum. Do you sing?"

"A little."

"Then you can have the drum, and sing with it. You don't want to hear me sing. I have a voice like a banshee!"

After lunch the woman taught Dominic to spin wool with a hand spindle. When he could do the work on his own, she poked about the house, working at other things. Within minutes she had crafted a rattle from the ram's hooves and hung it beside the mantle. Dominic couldn't help looking at it with a mixture of pity and revulsion.

The old woman admonished him: "What are you looking like that for?"

"I was looking at the rattle. I just . . . I remember the ram walking around on those hooves."

"Well, of course you do." She gathered more materials and sat near Dominic on the woolen blankets, and busied herself with sewing. "There's a lot to be done, still, with that ram. I'll make you a flask for carrying. When you set on your way, you can take some bread and fresh water for the journey—and a nice woolen sweater, for you're likely to get cold when you get farther inland."

Dominic looked at the woman reluctantly. He studied the pieces of soft hide in her hands. She was sewing the pieces together with a long thread made from dried sinew. "A flask made of ram skin?" he asked.

"Sure. Don't worry, it's sturdy as can be. The bladder is on the inside. That keeps the water from leaking."

Dominic felt his face pulling into an expression of disgust. "I don't know. I really wouldn't feel right, using something like that."

"Why not?"

"Well, partly because it's a *bladder*."

"Aha! You mean, because it had pee in it, once upon a time!" she laughed. "So what?"

"And because that ram . . . ." Dominic paused. "He was such a gentle, trusting animal. I suppose he affected me."

"Good for him. So why are you frowning and moping?"

"Oh, I don't know, maybe because he trusted me to bring him to a safe place and take care of him, and you chopped his head off."

"What a drama! Don't indulge in blame. Do you think he would approve of that? That ram gave his body for you. The rams have always given us food, and shelter, and tools, and company, and other things to live by. I wouldn't be alive without them, and neither would you. The rams warmed you with their fleece. And the one that you brought back, he fed you when you were hungry—and he'll do more for you than that, I reckon."

"I know, and I appreciate that. But he expected care. He didn't give up his life willingly."

The old woman looked surprised. "Of course he did."

"Oh, did he?"

"Sure."

"Really," Dominic said dryly. "And how do you know? Did he tell you?"

"Sure he did. He said that he was at the end of his life, and he wanted me to make a pair of flutes for the fine young man who freed him from the wire. So I took him to the guillotine. The guillotine works best; it happens quick that way."

Dominic stared at her.

"Oh, and he said that I should make you a stew from his meat," she added. "He was old, all right, but he made for a tasty stew! And come to think of it, he asked me to make you a belt—said you nearly lost your pants on the way here. I stripped some cord from inside his intestines; that'll make a sturdy belt."

"Are you serious?"

"Well I'm not saying it as a joke, am I?"

"A talking ram?" he said doubtfully. "It never said a thing to me."

"You could barely speak either, when you first showed up. I had to tend to you and give you a nice place to rest. And what do you mean, 'a talking ram'? You say it like you've never heard of such a thing."

"I haven't." Dominic paused. "Although . . . I guess I met a talking goat a few days ago. Or . . . a talking goat fish thing."

The woman looked befuddled. "A talking goat? What, you never heard a goat talk, either?"

"No. Seriously, a goat that speaks English?"

"Well they got voices and movements and expressions like us, don't they? And I got ears and eyes and a brain to understand—and who said anything about English?" She narrowed her eyes somewhat suspiciously at Dominic. "And you say you've *never* heard an animal talk?"

"No."

"Hmm," she said, and her eyes narrowed into slits. "Mighty peculiar."

By the next day, the woman had made a number of
gifts for Dominic. She had knitted a little woolen
sweater, soft and golden—even softer and brighter than
it had looked on the ram, because it had been cleaned
with such care. She gave Dominic the ram's-bladder
flask, and the belt weaved from gut, and a pair of warm
boots lined with wool. The two flutes had been tied
together with strips of hide, and a new wooden
mouthpiece fitted over them to make a double flute;
Dominic received that too. After the woman had given
all these things, she put on her heavy boots and her
shawl, and said that she had to walk "into town."

"There's a town?" Dominic asked.

"Of course there's a town! Now, if you find your girl
before I get back, you make sure she gets rested and fed.
Help yourselves to anything you need." The woman
looked toward the mantle contemplatively, and added:
"Take the flutes when you go. And maybe take the rattle.
You may not want it, but your girlfriend might like it."

Dominic started. "She's not my girlfriend. She's
eleven."

"Then she'll like it for sure." The woman went to the
window and gazed out, leaning onto the sill. "Well . . .
what in the world? Young man, I think the fence needs
mending again—in that same place where you found our
golden ram. Go out, would you, and see what's been
meddling with it. And take the flask. If the fence needs
fixing, you'll want water."

"Sure," Dominic said.

He put on the woolen boots and hiked out to the fence.
The boots were comfortable; he was glad of them, and
the woman's story about the talking ram had put a stop
to his revulsion.

At the boundary he noticed nothing unusual about the
fence. He walked along it one way, and after some
distance he turned and walked alongside it in the other

direction. The fence didn't seem to have suffered any invasion, but just as Dominic was about to turn back to the house, something else caught his attention.

A giant white bird was approaching over the ocean. Instantly, Dominic remembered the bird that had snatched him from the Aquarius chamber, and he was overcome by fear. As he shrank away, stumbling backward, his gaze remained locked on that creature—and he began to realize that it wasn't a bird at all. It was a horse—a winged horse, like the Pegasus!

The sight of that beautiful animal struck him with tender awe. It shone like a star, and the beating of its wings was both soft and powerful. It soared over the fence, and the movement of its legs as it landed on the soil was graceful enough to take one's breath away. Dominic could only stand frozen to the spot, staring at the elegant creature as it turned and stepped quietly toward him.

The shining brilliance of the animal increased as it drew near. Within that dazzling light Dominic could see the curves of its muscles and the wisps of its mane, and the softness of its wings as they folded along the horse's back. And then the entire form began to shift—and it did so quickly, neatly, without any of the thrashing and flipping that he had seen in his own transformation, and even in that of the Capricorn. The winged horse was changing into some other creature. Within the length of a second, it changed into a girl.

"Hannah," he breathed, hardly able to believe his eyes.

She was there in front of him, having undergone the transformation without breaking her stride. A smile lit up her face as she approached him. Hannah reached out her arms and caught Dominic in a tight embrace.

He was speechless for some time, merely looking at Hannah after she withdrew. How different she looked! She was the same eleven-year-old girl he remembered, with the long braids and red vest, yet something in her demeanor had changed. Her eyes were bright, her face was flushed with gentle radiance, and she stood straight and relaxed.

"What happened to you?" she asked. "Did you turn into a fish?"

Dominic had nearly forgotten. "Yeah . . . ."

"I knew it was you! Did you see me, under the water? I was a fish, too."

"Yes, I saw you," he said. "Where did you go? Did you get swallowed by . . . ."

"By Cetus! Yes, I did."

"How did you get out?"

"Oh . . . it took a long time. I felt like I was in there forever. Everything was dark, and after a while I started seeing things. I saw people I knew, and . . . well, I didn't see nice things. It was terrible, but I feel much better now."

Dominic beckoned her. "Come on. We can go to the house I've been staying at. There's a woman there who can help us. She said that when I found you, I should bring you back and get you something to eat."

"I *am* hungry. I didn't notice it before."

They started across the plain, and Dominic had to hurry to keep up with Hannah's springing steps. "You helped me get out of Cetus," she said breathlessly. "It was all dark everywhere, but I kept seeing all these bad things, and people being mean. I was mad at everyone, and sad, and . . . sort of disgusted with myself. And then I remembered the thank-you song that you were singing at the tree, and I tried to sing the same words. And after a while I started to understand what the words meant. I'm not sure how to explain it, but . . . the words helped me. I wasn't angry anymore, or sorry for myself, and I started to see people differently. I wanted them to stop sneering at me, but they didn't; and I waited for them to disappear, but they didn't. I couldn't make them go away, but I started to realize that I could change myself. And then I remembered how I had transformed into a fish, and back into a girl, and I knew that I could change into any kind of thing. At first I thought of changing into a bird, but then I remembered the enigma about Cetus—the one that we read in the Aquarius chamber. It talked about springing forth in beauty, and I remembered the story about Pegasus springing from the sea. And I thought about how beautiful it would be to become Pegasus instead. But I couldn't do it just by thinking about it. I had to change my feelings first, and I had to change the way I thought about people, and about myself. So I kept singing and singing, and I started to feel differently about everything. I just felt grateful. After that, I could change myself into Pegasus."

Dominic stared at her in quiet amazement.

"So what do we do next?" Hannah asked eagerly. "Did you find the next enigma?"

"Did I . . . no, I don't think so."

"Aries is next, I think, after Pisces."

He frowned. "What's Pisces? I thought we just came from Aquarius."

"Pisces is the two fish."

"Oh. So where was the enigma with two fish? I don't—"

"It was *us*! *We* were the two fish!"

"Ah . . . of course," Dominic replied sheepishly.

"And I bet Aries is next. I wonder if it's going to be a real live animal, like the Capricorn."

"What kind of animal would it be?"

"A ram."

Dominic was quiet for some time, thinking of the ram he'd released from the barbed wire. The one that the old woman had beheaded. Then, very casually, he said: "Would you be upset if I told you that I killed it and ate it?"

"That's not funny," Hannah said, giving him a nasty look.

"Fine. Sorry." He fidgeted uncomfortably, trying to figure out how to explain what had happened. "It's just that . . . ."

Hannah stopped. She was staring at Dominic with a suspicious light in her eye—not at him, really, but at his ram-hide boots, and at his leather belt. She riveted her gaze on the flask in his hand. "Where did you get those things?" she asked.

"What things?"

"Those fleece boots, and those leather things."

"Well . . . ." Dominic stammered.

"You *did* kill it!" she cried.

"It wasn't me," he protested. "It was the lady. She killed it while I was asleep, and she started making all kinds of things from its body."

Hannah's mouth hung open in astonishment. "But what if we needed the ram to solve the next enigma?"

Dominic shrugged. "I'm not the person to ask."

When they arrived at the house, the old woman was nowhere to be found. Dominic checked the barn and looked out at the fields. "She said she was going to walk to town," he told Hannah. "She probably left already."

Hannah regarded him suspiciously. "You're sure there was a lady?"

"I'm not making her up."

"What was her name?"

Dominic paused. "I don't think she ever told me her name."

"Well, what did you call her?"

"I didn't call her anything."

"After she took you in and fed you, and gave you all these things, and worked all day long with you, you never asked her name?"

"No, I guess I didn't, and you don't need to scold me for it," Dominic replied. "She never asked my name either. Come on, you can rest while I put a meal together."

Dominic got the fire gently burning while Hannah curled up in the woolen blankets. He went out to pick some berries and apples, collect a few eggs, and fetch some milk from the she-goat. He mixed the milk and eggs with flour to make little pancakes, and crushed the berries into some honey to make a jam, and then he sliced up the apples.

The scent of the jam filled his nostrils and made his mouth water. Hannah, too, was roused from sleep by it, and eagerly seated herself at the table. Dominic smeared the pancakes with jam and arranged the apple slices around them. He sat across from Hannah, and they ate happily, talking about their adventures over the past few days.

All afternoon and evening they waited for the woman to return, but she never came. Dominic and Hannah decided to clean the house for her, as a way of saying thanks. They shoveled ash from the fireplace and washed the floor and all the hangings, and scrubbed the blackened pots and skillets until their own hands were stained with soot. They set another fire burning before the daylight vanished. When the flames were roaring and dancing, Hannah and Dominic sat on the heap of blankets with the hide drum, the horn flutes, and even the hoof rattle. They made music until the fire burned low. Hannah sang without embarrassment now. She sang camp songs, and songs from her favorite records.

"I don't think the lady will mind if you sleep in her bed," Dominic said. "I doubt she'll come back tonight. If she's not here in the morning, we can just clean up again and look for the next enigma."

They lit a candle and went into the little bedroom. To

Dominic's surprise, he found a soft, child-sized nightgown neatly folded on the bedspread. Hannah held it up to her own body, and saw that it fit her just right.

"She must have left it for you," Dominic said. "There's no way it's her nightgown. She's too tall for something like that."

He left Hannah alone to change. In the other room, the fire was reduced to tiny flames licking among glowing cinders. Dominic sat on the hearth and held the woolen sweater that the old woman had knitted for him. He pressed it against his cheek. In his mind was the vision of those soft, intelligent eyes, those glorious curving horns, and the tender care that the ram had showed him every time he stumbled alongside it. And to think that he had just made music from the animal's horns and hide! It was almost too strange a thing for him to grasp.

Hannah came out to bid him goodnight. In the dying firelight Dominic could see that she wore a small pendant, hung from a cord around her neck. "What's that?" he asked, beckoning her closer. "Is that yours, or did you find it?"

"It's mine. My dad gave it to me." She sat beside him and turned the face of the stone pendant toward the light. Etched into it was the figure of a young deer. "It's his clan symbol."

"Navajo?"

"Yeah."

Dominic peered at the stone. "Deer clan? Which one?"

"Ummm . . . I don't know. Is there more than one?"

"Sure. There's Little Deer, Spring Deer . . . ."

"I don't remember. My dad doesn't really talk to me anymore."

Dominic hesitated. "Do you know where he is?"

"Yeah. I get to see him sometimes." She lowered her eyes and bit her lip. "My dad got hurt when he was in the war. He lives at a care center in Phoenix."

"Oh," Dominic said.

"He can speak a little bit, sometimes, but he's confused. I don't think he remembers who I am. He recognized me at first, but the nurses said it wouldn't last very long, and . . . they were right."

Dominic was quiet. Hannah dropped the pendant against her nightgown, sitting with her gaze lowered. Her eyes began to fill with tears, and when Dominic saw them full and glistening, he put his arm around her shoulders and gave her a gentle squeeze.

"What about your mom?" he asked. "Is she . . . ."

"She lives in Costa Rica."

"Do you have other family? Relatives?"

"No. My grandma died when I was six. A lot of my dad's family got sick from uranium poisoning. I don't think there's anyone else now."

"When we get home you should get in touch with some people from your clan. Those people are your brothers and sisters."

"It's my dad's clan, not mine."

"Sure it's yours. You're born to your mother's clan and born for your father's clan."

"My mom doesn't have one. She's Greek . . . Greek and German."

"It doesn't matter. You were still born for the . . . ." Dominic paused, scrutinizing Hannah's pendant. "Something Deer clan. Tell you what; when we get back, I'll help you figure out which clan you belong to, and we can find some of your relatives."

"Don't bother." Hannah wriggled farther away from him. Her face was fixed in an expression of gloom. "They probably won't like me."

"Oh, baloney. Why do you think they wouldn't like you?"

"People think I'm too sassy. They call me 'Miss Sassy Pants' and 'Smart Mouth.'"

Dominic chuckled. "Hannah Smart Mouth. You *do* have a smart mouth. That's not a bad thing, though. I like that about you."

"Nobody else does. Even the people who take me to live in their houses don't like me that much—and I can tell when people don't like me. They just put up with me because they don't want to be rude, and that just makes me feel worse. So I decided to stop hoping that people would like me. That way, I don't feel as bad."

"Hannah . . . ." Dominic looked over her for a moment, remembering the radiance with which she'd come upon the shore. *This girl was a Pegasus only hours ago. She flew from the mouth of a monster, over the ocean and into the sky, and changed back into a girl like it was nothing at all.* That radiance was waning now, fading beneath a rising grief. "*I* like you," he said. "You're a perfectly likeable kid. You're smart. You're conscientious."

"I don't know what that word means," Hannah mumbled. "And I'm not that smart. I'm bad at math, and I always get into trouble for not paying attention in class."

"So you're smart in other ways. If it wasn't for you, I'd still be lying by the scorpion bushes, whining and feeling sorry for myself. Right?"

Hannah shrugged. "Probably."

"Let me at least find some people from your clan—not just for you, but for your dad. Okay? I'll start looking as soon as we get back. If we're not dead."

She folded her arms, slumping back against the stone hearth. "No, you won't. You think you will, but you'll forget. My foster families tell me they'll keep in touch, but after a few weeks they forget about me."

"I won't forget. I promise. I rarely ever make promises, and when I do, I don't break them." He gave her another squeeze. "I know what it's like to stop hoping anything will turn out the way you want, and I know what it's like to feel like you don't have any real friends. But you'll get older, and you'll go out on your own, and you'll be able to find people who have things in common with you. And in the meantime, you'll meet a few people who will turn out to be friends. What about the foster parents you have now, are they all right?"

"They're nice. Andy is at work a lot, but Carmina takes me places, and she lets me work at the community gardens with her—and I like it a lot."

"Good. That's three people you can count on, at least."

"That's only two."

"I was counting myself. And even if you feel let down by people, you just have to remember that you're the girl who can turn into Pegasus."

She smiled.

"You can count on yourself," Dominic reminded her, and gently added: "But that doesn't mean that you have to go through everything in life alone."

Hannah stared at him in silence. At length she held out her hand and said: "Shake on it. And it has to be a fancy handshake, not one of your boring handshakes."

So they shook hands, in Hannah's peculiar way of shaking hands. And Hannah went to sleep in the comfortable bed, dressed in the soft gown, and Dominic curled up on the heap of fleece blankets and watched the cinders fade into darkness.

8: Taurus

In the morning, Dominic shoveled the fireplace and carried the ashes outside to the compost pit. As he stood, turning the shovel into the pit, he lifted his gaze to the sky. There was ever a strange haziness about it. There was not a cloud there, and of course not a sun. Their absence caused a panic to stir within him. *I don't belong here. I've been here for days and I am still here. I will never get home again, never see my family . . . .*

He shook himself, clanging the shovel against the ground to shake off the loose ash. Hannah had come out of the outhouse, still wearing the soft golden-brown nightgown; she had her pants underneath it and her red vest zipped over the top. She drew a bucket of fresh water from the well and returned to the house.

A minute later, she hollered: "DOMINIC!"

He came running. Hannah stood at the dining table, staring at it in awe, the water bucket forgotten at her feet.

Dominic immediately saw what had startled her. That bare wooden table, which he'd taken his meals on over the past few days, was bare no more. Its surface was covered with a large ornate inscription, carved all over with symbols and little pictures. There were colorful shapes, and different plants, and many kinds of animals—even a goat-fish and a sea monster. And in the very center of all that was a little poem written in elegant cursive:

Two simple pairs begin the dream
while all the rest remain unseen.

Fate, Fortuna, cast your spells;
Tame your goblins, send your elves.
Do you write legends in the stars,
or are you just a spinster's farce?

"What in the world," Dominic whispered.

"Isn't this the same table we ate on last night?" Hannah asked. She stood back and inspected it, and found that aside from the inscription, the table looked the same. "How is that possible? Someone would have to have done it while we were asleep."

"No, someone would have to have done it while we were outside. The table was blank when I woke up. I looked at it."

In silence they studied the words and the little pictures. At last Hannah shook her head and said: "I wonder what it means. I think that some of these are constellations. Here's Orion facing the bull, with his two hounds— Canis Major and Canis Minor. And . . . this must be Monoceros." She pointed to a vague figure running between the two hounds.

Dominic leaned forward and peered at the image. "What's Monoceros?"

"Plancius said it was a unicorn."

He raised his eyebrows at her.

"He was an astronomer," Hannah added. She studied the poem again. "I can't see what the poem has to do with the symbols. Two simple pairs . . . ."

Dominic glanced around the room. "Is anything else different? Or is it just the table?"

"I don't know. I didn't look."

They made a careful examination of the space around them, and found everything else quite the same. Hannah

was about to turn back to the table when she noticed a
dusty book sitting on a shelf between two tins. The book
itself had always been there; Hannah had seen it before.
But now she realized that the cover of the book bore
many of the same symbols and pictures that were
engraved into the table.

She pulled the book from the shelf, blew the dust off
and wiped it with her skirt. In bold letters across the
cover were the words: *FAIRY TALES*.

"Look at this." Hannah set the book on the table,
sliding it towards the place that had the most matching
symbols. Both the book and table had a picture of a
woman wearing a jeweled crown. She stood beside a
small human figure leaping over a bull. Hannah ran her
finger along the vivid illustrations. "They're the same."

She opened the book, flipping pages and looking
through the dazzling illustrations. Dominic climbed onto
a chair beside her, waiting patiently while Hannah
skipped back and forth between stories; and then she
turned back to the first one and began to read.

Hannah recognized the story. It wasn't a fairy tale, at
least not to her way of thinking. There were certainly no
goblins or elves among its pages. It was the Greek myth
of Theseus and the Minotaur.

Theseus was a prince of Athens, famed for his athletic
skill. Across the southern seas was the island of Crete—
home to King Minos, who demanded that every nine
years, Athens send seven of its young women and seven
of its young men to be sacrificed at the Minoan temple.
Theseus heard of the blood debt and immediately
volunteered to be one of those sacrificed. Each of the
fourteen youths would be sent unarmed into the great
temple labyrinth. At its center they would face the
Minotaur—a giant, brutish creature, half man and half
bull, who would inevitably kill the defenseless youths.

Minos' daughter Ariadne fell in love with Theseus. She

helped sneak him out of the Minoan prison; she gave him a sword to slay the Minotaur; and, to help him find his way out of the labyrinth, Ariadne gave him a long thread that he could follow back to the entrance.

Now Theseus could hear the breath of the hideous beast, and he readied his sword. He crept around the last corner of the labyrinth—and there in the center was a giant brute of a bull, its legs malformed so that they looked like human thighs with a bull's calves, and a breast that looked like a man's breast, and his eyes were like a man's eyes. Theseus was for a moment so horrified by creature's appearance that he could not move; but, driven both by spirit and revulsion, he burst forward and leapt onto the monster's back, driving his sword across its neck and rendering it helpless. He drove his blade into the beast's heart and slew it. Thereupon he followed Ariadne's thread back to the beginning; Ariadne, who held the spindle and who had command of the thread, he sought and found. . . .

The second tale was similar. This, too, was a richly illustrated account of the slaying of a bull. It told the story of the Sumerian king Gilgamesh, who slaughtered the "bull of the sky" after it descended and trampled the earth. A jealous woman had sent the bull to attack Gilgamesh: *Thus came Inanna, the lady to whom was given the weaving of threads—who held the spindle and tangled those threads which were straight, and straightened those that were tangled. Called down she the bull of the sky to trample its hooves upon the earth. . . .*

Hannah frowned as she read on. She recognized two of the names in the story: Gilgamesh and Enkidu. She was certain that the Capricorn had used those names in one of its stories. *Enkidu flung himself onto the bull; he seized the great bull by its horns and seated himself on its back. He slashed the beast across the back of its neck,*

*and it bellowed in pain. Its head hung uselessly.
Gilgamesh seized the bull by the thick of its tail, and
with all of his might he flung it to the ground. The great
bull fled, but Enkidu gave chase, and with another leap
he mounted the bull and gored it again, and again
Gilgamesh got hold of the tail and flung the beast to the
ground. When its breast was exposed Gilgamesh
plunged in his sword and cut out the heart. . . .*

"Gross." Hannah frowned and closed the book. "I
don't like these stories."

"Since when? I thought you loved reading this stuff."

"I do—when I know it's not real."

Dominic looked at her cautiously. "You're worried that
this might be real?"

"Yes, because I think the next zodiac symbol is
Taurus," Hannah said. "Taurus is the bull."

"I see. I hope it's not as hideous as the one in the
book." Dominic paused, and added, "And that we don't
have to kill it."

"Maybe we will. I can't see what we're supposed to
do." Hannah made another examination of the table, her
eyes roving over its characters and strange symbols.
"The enigma says to look for two pairs of letters at the
beginning of the lines, so I thought maybe the answer
was *fata*. That's Latin; it means 'fate.' But I don't know
what we're supposed to do with it."

"I thought you didn't speak Latin."

"I don't. I just know some mythology stuff . . . and the
words to some Catholic songs, because my grandma was
Catholic."

"Hang on a second," Dominic said. He moved the book
so that it sat beside the poem. "I think it's telling us to
look at the book."

Hannah frowned, studying the inscription carefully.
"Where do you see that?"

"Look." He pointed to the book's title. "F-A- begins

the word 'fairy,' and T-A begins 'tales.' The rest of the letters are unseen, and the poem talks about fairy tales—farcical legends about elves and goblins."

Hannah gasped. "You're right. Oh, that was a hard one . . . what's 'farcical'?"

"Fake. Made-up."

"See, Dominic, I told you that you can solve the riddles. I hope they don't keep getting harder. I think we're only halfway through the zodiac." Hannah opened the book again, flipping pages. "We already *did* look at the book. So . . . ."

"Let's look more carefully. Maybe we missed something in the other pages."

Two other stories were found within the volume. The Greek hero Heracles, seeking repentance from his crimes, vanquished the wild Cretan bull: *Here the bull trampled the earth, devastating what man had built and ruining the crops. Heracles covered himself in skins to mask his scent. He snuck upon the bull and pounced, and, wrapping his powerful hands around the bull's neck, he strangled it.*

And then there was another tale about Theseus, who, before facing the Minotaur, had subdued yet another savage bull: *Just before he arrived at Marathon, the place of the fennel staff, a storm began to rage. At the crossroads Theseus was forced to take shelter. There he came upon a small hut belonging to the weaver Hecale, who opens her home to travelers and to whom the underworld road is known. She took the stored wood and piled it in the fireplace; she cooked a hot stew; swiftly she brought down the boiling pot and filled it again. From the bread box she took and served loaves in abundance. She weaved together a shirt of bull's hair to hide the young man's scent. . . .* After a brief respite with Hecale, Theseus went on to capture the bull. He brought it to Athens and killed it there.

"Wait a minute," Dominic said, alarmed. He peered hard at the illustration of Theseus and Hecale. "How come Theseus is so small?"

Hannah looked at him questioningly.

"Is that supposed to be me?" His voice was edged with worry. "Look, the old lady is a giant compared to him. And here he is with the bull . . . ."

Hannah looked at the image of a tiny Theseus straddling the back of a giant, heaving animal. "Well, it was supposed to be a giant bull," she said.

"But it *looks* like me," he insisted. "And this lady . . . she reminds me of the old woman. The one who lives here. She gave me stew and bread, and she made me a sweater from the ram's wool. And she was even wearing a dress and boots like that."

"You should wear the sweater," Hannah suggested. "If she made it for you, it's probably important."

Reluctantly, Dominic picked up the sweater from among the woolen blankets. He slipped it on over his T-shirt and tied the belt around his waist.

Hannah kept turning the pages back and forth, looking at illustrations. "I wonder if the woman is important. In three of the stories there's a woman who weaves . . . ."

Dominic grabbed the text and pulled it closer. His gaze fell on a small illustration of the Minoan palace. Though the story described the labyrinth as a branched structure in which one could become hopelessly lost, the picture showed a simple labyrinth with a single path; it looped and curved around several times before reaching the center. The tiny figure of a bull was painted in the middle.

"Actually, I recognize some of this." Dominic tapped his finger against the image. "See this one, I've seen this before. It's—"

"It's the cornfield!" Hannah blurted. "The cornfield is a labyrinth. I bet that's where we're supposed to go next."

"What cornfield?" Dominic asked. "You mean the one right out here?"

"Yes, I saw it when I was flying," Hannah said excitedly. "You probably can't tell from the ground, but from above you can see that there's a passageway inside of it." She pressed a finger to the illustration. "It looks just like this."

"All right, then . . . ." Dominic frowned, flipping through the pages again. His eyes rested on the figure of Theseus drawing his blade against the bull's neck. "I would say 'let's go,' but . . . I'm worried about what I might have to do once we get there."

"Well," Hannah said, "Maybe there are more clues inside the labyrinth. Let's just go, and see what we find."

Dominic glanced at her reluctantly.

"Come on, let's just look. Let's take everything we might need, in case we can't get back to the house."

Dominic nodded at the golden-brown dress that Hannah still wore beneath her vest. "You're going to take that nightgown?"

Hannah fingered the cloth contemplatively. "Yeah. I think . . . she made it for me."

"All right." Dominic was tying together the laces of the ram-skin boots. He didn't want to leave his own shoes behind, but decided to take the boots along as well— simply because the old woman had told him to. He filled the flask with fresh water and looped the handle around his shoulder, tied the double flute into his belt, and grabbed the boots by the laces. "I think that's everything," he said, taking a last look around the cozy room.

They set off toward the cornfield when the day was still bright. Behind the yard and barring their way was a shallow stream, not quite narrow enough to leap across. Hannah and Dominic removed their socks and shoes before stepping carefully into the water. Dominic emerged with soaked pant legs, and Hannah fared a bit differently; she stumbled on a slick rock and lost her balance, landing on her butt in the middle of the stream, dropping her shoes in the water. She sat there with her mouth open in surprise, astonished by the fact that she'd fallen.

Dominic couldn't help laughing. "Are you all right?"

"Ah . . . sure. It isn't cold." She stood and shook the water from her shoes.

Hannah was excited to see what lay within the rows of corn. She skipped ahead, her long braids bouncing along her back and her wet skirt sagging, and Dominic repeatedly asked her to slow down. He trekked across the field with much less enthusiasm, thinking of those drawings of ancient heroes slicing through the flesh of a wild bull—and of the small figure that looked so much like him. As he walked he kept searching the horizon for signs of the old woman. But the land was flat and bare, and the only thing rising out of it now was the cornfield.

"My scorpion sting is getting better," Hannah said. "Look." She thrust the arm toward Dominic. "You can just see a little mark where the stinger got me." She examined the arm again, adding, "I wonder how many other people this has happened to. I bet there are other people who have been here, and they never tell anyone about it. *You're* not going to tell anyone, are you?"

"I don't know. I haven't thought about it." He paused. "Probably not."

"I think we've been through . . . ." Hannah counted on her fingers. "One, two . . . three was the Capricorn . . . Aquarius four, Pisces five . . . Aries six, and this is going to be seven." She frowned. "Only seven? We're only halfway through. I feel like we've been here forever."

"Yes, well, at least you're having fun."

"It's not *all* fun. Cetus was horrible. And I hated

changing into a fish."

"I didn't mind being a fish so much. It was . . . pretty. I remember everything in the ocean being really beautiful and fascinating." Dominic paused, thinking back. "That's funny . . . I don't remember it so well now."

"I only got to be a fish for a few minutes, and then I got swallowed by a monster," Hannah said.

"Wasn't it worth it?"

"You mean, because I got to be Pegasus? That was the best part. It was dark for such a long time, but after I started singing, and after I got used to the dark, my body turned into light—and then I could see all around me."

"Your body turned into light?"

"Yes, and I could see that there was just a round space around me, like I was inside a giant egg. And I thought of being a butterfly in a cocoon—except, instead of a butterfly I could be a bird, or a horse with wings. And when I became Pegasus, I was big enough that my body pushed against the walls of the egg, and I kicked out the eggshell, and I opened my wings up and flew. And it wasn't like changing into a fish at all! That was something that *happened* to me; but Pegasus was something I *did*. And it felt like the most wonderful thing I've ever done."

Dominic's feet seemed to grow heavy as the labyrinth loomed before them. He stopped some distance from the rows of corn and looked them over. The husks were dry. Having lost their greenness, they gleamed like gold in the daylight, and the stalks stood so close together that they made up a curving golden wall.

The entrance was directly before them. The ground was covered with strips of dried husk.

"I'll go in first," Dominic said.

"No, walk next to me," Hannah replied. "We'll go together."

The plants smelled sweet and dry. Dominic found the

scent somewhat comforting as he crossed the threshold, and he was soothed by the sounds of the plants shifting in the soft breeze. But he had only seconds to enjoy the tones of nature. He and Hannah had taken a sharp right turn into the labyrinth, and after several paces the labyrinth looped around to the left—and as they came around that first loop, they were met by a puzzling scene.

Two pieces of metal armor hung from the stalks of corn. Each was a type of breastplate, stamped along the edges with various embellishments and symbols. One had a sheet of silver that hung over the chest, attached by chain to another sheet to hang down the back. The other was loosed by hinges, with the pieces swinging together to enclose the entire torso in a suit of gold. Between them hung a weathered parchment that read:

Choose wisely, now, what you would wear
upon your heart of strength and care.
Which armor would the hero claim
with ardor and with purest aim?

"How should we know?" Hannah said softly, studying the breastplates. "They look the same. They're just different colors. And they have different designs on them, but . . . ."

Dominic peered hard at both pieces of armor. "Well . . . is one of the designs *bad*?"

"They don't even seem that different. One is a loop and one is a wave. Is a loop better than a wave?"

"Maybe it's the loop, because the labyrinth loops around."

"It's not that kind of loop."

For some time they puzzled over the armor. Neither seemed particularly formidable, nor glorious. After a thorough study, Dominic said, "Let's take them both.

You carry one and I'll carry one."

"But what if one of them is bad?" Hannah asked.

"Then one of us is in trouble, and the other isn't."

They gathered up the armor and continued down the gold-hued path, curving around and approaching the next bend with apprehension. Their expectations were well met: two belts, strung all around with ornate metal plates—one all silver, the other all gold—hung along the corn stalks. And between them was another parchment:

Which plated waistband of this pair
can serve you in the wild bull's lair?
And what shall gird you round your frame
to make the beast forever tame?

"Maybe gold is right, because it matches the cornfield," Dominic suggested.

Hannah's look told him that she didn't agree. She studied the little decorations on the plates. There were little squiggles, and etchings of little people—some sitting, some standing, some holding little objects in their hands. None seemed any more important than the others, and neither Hannah nor Dominic could detect any particular meaning in them.

"We'll take both." Dominic removed his ram-skin belt. "I have a feeling we're going to end up with a full suit of armor—five more pieces, at least."

"Why five?"

"The labyrinth has seven turns."

Hannah looked at him dubiously. "How do you know?"

"I know the labyrinth. I've seen it before, it's a Hopi labyrinth."

"It's a Greek labyrinth," Hannah protested. "No, wait . . . it's Minoan, not Greek. It's supposed to be King Minos' labyrinth."

"Oh, you're sure of that."

"Yeah, I've seen it lots of times. What's it supposed to be in Hopi?"

"It's . . . I don't know." Dominic pulled the gold-plated belt around his waist, and he secured the breastplate around his chest. The belt hung loose and heavy. Hannah's was worse. They wore the belts anyway.

At the next loop they stood and stared at four metal boots lined up along the ground. Both pairs were open-soled, the metal plating attached with hinges and fastening over the feet and around the ankles with metal clasps.

"Let's just put them on and go," Dominic said. "I'll take all the gold, you keep taking the silver."

In this way they traversed the rest of the labyrinth—taking up the armor and helping each other put it on, until they were clinking and clanging their way past rows of corn. Both of them were too small for the armor they wore. At the next turn they picked up shin guards, and then heavy shields—and then they came upon two weapons leaning against the plants. One was a long, wooden spear with a silver tip; the other, a gold-hilted sword.

"This is ridiculous," Dominic said, dropping his ram-skin boots and flask. He set his ram-gut belt and flutes gently on the ground. "I'm dying under all this stuff." He pulled off his sweater and set it on the boots, and put the breastplate on again. He weighed the sword in his hand. It was an impressive instrument: light, with curling embellishments along the hilt and blade, and dangerously sharp. "You take the spear," he commanded Hannah. "If we come across any kind of dangerous animal, I don't want you going anywhere near it. You can stand back and throw this."

"What if I miss?" Hannah asked.

"Please don't."

They tried to move quietly as they approached the middle of the labyrinth, but the ill-fitting armor jangled loudly. Scraps of corn husk crackled under their feet. The final bend was littered with a heap of metal helmets—some rusted, and some that shone with a clean brilliance; some covered with gleaming chainmail, and others with double visors to cover the face—and several other pieces all jumbled together. Hannah lifted a heavy one and let it drop over the top of her head. The space inside the helmet was too large; the metal hung down over her eyes, so that Dominic could just see her nose sticking out. After a moment the visor swung down, hiding the rest of her face.

Dominic lifted the visor and chuckled. "We're doomed," he said.

Hannah pulled off the helmet. "Let me try a different one."

She found a silvery wing protruding from one of the helmets and pulled it out. The helmet was light and simple. It covered just enough of her head to stay put, and on each side was attached the gleaming shape of a bird's wing.

"It's Mercury's helmet," she said.

Dominic glanced at the poem above the heap:

With what cap would you crown your head
while walking in the hero's stead?

He asked quietly: "You think that's the right one?"

She shrugged, and said just as softly, "I like this one best."

Dominic didn't like any of them. But he picked up the one that looked the least uncomfortable—an ornate golden kabuto that left his face uncovered.

Now Hannah and Dominic moved slowly, and with utmost caution. The labyrinth was laid out just like the symbol in the book. They had passed around all seven loops, and as the walls curved onward toward the central chamber, they came upon a final riddle set upon the dry stalks:

TAUROS

Before you waits the horned calf;
look again, and see my staff.
Be not gored by your own fear;
seven stars shall then appear.

"The seven stars are probably the Pleiades," Hannah whispered. "It's a constellation inside of Taurus."

The words "gored" and "fear" made Dominic's stomach turn. He looked at Hannah with helpless anticipation, and whispered back: "We're supposed to read about being gored, and not feel scared? That doesn't seem fair to me."

Hannah pressed her lips together and didn't reply, but Dominic could see the concern in her eyes.

Together they stepped forward, peeking from the passageway into the central chamber.

What they saw gave them such a shock that they stood frozen for some time. The center of the labyrinth was impossibly large. Hannah had seen it from the sky, and she knew that the central chamber shouldn't have been much larger than the passageways. Yet it was wide and circular, and in its very center was the strange-looking figure of a bull. It stood facing them, its forelegs and broad chest gleaming like dark polished wood. Two horns protruded from the sides of the head, mottled dark blue and gold, the tips narrowing into sharp points—but the most frightening part lay between the horns.

Over its face the bull wore a hideous, frightening mask, smeared with red streaks that might have been blood.

Matted feathers were plastered around the ears and jaw, and the patches of its unpainted flesh shone with that same appearance of polished wood. Four long teeth protruded from its curling lips. Two eye holes were positioned at the front, so that they looked like human eyes rather than a bull's eyes. The figure stood without moving. For a moment Hannah thought it was a statue—but as she gazed through the eye holes, she became certain that the bull was looking back at her.

She shuddered. *Look again, and see my staff . . . what staff? Where is it?*

Dominic took a breath and stepped forward. "Stay here," he hissed at Hannah.

"Do you see a staff?" she whispered back.

He didn't move.

"The riddle said to look again and see a staff," she reminded him.

Silence. Dominic may have been looking for a staff somewhere in the chamber. His eyes flitted back and forth.

"I'm going to get closer," he whispered.

Hannah squeezed his arm. "Try to be brave."

"Right."

Each step seemed a challenge. Hannah watched, holding her breath, as Dominic placed one foot forward, and finally another, making his way toward the daunting figure of the bull.

The bull didn't move.

Dominic stopped. Hannah released her breath, waiting—and then Dominic took several quick steps back, coming to a halt beside her.

"I don't think I can do it," he whispered. "I mean, I don't think I can do it physically, and even if I could, I wouldn't." He gestured impatiently to the bull. "It's not even doing anything. It's just standing there."

"Good," Hannah whispered back. "Would you be

happier if it was attacking us?"

"No."

"It will probably attack when you get closer."

"Great. Have you noticed anything else—another rhyme, an object, anything?"

Hannah scanned the golden circle of corn. "No. Maybe there's something behind the bull?"

"Maybe."

"Maybe we don't have to go through the bull. We can try going around. There could be something behind it."

They talked in whispers for some time, and formulated a plan: Dominic would approach the bull, slowly, while Hannah went around the edge of the circle toward the other side. Perhaps if Dominic got close enough to the bull to distract it, it would give Hannah some time to look for other clues within the chamber.

The strategy seemed to work well enough. As Dominic ventured back into the arena, the bull stood with its gaze fixed on him, ignoring the girl who slipped around the chamber's circumference. Dominic got halfway to the bull and edged even closer, slowing his pace to give Hannah more time.

The bull's foreleg moved, and Dominic froze. For just a moment, as it shifted its position, the bull's form seemed to fragment; its front legs seemed disjointed. But it quickly corrected itself and stood strong.

What is it? Dominic wondered. *A weakness? A good moment to attack?*

A closer look at the animal revealed the details in its wood-grained mask. It covered the creature's face almost completely. The mouth and nose were stylized— the nostrils painted into spirals, the mouth grinning broadly around curving teeth. But through two small holes Dominic could see the eyes looking back at him. Those eyes seemed familiar. They were a deep brown, and seemed remarkably calm and soft—a stark contrast to the vulgar mask. *An animal's eyes.* Perhaps they simply reminded him of the ram. Yet they couldn't have been a ram's eyes, or even a bull's eyes, because of their forward-looking position.

Dominic tried to push aside his hesitation. He lifted the shield a bit higher and extended the sword.

Hannah, meanwhile, had noticed something that made her stop only halfway around the chamber. As she drew farther from the entrance, the bull's form seemed to come apart, shifting and thinning out. The illusion of its breadth vanished—and now, looking at it from the side, it was obvious that what Hannah had seen from the chamber's entrance was an illusion. The "bull" was actually standing upright on two legs. From this angle it looked much like a human being in a strange costume, holding two staffs in front of it that could have been mistaken for bull's legs. The appearance of the bull's wide, muscular body was created by a flat sheath that dropped in front of the figure's body.

Hannah stared. *That's not a bull at all! It's a person—a person with a bull's costume!*

Dominic was eyeing her, waiting for her to continue. She hurried around the rest of the circle, glancing along the wall for other clues, but she saw only blank rows of dry corn. The only other object in the arena, aside from Dominic and the "bull," was a short golden hedge of cropped corn stalks, rising only as high as Hannah's knee. It was arranged in a sort of X shape. Hannah recognized it; it was the cross-section of the labyrinth, the spot that marked the very center. The bull figure stood just in front of it.

When Dominic saw Hannah retreating to the entrance, his stance faltered. He lowered the sword. Then, abruptly, he turned and sprinted back to Hannah, trying to peer over his shoulder at the motionless bull. The armor rattled noisily as he went.

"Did you find anything?" he asked breathlessly.

The creature was still facing them. Hannah could no longer see the length of its body; again it had the convincing appearance of a strange bull. "Dominic," she said, "that isn't a bull. I think it's a person."

"A person?"

She leaned toward Dominic's ear and lowered her voice to a soft whisper. "Wait, and I'll go toward the middle instead. You walk around to the side like I did. If you look at it from the side you can see that it's not a bull. It's only standing on two legs, not on four. It's wearing a costume and holding two sticks that look like bull's legs."

Dominic looked doubtful. "Hannah . . . ."

"I'll be careful. I don't think it's going to hurt us."

"All right, I'll be quick."

It was Hannah's turn to approach the bull with a heart full of anxiety. What was it that was smeared along the mask? Was it blood—blood, gore, and feathers? Had it attacked others and devoured them? *Will it attack me if I'm too scared?* Was that the meaning of the rhyme— that if she was scared, the bull would charge?

She had seen videos of people being gored by bulls— during bull fights, bull runs, anything ending in such disaster that it appeared on the international news. Bull's horns were even more dangerous than they looked. And if this creature wasn't a bull, the horns might still be fatal.

Be not gored by your own fear . . . .

Hannah took a deep breath, tried to calm the pounding of her heart. The eyes that looked back at her weren't the eyes of a human being. The irises were too large, so that as she got closer, she could barely see the whites around them, and the creature's gaze was so soft that she could see its gentleness even in the midst of the grotesque mask. It was the sight of those eyes that softened

Hannah's heart. She began to relax as she realized that the bull was relaxed; its muscles never stiffened, its gaze never sharpened. A few yards away she stopped. She turned the point of her spear upward, standing the shaft on the ground beside her—but kept the shield positioned before her, just in case.

"Hi," she said softly.

The terrifying creature stared back at her with its strange eyes. Seconds ticked by. Then, a muffled voice replied: "Hi."

The two of them looked at each other in silence. Dominic stood frozen at the edge of the chamber.

"Are you going to hurt us?" Hannah asked at last, at a loss for anything else to say.

One of the bull's legs lifted high; fingers sprung from it, and Hannah saw that the leg was really some kind of staff, and that a man's painted hand had indeed been clutching it. A finger and thumb grasped the feathered mask and pulled it away from the face. And it was true—the creature had a man's face. Wisps of dark hair curled down over his forehead, and his ears and nose and mouth were like that of a man. But those eyes! Everything seemed human except the eyes, which had the look of an animal's eyes.

"No," the bull-man replied. He gestured to the spear in Hannah's hand. "And are *you* going to hurt *me*?"

Hannah paused. Setting down the spear and sword, she said, "No. We didn't know you were a man. We thought we were supposed to . . . ."

He raised his eyebrows. "Supposed to what?"

"We thought that you were a bull and we were supposed to kill you."

"I see. And what led you to believe such a thing?"

"We read a story about you—about how you were a wild bull who lived in a labyrinth and trampled crops, and . . . ."

"Hm. Well, suppose I *am* a wild bull, of sorts. And here you see me at the center of a labyrinth, and I may have trampled some crops."

Dominic walked up beside her. He stood a couple paces in front of her, as if to put himself between her and the celestial creature, but the bull-man ignored him and nodded to Hannah. "Give me your helmet," he said.

Hannah removed the silver helmet. Hesitantly she stepped forward and stretched her arms to him, afraid to draw too near.

A tiny smile played on his face. His right hand appeared from behind the costume, and he took the helmet and studied it. "Will this piece of metal help you to understand what's in my mind?" he asked, lifting his gaze to meet hers.

"No," Hannah said softly.

"And your breastplate, will it connect your heart with mine?"

"No. . . . ." Instinctively, Hannah placed a hand over her heart. Something stirred there as she looked into the bull-man's eyes. She thought she felt the emanations of his own heart, of his own spirit—gentle like those eyes, and with a love that was at once entirely calm and immensely powerful.

He lowered his eyes, focusing on the awkward metal boots. "And those boots, will they teach you to walk in another person's shoes?"

"What are you?" Hannah asked.

He shrugged. "Oh, I'm no one special. And what are you?"

Likewise, Hannah shrugged. "No one special, I guess."

"Really. Well, that's something we have in common." The bull-man placed the helmet on her head and continued: "These metal scraps can't give you powers of truth or insight. Can they?"

Hannah shook her head.

"But tell me this: what made you stop and speak to me, instead of rushing at me with violence?"

"I . . . saw your eyes."

"You approached to look more closely, and you looked into my own eyes, and you spoke to me," the bull-man said softly. "But you did more than that. You chose to look from more than one angle, and to take care about the fabrications you read."

"About the . . . the what?"

"The stories. The tales that people make up to tell other people what they saw, or what they thought they saw— what they fear, what they hope for, what they believe, what they'd rather not see."

Hannah was silent, considering.

"And for your efforts . . . ." Again the bull-man pulled his hand from behind the disguise. "Seven lights to help guide you through the darkness."

Hannah gasped. Suspended there, just above his palm, seven silvery-white lights shone—a central light surrounded by six others, gleaming steadily.

"The Pleiades," Hannah said.

"Call them what you will, but remember that these objects you've uncovered will only serve you as symbols." The bull-man swept his hand quickly behind the costume, and the lights vanished. "They aren't magic keys that will unlock the secrets of the universe—but they will at least unlock the next few gates. And so you, young lady, will need to take them with you."

Hannah reached out, as if to carry the little bundle of lights in her hand.

The bull-man moved forward and delicately tapped Hannah's winged helmet. "They're here."

She grasped the headpiece and lowered it. Her eyes beheld a delicate metalwork over the forehead: a silvery, eight-petaled flower surrounded by thin vines and leaves. Set in the midst of that flower was a T shape like the one on the bull's mask. The curving delicacy of the design was lovely and ornate, but what made Hannah's breath catch in astonishment was the sight of seven glowing lights set into it—four into the petals, and the other three placed along each end of the T.

"Return the other pieces of armor, Hannah, but keep this helmet."

She looked up at the bull-man. "Thanks, but . . . I wouldn't feel right, wearing this."

He gazed at her for some time. Then he asked: "Why not?"

Hannah's thoughts turned to her ordeal within the belly of Cetus. She remembered how people had sneered at her. She remembered seeing the other Hannah, mean and bumbling, and she remembered feeling ashamed of herself.

The bull-man saw her thoughts. Hannah could tell by looking into his eyes that he knew what she was remembering.

"It's not just that I feel like I don't deserve it," she said. "It's just . . . it doesn't seem like something a person should wear."

"I see. Do you think so little of human beings?"

Hannah lowered her eyes.

"You needn't reject it out of humility," he said gently. "This crown isn't something that a person can wear out of vanity and pride. It represents the principles with which you can discern the specter of the bull."

He reached out and plucked a light from the topmost petal, turning it between his finger and thumb. It glowed like a luminescent gemstone. "This isn't a sacred object," he continued. "It's a reminder of something sacred."

"But . . . what's it supposed to remind me of?"

"That's up to you to. As you're walking through the next realm, think of the things you've learned. Think of what you discovered in Cetus, or in another realm, and attach those lessons to one of the lights. Even after you give them up, you'll still remember that each of your seven lights is a symbol of something important."

"I have to give them all up?"

"Yes. They aren't anywhere near as important as the lights you carry within you, but you will need them to continue along the road." He pushed the shining sphere back into place, and then he took the helmet from Hannah's hands and placed it on her head.

He turned to Dominic. "And you, sir, already have what you need." The bull-man gestured to the passageway, where fleece and hide lay scattered along the looping path. "Those were the garments by which you may have identified with me; they are of the same flesh, and they were given to you for a reason. With them you might even have recognized me. Be sure to take them with you when you go."

"Go where?" Hannah asked.

"Farther into the labyrinth. Always go there." He smiled and spoke light-heartedly, as if he was telling a joke. "Right now, you're standing in a labyrinth within a labyrinth. This universe is a labyrinth, and your world is a labyrinth, full of turns; you've been to the edges, like an exploded universe, and there's a gravity always pulling you back toward the center, however slowly. And at each turn you'll face something new, and yet old. You'll stop there, and sometimes you'll move on easily, and sometimes you'll get stuck, and not everyone gets stuck at the same place. But know this: when you've left this labyrinth, you haven't really left the labyrinth. You will seek the center of the labyrinth and meet me again, because you are center-seeking creatures. All human beings are."

Hannah couldn't hide her disappointment. "That doesn't tell us anything!"

"It's a riddle," the bull-man replied, and waved them away. "Go on now, gather your ram-things, remember what I said, et cetera. And—wait. What did you bring?" He cupped his chin and gazed at the passageway. "A shirt, a belt, two boots, a double flute, and a flask . . . you didn't bring the hoof rattle?"

"No," Dominic said.

The bull-man gave him a small, wry grin. "Hmm. You'll be needing that. You'll have to go back and get it."

"And then what?"

"And then come here, to the center."

They retreated. Hannah glanced back as she and Dominic entered the passage. The strange man was in his bull guise again, the mask over his face, the staff held carefully in place.

"He said *et cetera*," she said. "That's Latin, too."

"I think I like it better when they don't talk." Dominic dumped his helmet on the ground.

"You shouldn't say that. He was—wait! He said to take your ram things."

"I'll grab them when we come back. All these extra clothes are killing me." Dominic dragged the sword as he retreated, uncovering a line of dirt through the husk scraps and other debris. The shield drooped in his other hand. "I'm out of shape. I'm working full-time—well, I *was* working full-time, and going to college, and it's a lot to keep up with. I spend my time sitting in a chair, doing homework and eating take-out."

Hannah didn't like the armor, either, except for her helmet. As she walked she tried to imagine what the little lights looked like, glowing star-like on her forehead. "That one was easy," she said as they left the labyrinth. "We didn't even have to do anything."

"It was as anti-climactic as I wanted it to be," Dominic said. "I hope—"

He was cut off by a strange cry—a long, low cry, like the baying of a hound in the distance. Dominic looked at Hannah with trepidation. "What was that?"

She shrugged.

Dominic surveyed the landscape, saw nothing of note. Still, the sound made the hair rise along his arms. He shuddered. "Let's get to the house."

They walked faster. Hannah outpaced Dominic; she could see that he was tired, that he couldn't walk as fast as he would have liked. "I'm not tired," she said. "I'll run and get the rattle."

"Sure. It's hanging by the fireplace."

Hannah plunged through the little stream, then broke into a run.

Dominic watched her and suddenly felt wistful. She ran so lightly, so easily, that she reminded him of the Pegasus. He remembered her shining in the air, the soft wisp of her mane, the way her face was lit with something even more powerful than happiness.

It wasn't until Hannah disappeared into the house that Dominic saw the dogs.

First he noticed a movement in the corner of his eye. He looked to his left and saw what looked like two dogs running in the distance, a large one followed by a smaller one, and he thought: *Oh, cute, a mom and her puppy; I wonder if they're the old lady's dogs*, and he smiled.

Then he noticed how skinny they were, and his smile faded. He wondered if they were hungry. They jerked erratically, haltingly, as they made their way across the plain. Dominic thought they might be rabid. One of the dogs looked at him.

"Hannah!" he called.

The open-mouthed beasts had large, blazing eyes. Their scrawny bodies were a strange color—a very dark red, or maybe a dark purple or blue-black, or all of those colors steaked together. Their sharp teeth and drooling lips were profiled clearly in the daylight, and when the larger dog's cry rang out, it seemed accusatory and outraged.

They were the most frightening animals Dominic had ever seen. And though they changed direction several times, they seemed to be heading for the house—but when Dominic shouted, the dogs stopped. They turned around.

Perhaps "around" is the wrong word, for there was something difficult in the way they changed direction. The dogs moved their heads first, so that all four blazing eyes were focused on Dominic. They ran several steps and then turned slightly, and ran again. They ran in a seeming haphazard pattern until they were pointed in Dominic's direction, and then they came for him; but even then the dogs veered from side to side, tracing angular paths across the field as they made their way closer.

"HANNAH!"

Hannah was already in the yard. She stopped when she saw Dominic fleeing toward the labyrinth.

Dominic yelled: "Stay in the house and close the door!"

Hannah couldn't hear the words from where she stood, but she wouldn't have listened anyway. She knew that she could easily hide inside the house, that she could find weapons to defend herself there. But Dominic! He had nothing, and Hannah could see that he wouldn't be able to outrun the racing hounds.

She picked up a rake and ran close to the stream. She waved the rake over her head. "Hey, over here!"

But they were going after Dominic, their bodies heaving, eyes burning like white-hot fire as they charged across the field. Hannah thought they must be blind; they turned aside again, straightened again, covered swaths of field as if they were afraid of missing their prey. And poor Dominic—he looked like a doomed man. He ran, but the field was so vast, and the phantom hounds so quick in spite of their strange movements. Hannah saw Dominic glance over his shoulder. He saw the hounds coming, and he yelled something, but Hannah still couldn't hear what it was.

"Dominic!" she cried, chasing behind them. "Dominic, go back into the labyrinth!"

He didn't heed her warning. He was running toward the side of the cornfield, as if he meant to go around it, and the hounds were quickly gaining on him.

She shouted at him again.

But the dogs were too fast. Even if Dominic had followed her advice, he would never make it. The hounds would be on him in seconds. They would tear him to pieces. *Or worse. Something worse . . . .*

Desperation moved in Hannah's being. She sensed something terrible about to happen to her friend—*and whatever it is, I will not let it happen. I will not!*

It was the experience with Cetus that led her to do what she did next. Within Cetus, she had realized a sudden necessity for transformation. She could not have survived by hanging onto her old way of seeing other people, or of seeing herself. Through that knowledge she had transformed into Pegasus. And she would need to transform yet again. She could not help Dominic as she was—and yet it was more than that. Hannah knew what she had to become. She remembered the inscription on the table—the painted figures of Canis Major and Canis Minor, the hunting dogs that followed at Orion's heels. Between them ran Monoceros, the unicorn. No one, not even the hounds of the stellar borders, would dare harm a unicorn. And the unicorn was fast. Faster than the hounds . . . .

Hannah ignored every signal of alarm that her body

sent as the mutation began. Boldly, she assured herself: *I am a unicorn. This is how I'm supposed to feel.* Faster and faster she ran, the sound of her beating hooves mingling with the cries of the dogs. In a second she was upon them; she raced past and turned on them with a sharp jab of her horn. Her hooves kicked at the air an inch from the larger dog's face.

The hounds instantly hung back. Their jaws snapped; they growled viciously and tried to charge around the great unicorn, still moving in their strange angles. Hannah lashed at them over and over again, hoping to give Dominic more time.

She dared to glance back and saw him still running in the wrong direction. *Where does he think he's going?* The farther from the labyrinth's entrance he got, the more danger he was surely in. Hannah left the hounds and went to fetch her friend before he ran off into an even more vulnerable place.

Dominic didn't seem to realize that Hannah had become a unicorn. As she galloped up behind him, she heard him still screaming, bursting with words of fear. She ran around him, facing him and bringing him to a halt; and before he could get over his surprise, she carefully dipped her horn between his feet and lifted him up, so that he sprawled awkwardly along the length of her neck. She felt his fingers clutching at her mane as he rode, face down and backwards, back toward the labyrinth, while the hounds came ever closer.

The entrance was too small for Hannah to run through as a unicorn. She stopped and lowered her head, sending Dominic tumbling to the ground—and without a pause she became a girl, stumbling into the labyrinth on her two small legs. She grabbed Dominic by the arm, dragging him away from the snapping jaws of the hounds.

Hannah and Dominic clutched each other as they ran.

Behind them was the terrible sound of bodies crashing against rows of dry corn. There was the smell of wet fur, of dogs dripping with steaming sweat. The hounds bucked their heads this way and that, throwing themselves from side to side, and between each ripping crackle of dried stalks Hannah could hear the beasts grunting and growling. But the curving passageways proved to be too much for them. The corn walls wouldn't give way, and the hounds fell behind, unable to navigate the curving labyrinth.

Only at the center did the noise fade into silence. The central arena was still and empty, the bull figure nowhere to be seen.

Dominic and Hannah stood hunched over, catching their breath. Finally Dominic said: "Did you get the rattle?"

Hannah shook her head.

"Well, never mind it now." He straightened up and laughed. "All that, for a creepy hoof rattle that I can't stand to look at. What next?"

"Back there." Hannah pointed at a small sign hanging opposite the entrance. "I think it's another enigma."

Dominic started forward, but Hannah said, "Wait! Get your ram things."

"Right." He fetched the boots, flask, and other things from the passage, and hurried to meet Hannah.

The sign at the rear of the arena had four symbols on it. When Hannah moved closer, she realized that the symbols were letters, and that the sign simply said "PUSH."

She and Dominic looked at each other. Then Dominic pressed his palm against the wall of dry stalks.

A rectangular section fell away. It landed with a loud thump, sending bits of corn husk into the air. Hannah expected to see another walled path beyond it, but she was surprised again. The rough doorway opened to a vast open space. Beneath the broken stalks, and stretching far across the landscape, was a stone path.

"That was easy." Dominic started through the opening. "Here . . . be careful." He extended his hand and helped Hannah over the debris, and together they entered the next realm.

9: Gemini

Outside the labyrinth, the world looked quite strange.
Gone were the fields, the dry grasses and the haze of the
blue ocean in the distance. The grass was now a deep
green, neatly shorn and stretching for miles around the
path that sloped upward and down again over rolling
plains. It reminded Hannah of phony grass from a mini-
golf course. The sky was a bold blue, sunless and bright,
like the sky in a child's painting. A wooden sign along
the road read: *Welcome to Gemini. Population: 2.*

Hannah followed the bull-man's advice as she walked.
She thought of the glowing spheres in her helmet, and
she attached memories to each of them. The central
light—that would remind her of the thank-you song, of
being grateful and remembering to give something back.
The light at the bottom of the T shape—that would
remind her to be kind, and to speak up for people, the
way she should have spoken up for Annabelle.

She didn't think about these things for long, because
the road soon branched into three dirt paths. Just before
the branching was a sign, a slightly tilted face upon a
thin pedestal, like the trail maps that Hannah saw when
she went biking at the park. At the beginning of each
new road was a stone post with a large petroglyph
carved into it. Even before she drew near to them,
Hannah could make out the images: a pair of scales, a
crab, and a lion.

"I think we have to choose which constellation to go
into next," she said. "The one on the left is Libra. Then

there's the crab and the lion, but I don't know which one comes next."

"And this must be our enigma." Dominic stopped at the sign.

The surface was painted with words and brightly colored figures, animals and human figures with featureless faces. At the top left was a goat with a fish tail, which Hannah recognized as the Capricorn. She saw a ram, and an armored figure that was utterly surrounded: a unicorn and a pair of dogs at its back, while before it was a large bull and a ribbon of stylized water that rushed against its knees. Each image was marked with small luminescent dots. Hannah recognized the constellations and their stars. She even recognized the Gemini constellation, though it didn't look as she'd expected. Its stars were laid over two human figures—one in a red vest, with two dark braids trailing down its chest, and the other with a T-shirt and blue jeans.

"It's us," Dominic said.

The words were arranged in two passages, the first scrawled among the figures, the other set to the right of them. The first read:

Here the goat and fish is beckoned for one wish, and stays the second.
Next we see two wandering lambs with gifts from a celestial ram. One remains dressed, one sheds the rest. Hounds of the barrier circumvent the path of him with Earthly scent. If one would seek, and traverse there, with deference one must prepare.

Hannah was quiet for some time, trying to discern the meaning. At last she asked: "Do you understand it?"

"The hounds chasing a guy with earthly scent—that's obviously me. And I think we're the wandering lambs. We had gifts from the ram."

"You took off your ram things. Maybe that's why the dogs went after you. See, because he was a *celestial* ram, and he has the scent of this place. I was wearing my nightgown, but you were just wearing your Earth things."

Dominic took a deep breath. "My Earth things," he muttered. "I hate this place. I want it to be over."

"And remember the fairy tale book—there was a man who wore animal skins to cover up his scent. The one who *looked like you.*" Hannah touched the larger of the two dogs, tracing a line between the glowing spots. "See, this is Canis Major, and that's Canis Minor . . . the hunting dogs." Her finger stopped at the largest, topmost dot. "Here's Sirius, the dog star. These are supposed to be Orion's hunting dogs. But . . . maybe they're hunting *him.*"

Hannah's gaze fell on the other piece of text.

An acrostic riddle:

Sideways walkers stop and stand
in the space above the land.
From the sunset until rise,
squares have not four, but six sides.
Day and night have equal length;
threads are intertwined for strength.

"These *are* getting harder," she moaned.

"What, the word puzzle? You don't know how to solve it?"

"It's not just an acrostic. It's a riddle. You have to guess which words the poem is talking about, and then you use the first letters of each word to spell the answer." She glanced at the three pathways, at the emblems engraved into each post. "And I bet it tells us which road to take."

Dominic shook his head at the inscription. "I wish
Chad was here. He likes these kinds of puzzles, and he
reads a lot about mythology, and he studies all kinds of
ancient glyphs from all over the world. I think he would
recognize some of this stuff." He looked at Hannah.
"Chad is the guy who was at Wupatki with me. You
remember him? The guy who asked you to stand on the
blowhole?"

"Yeah, I remember. I thought—"

Hannah broke off, distracted by a sudden, rhythmic
sound behind her, like the sound of footfalls. She looked
over her shoulder, and Dominic saw her face become
deathly afraid.

"What's the matter?" he asked. He followed her gaze,
tensing himself for whatever surprise waited behind his
back.

Chad was strolling along the path toward them. He still
wore his sunglasses, and below the dark glasses his
mouth was curved in a relaxed grin. "Hey," he said.
"What are you guys doing here?"

Neither Hannah nor Dominic could reply, so Chad
continued: "That blowhole has some serious fumes. As
soon as the air started blowing out, *wham*—I'm
hallucinating. You must have cracked open a
passageway to some seriously pent-up gases."

"Oh, no," Hannah said, her voice full of dread. "It's . . .
it's your wish."

Chad thought that sounded hilarious. He leaned
forward, stumbling a bit as he cackled at Hannah's
words. "Well I didn't wish to breathe cave fumes and go
into a full-blown phantasmagoria, but whatever."

Hannah pulled on Dominic's arm. "You just wished for
Chad to be here," she whispered. "The Capricorn said
she would help grant my wish, but you never made one,
until just now."

"Chad?" Dominic asked.

"Dom, what's up?" Chad slapped him on the arm, looked around, and put his hands in his pockets. "So what're you doing out here? Man, this place looks like Candy Land. I'm waiting for Princess Lolly to jump out at me. Or Queen Frostine. But I think I'd have better luck with Lolly. What's with the ridiculous helmet?"

Hannah raised her hands protectively to the sides of her winged helmet, as if to keep him from taking it. "It was a present. Taurus gave it to me."

"Who?"

"We're trying to get to . . . ." Hannah paused. "We're on a zodiac road, and we need to solve this riddle, so we can figure out which road to take."

"What riddle?" Chad peered at the post. "This? What's this?"

"It's an acrostic riddle," Hannah said hesitantly. "Have you done acrostics before?"

"Acrostics? Sure. Wait, what do you mean, it's a riddle?"

"There's a one-word answer for each line, so you have to guess all the words, and then you have to take—"

"Sure, sure. And you think the answer will tell us which road to pick?"

"Yes. Probably. We're in Gemini now, and we have to figure out which is the next zodiac sign."

"Hmm," Chad murmured, looking over the poem. "And, what do we need to do with the words?"

"The first letter of each word will spell the answer. So, it's like . . . ." Hannah paused, frowning at the riddle. "What's a 'sideways walker'? Never mind that one. 'The space above the land'—that could be 'sky.' Sky starts with *s*. And then you have to find the five other words and their first letters."

"So the real answer is a six-letter word."

"Yes."

Chad glanced at the posts, and then back at the

acrostic, and laughed.

"Sunset until rise," Dominic mused, "would be night, right?"

He and Hannah discussed the possibility of an answer that was spelled something-S-N-something-something-something, but Chad was already approaching the post marked with the symbol of the crab. He spoke to them over his shoulder: "It's Cancer, dum-dums. Cancer the crab."

"Wait a minute," Hannah protested. "Tell how you figured it out."

Chad came back to the stone inscription. "Sideways walkers—crabs," he said. "They walk sideways. The space above the land is air. From sunset to sunrise is night. What kind of square has six sides?" He looked pointedly at Hannah.

"A square always has *four* sides," she replied. Chad just stared at her, so she thought about it and said: "A cube?"

He nodded. "Day and night have equal length at the equinox, and threads intertwine to make a rope. Crab, Air, Night, Cube, Equinox, Rope. C-A-N-C-E-R." He smirked and added, "I knew it was Cancer anyway because it's next to Gemini in the zodiac, and it was the only six-letter answer. Leo and Libra didn't fit."

"You know the order?" Hannah asked. "So, what's next after Cancer?"

"Well, if we're going away from Gemini, it's Leo and then Virgo."

Hannah felt a tiny surge of hope. Perhaps Chad could help them get home after all. She and Dominic exchanged silent glances, and then they followed him down the middle path.

"Keep talking," Chad ordered them. "Don't get quiet on me. I'll start freaking out. Talk, keep me focused on something."

So Hannah told him about some of their adventures—about riding on the Capricorn's back; about being a fish and sitting in darkness within the sea-monster's belly; about Taurus and his kind eyes, his gift of seven stars and his strange words. "He said that we're in a labyrinth inside of another labyrinth, and that we're always making our way toward the center."

"That's true," Chad replied. "We're *centripetal*. It's like we're in a great cosmic mandala. Have you seen mandalas?"

"No."

He spoke rapidly, so that Hannah struggled to keep up with his words: "They're kind of like labyrinths. We experience pain and grief along the outsides, and as we get farther in, we get closer to peace; but we have to get through a lot of turns and curves to get there. It's a law of motion. See, balanced objects tend to travel in straight lines, and you need an unbalanced force to make it move in curves. We don't get anywhere by going straight. We have to curve into all these different places, experiment, play around. And the longer you stay unbalanced, the more places you get to experience. That's why it's better to stay unbalanced."

Hannah gave him a puzzled look, and Dominic said: "Don't ever take advice from him."

Chad shot him an annoyed look. "And what have *you* ever done to merit giving advice?"

"I'm not supposed to be talking to you anyway," Hannah said. "Taurus told me to think about my seven stars."

Chad laughed. "What, you can't think and talk at the same time? You're trying too hard. That's the problem with people; they duck their heads and focus on one thing that they're worried about, and they miss everything else. . . ."

Hannah found it hard to focus on the stars.

As the three travelers followed the dipping and curving path, Chad continued to explain the problem with people. "Our society takes people in their prime and exposes them to all these debasing, spirit-draining ideas. People are trapped in this guilt-ridden delusion where they *think* they can only learn and secure things through struggle. But life isn't meant to be like that. Everything can be easy."

"But, what if you *need* to go through something hard, because it teaches you something?" Hannah asked. "If I had never been inside of Cetus, I would have never learned how to turn into Pegasus."

"Yes, but it took you a long time to do that because you thought you had to suffer first. You could have just done it instantly, by refusing to suffer."

Hannah frowned. His words didn't sound quite right to her. "I didn't think I *had* to suffer."

"Then why did you? And what good did it do? Can you turn into Pegasus *now*?"

She bit her lip, considering. "No."

"Ha, that's because you believe that you can't have anything good unless you suffer first."

"That's not true," Hannah protested. "I don't *need* to turn into Pegasus now. It was something I needed to do when I was in Cetus. And I turned into Monoceros to save Dominic. It's not some kind of trick that I can perform whenever I want."

"Why not?"

"Because . . . I don't know how to explain it. The Pegasus constellation was back there for a reason. I don't need it anymore. And changing into a winged horse wasn't important; changing my *feelings*, and the way I saw things, was important."

"You're making that up to justify your ideas," Chad replied with a smirk. "See, you're in control of your abilities. You were in control of everything that whole time, but you suffered because you believed that you had to. People have been duped into thinking they can never have anything good unless they experience some kind of discomfort first. We toil at these nine-to-five jobs and come home to a stifling life that kills our spirits. We have this natural drive to go out and explore everything about the world around us, but we get trapped into these dull routines. We end up with obligations to other people that prevent us from honoring ourselves."

"But people can't just do everything for themselves," Hannah protested. "What if you have a baby? If you have a baby, it depends on you to take care of it. That's a routine. You were a baby once, and someone took care of *you*."

"Sure. My mother did that. But it wasn't an act of selflessness, because she got something from it. She got love. Love is a natural part of life; it's the greatest thing. But you have to love yourself, too. And when you realize that life isn't about suffering, you have to honor yourself by refusing to fall into this toil-and-guilt routine that everyone else is wrapped up in. Take my parents, for instance. I can take what they earned and use it to my advantage, but that doesn't mean I have to do the same thing. I can just live off of it until I find a way to sustain myself without labor."

"You just live off your parents while you figure out how to not work?" Hannah asked. "That's like not believing in growing up. You sound like you'd rather just stay a child and let someone else take care of you."

"It's not the same," Chad snapped. "I'm talking about society and the concept of hard, toiling, energy-draining work. We're not meant to work; we're meant to enjoy life to the fullest. But there will always be people trapped in this delusion about following orders and working hard, and they get whatever they believe in. I have a better mind than that; I'm *creative*. So I can get *them* to do all the work while I channel my energies into something greater. That's the key to enlightenment. It's knowing the truth, and getting that inner peace, while the people around you are still stumbling around in the darkness. It's about getting that freedom from guilt."

Chad kept talking about peace and enlightenment. He spoke with a great deal of enthusiasm, but Hannah turned to Dominic with a frown, murmuring: "Your friend sounds like a jerk."

"No comment."

Chad's head whipped around. "What'd you say?"

"I said that you talk a lot," Hannah replied.

He looked suspicious. "Oh, is that all?" He shrugged. "All right. It's not like I care about the opinion of a ten-year-old."

"I'm eleven," Hannah said flatly.

"You guys, don't start arguing," Dominic warned as they reach the top of another hill. "Look, this path could go on for miles. I don't want to spend the whole hike listening to you two bickering."

But Hannah and Chad bickered anyway.

At the next hill they were still bickering, and when it seemed they'd walked a mile they were still exchanging sharp words.

"Enough already," Chad demanded. "I'm forty-four years old, Hannah. I've got a few decades on you at least, so I don't need your life lectures."

"You're forty-four and you still live off your parents?" she asked.

"I don't live off my parents, I work at a record shop. Dominic does all the crap work, and I get the fun jobs."

Hannah looked at Dominic. "Doesn't he bother you?"

"Yes, he does," Dominic replied. "So do you. You're *both* driving me crazy."

"*Me?*" Hannah looked at him in surprise. "What am *I* doing?"

"You keep arguing."

"He's being a jerk."

"So ignore him."

"I shouldn't have to!"

"Hannah . . . didn't I say I can't stand the sound of kids whining?"

"So ignore it," Hannah replied coolly. "What, you can ignore the sound of Chad being a jerk to everyone, but you can't ignore me complaining about it?"

Chad sneered down at her. "Am I being a jerk to Dom? He's fine with me because he's not a whiny, know-it-all kid getting on my nerves."

"I wish you hadn't come here. I don't want to walk through the zodiac with you."

"So get lost," Chad snapped. "Three's a crowd. We're in Gemini, there's only supposed to be two of us."

"Yeah, me and Dominic."

"Says who? Gemini is the constellation of the hero twins. Practically every culture has a story about hero twins, and it's always two guys. You must at least know the Navajo hero twins, Monster Slayer and . . . Water Boy, or whatever his name is."

"The riddle says it's us. There was a picture of us together—me in my red vest, and Dominic with his shirt and jeans."

"Oh yeah? Well, look." Chad stopped and scratched some lines into the dirt with his boot, making a tall stick figure and a shorter one beside it. "Different place on the path, different picture. It's me and Dom now. So, beat it. Go and do your own thing."

Hannah looked pleadingly at Dominic. "Aren't you going to say anything?"

"I'm not talking to anyone."

"If you were my friend, you would stick up for me."

"You think Dom is your friend?" Chad smirked. "Maybe if you were ten years older and more developed,

and not dressed in that ridiculous-looking nightgown. I
guess you're about the right height, though."

"You look ugly with that stupid smirk on your face."

Chad balked; the smirk vanished, but he quickly
recovered, speaking with pure anger rather than sarcasm.
"Yeah, and you just look ugly. I don't want to walk
through the zodiac with an ugly, whiny kid."

Again, Hannah looked at Dominic. He ignored her,
focusing on the path ahead.

They stopped talking then, because they were coming
to a new place. At the bottom of the last hill stood a
large archway of deep-blue stone, and across the arch
was inscribed: GATE OF CANCER.

Just beyond the arch was another labyrinth, walled
with the same blue stone, vast and curving. As the three
came closer, they saw that the entrance was barred by a
tall metal gate—and behind the bars stood a small, thin,
goblin-like creature, a few strands of white hair
streaming from its greenish-gray head, a grin on its dry
and cracked lips, and small dark eyes that gleamed
merrily.

"Well, *that's* ugly," Chad muttered, loud enough for
the creature to hear.

"How do we get through?" Hannah asked.

The creature pointed to the arch. Hannah spotted some
words carved into one side of the blue stone, and she
moved closer to examine them. Up close she saw that
the stone was streaked with gold, flecks sparkling within
darker gold clouds that swept across the stone's surface.
She thought of stardust in a dark blue universe; she
admired the stone's beauty. Then she remembered Chad
and Dominic, and her mood fouled.

An acrostic:

"It's the Pleiades," Hannah said dully.

"How do you know?" Dominic asked.

She glared at him, but pointed out the first letters of each line: "P, L, E, I, A, D, E, S."

"That's a lazy way to do it," Chad said. "There's more to a riddle than just finding a word. We have to figure out what to do with it."

"I already know what to do, because Taurus told me. We have to use my seven stars to get through the gates."

"*Your* seven stars, huh? Do you actually know about the Pleiades? I happen to know a lot about them. They're actually really fascinating." Chad stepped closer to the arch and ran a finger over the words. "You see here, where it's saying that the stars are lowered into winter's gloom—that's a reference to the way people have used the Pleiades constellation to mark the seasons. Up here—I mean, in the north—after spring arrived, the constellation would rise above the horizon just before dawn. In the fall it would set at dawn. People based their farming cycles and their other seasonal routines based on this constellation . . . ."

He went on, explaining how the position of the constellation made it visible nearly everywhere on Earth, and thus susceptible to widespread mythology; and then he talked about the heliacal rising of other stars.

"Chad," Dominic interrupted at last, "I'm not in the mood for an astronomy lesson, and I'm sure Hannah isn't either. We both have scorpion stings, and mine is starting to throb again, and we need to get through this road to find the antidote."

Chad laughed. "Oh, is that your story? Where's your—" He turned to address Hannah, but broke off when he realized she was no longer standing beside him. He looked this way, and that, and said, "Where'd she go?"

Dominic didn't see her either, but he knew perfectly well where she was. He knew because the strange-looking gatekeeper, still poised just beyond the gate, stood admiring something in its hand. Within that thin-fingered grasp was something that looked like a tiny glowing star.

10: Cancer

"She went in without us," Dominic said in disbelief.

"What a little turd! Well, what do you expect from a twelve-year-old?"

Slowly, Dominic approached the gate. "What are we supposed to do now? I can't believe she left us here." He shot a dark look at Chad. "Great job. You know, you could stand to be a little more civil to a kid."

"Don't blame *me*. She's determined to do her own thing, so let her go. She'll have to learn things the hard way like everyone else."

Dominic looked at him for some time, and replied: "I'd feel better going in with Hannah." He sighed and addressed the gatekeeper. "Hey. Is there another way to get through, without using the little star things?"

The gatekeeper stretched out a bony hand.

"We have to give something," Dominic said. "Can we give other things?"

The creature grinned and didn't answer.

The ram-skin boots were still lying near the stone arch, where Dominic had dropped them. He untied them and brought them to the gate.

Dominic barely stuck the first boot through the bars when the creature snatched it. It curled its fingers into the woolen lining with one hand and opened the gate with the other. From its little mouth came a strange little chuckle.

The two men started tentatively onto the walled path, keeping their distance from the gatekeeper. The deep-blue passage curved slightly and came to a loop, and as they rounded the loop the men came upon another gate. And there, behind its metal bars, was another little creature with sparse strands of hair and beady little eyes.

Dominic looked on with disbelief. "Aren't you the same guy we saw at the last gate?"

It grinned and held out its hand. Dominic pushed the other boot through the bars, and the gate opened noiselessly.

He knew what they would find ahead. Again the path curved into a loop, and again they came to a tall gate. Again the same gatekeeper stretched out its hand.

"We don't have enough things to give," Dominic said.

Chad nudged him. "Sure we do. Give him your flask."

Dominic hesitated, eyeing the soft ram-skin vessel. "I'm not sure I'm supposed to give these things."

"Well, don't look at *me*. I have empty pockets."

"You have something. You had cash in your pants pocket."

"Not anymore. I checked. Everything must have fallen out. Or it's not part of my hallucination, or whatever."

"Fine." Dominic passed the flask through the gate, and the little creature grabbed it.

Dominic searched his garments for something else to give. He didn't want to lose the flute; it was precious to him. He found Chad's flashlight in his pocket, and before Chad could protest, he handed that over instead. With another little chuckle the creature allowed them to pass.

Dominic continued to rifle through his clothes as they walked, counting under his breath.

"That was *my* flashlight you gave away," Chad scolded him. "You could have at least asked for permission."

"We have to come up with three more things to give."

"How do you know?"

"Three more gates. Seven gates total. Remember the

riddle?"

Sure enough, they soon came to the fifth gate—and there again was the strange, smiling gatekeeper. There Dominic handed over his belt; and as they proceeded through the last two gates, he gave up his woolen sweater, and finally the horn flute.

"I should've grabbed that hoof rattle," he muttered. "That, I wouldn't have minded giving up."

The gatekeeper seemed to think that was funny. It laughed—and to Dominic's astonishment, it spoke. "The underworld queen is busy," it said in a wheedling voice. "She's with a young girl who just came through. You'll have to wait."

"The underworld queen?" Chad peered at the path before him. It opened into a wide plaza of cobbled stone and mortar. A small sphinx-like figure, a lion with a woman's face, crouched at the opposite edge, and beyond the sphinx was a remarkable dome of blue stone.

"You may have to wait for eons," the creature said. "Or . . . you can pass through over there." It pointed to the right, where another path sloped upward toward an angular stone tunnel. "It's the long way, but it's easier, and it will take you where you need to go."

"Better up than down," Chad said. "Although I wouldn't mind getting a look at the underworld queen. Then again, she might be someone we want to avoid."

Dominic sighed and walked on. "Let's go."

They followed the tunnel into a small square room, dimly lit by an opening in the ceiling. A rough wooden ladder, bound together with thick fibers, rose through the opening into daylight. Chad gestured to Dominic. "Onward. You first."

Dominic hoisted himself onto the ladder. He wouldn't have minded the rungs being closer together, or the wood being sanded—but the difficult climb eventually brought him into another square room, a room with a significant difference. It had a door. And through the doorway Dominic saw a familiar, comforting sight: shrubs and pines stretching across a vast plain, mountains visible in the distance, and over all of it a light blue sky . . . a sky with wispy white clouds and a blazing sun.

"How is it?" Chad asked from below.

Dominic breathed the pine-scented air. "It's beautiful."

A dirt path cut through the shrubs and weeds from the doorway, as though it had been worn down by frequent walking. Dominic stood and admired the landscape more deeply than he had ever admired any place.

"Did you see this?" Chad's words were followed by a deep pounding sound. Dominic turned and saw him holding a small frame drum in one hand, a wooden drumstick with hide padding in the other.

"Where did you get that?"

"Right here." Chad gestured to a wooden bench. "Look, the stick has symbols carved all over it. I bet it's a clue."

He banged the drum again.

"I wouldn't do that," Dominic warned.

Chad rolled his eyes. "Relax. Maybe we're *supposed* to play it. Let's take it with us. Even if it isn't a clue, we could use some music." He stepped outside, into the sunlight, and peered at the symbols. Chad and Dominic studied the spiral shapes, the carvings of little people and animals, griffins and birds and crabs—but they couldn't make anything of it. So Chad pointed to the path and said, "Let's see where it leads."

As they walked, he asked: "Doesn't this remind you of Chaco Canyon? It's just like Chaco, except . . . ." He looked down at Dominic. "Come on, you've been to Chaco, we went there together. That place was set up with all sorts of astronomical measurements. Maybe there are dimensional portals there, leading to the stars, and we've gone through one of them, right back into our own world. Maybe we've come back in another *time*. I mean, look at this place. Doesn't that look like Fajada Butte?"

"This isn't Chaco Canyon. The landscape is different."

"Exactly. We traveled through time."

"I think the sun is setting."

"So what, you want to head back?"

"No. I don't think we're really on Earth. I want to get through this place, whatever it is, and I want to go home."

The worn path led far across the pine-dotted basin and up into rocky terrain. The two men followed as it cut into the side of the mountain; they enjoyed the fresh air and warm sun. But the sun was, indeed, setting.

"Guess we'll have to camp out," Chad said. "Too bad we can't make a bonfire." He sat against a flat rock and placed the drum upright on his lap. And then he banged on it, loudly and steadily, for a long time.

"Please put the drum away," Dominic pleaded at last.

"I actually have an amazing sense of rhythm. I could go on like this for hours. Have you ever heard of trance drumming? You can drum a certain rhythm for so long that eventually—"

"You shouldn't be playing it here. I don't want to draw attention."

"That's because you're looking at things through a lens of fear, and expecting the worst," Chad said. "We'll probably draw *positive* attention. I really wish I could remember some of those songs that Ben sings with frame drum. How does that one go—I can't remember the actual words, but there are some vocables . . . *ohhh . . . hey-oh hey . . . .*"

"Please don't sing those songs, they're sacred and you're not in ceremony."

"I'm *always* in ceremony."

"You're just sitting there talking about what a great drummer you are." Dominic grabbed at the stick, but Chad snatched it from his grasp.

"Now look what you did. You threw off my groove." Chad started again, tipping his head back and singing along: "*Heyyy, oh hey-oh* . . . ."

Dominic leaned his head against the mountain and stared at the featureless black sky.

By the time daylight returned Chad had fallen silent, sprawled against the rocks and snoring. He woke with a start, moaned as he twisted upright. "Still here? That's great; that's awesome." He pressed one hand into the base of his back. "Ah, that's going to be sore. What I wouldn't give for a . . . ." His voice sharpened. "Where'd you put my drum?"

Dominic spoke groggily from his own rock. "I didn't touch it."

"It was right . . . what is *that*? You've got to be *kidding* me."

"What's wrong?" Dominic struggled to rouse himself, carefully turning his aching head on his stiff neck.

A large crack had opened in the stone floor—perhaps two feet wide, and a few feet in length. Chad was leaning forward on his palms, craning his neck, trying to peer into the chasm. "It's down there. I see it, but it's too far down to reach."

"Good."

"You have to climb down and get it."

"No."

"You're the only one who's small enough to fit inside."

"Don't start that again."

"It's true. We *need* that drumstick, Dom, it's our map. It has all the inscriptions on it. It's probably our next riddle."

Dominic ignored him. His shoulders and back ached

from his rest upon the unyielding rock. He slowly tried
to stretch his body.

"All right, listen: I swear I won't play the drum. And
I'll make more of an effort not to act like a jerk. It's just
. . . you know how I get. It's all about the distractions."
Chad tapped his fingertips rapidly against the flat stone.
"When things get tough, the distractions keep me sane."

"Yes," Dominic said dryly, "I've heard your 'It's all
about the distractions' speech before."

"It's true. I mean, this is great, it's an amazing
adventure, but it's *crazy*. If I stop to think about it too
much, instead of focusing on the distractions, I'll go
nuts. I mean, really, without our coping mechanisms, can
you imagine what would happen to our *minds*? It's the
same with being a jerk. I'm afraid to get close to people;
the closeness terrifies me. Being a jerk keeps people at a
distance. It helps me cope with the terror of being a
human being."

"I've heard this one, too."

"I'm serious. I've been trying to cope with all this by
going with the flow, but I'm starting to feel like we're
stuck. I'll never get back to my apartment. I'll never get
back to my . . . my *things*. My parents will never know
what happened to me." Chad leaned close again and
stared into the opening. "That stick *is* our map. If
Hannah was here . . . ."

"Since when do you care about Hannah's role in all
this?" Dominic crept to the other side of the chasm and
studied the drop.

"Dominic, if you bring it back, I will be seriously
grateful to you, and I will try harder not to freak out. I
swear it. Look, there are little ledges that you can use for
steps, and it's not far down. Just climb a few feet and
you'll have it."

It sounded eerily like what Dominic had heard just
before his fateful decision to climb into the hole at

Wupatki. But Chad was probably right about the stick: it was important, it was a piece of the puzzle. And Dominic needed to find his way forward—not just to get home, but to find the cure for the scorpion venom. *And probably to catch up with Hannah.* Dominic wondered how far she'd gotten, if she was still safe, if the venom was still dormant in her body.

So he made the short climb downward. The ledges made it easy. Dominic could rest his back against one side of the chasm and step onto the ledges on the other side. He scooted a few feet downward. The drum was just below him, stuck on a couple of perpendicular ledges, but Dominic had no intention of retrieving it. He grabbed the stick.

"Got it," he said.

And then the ledge broke beneath his feet, and he fell.

Once again Dominic dropped through a short tunnel onto a hard floor. His legs buckled and his body lurched forward as he struck bottom; he sprawled face-down, barely managing to avoid knocking his teeth against stone. Almost immediately Dominic became aware of a peculiar buzzing sound. He tensed, remembering the buzzing that had filled his ears when the giant bird-thing had descended on him, the buzzing that intensified as he transformed into a fish—and all he could think was *Please don't let me transform again, please let me stay a man.*

But when he lifted his face, he felt relieved. The buzzing came from a fly: a simple, harmless, wandering housefly. It perused the area around Dominic's face, then lost interest and disappeared into a large rectangular passageway.

Dominic dared to hope that he had landed back at one of the Wupatki ruins. The cavern around him was solid stone, yet it had been cut into angular forms: a square room, three dimly lit corridors. Dominic stood and

listened, focusing on faint sounds of movement—
footsteps, maybe. He ventured into one of the halls,
forgetting to inspect his new scrapes or to check his
aching feet. He forgot to call out to Chad. He forgot
about the drumstick that had rolled against the wall, the
drum that lay scratched but intact behind him. With a
slight limp Dominic crept down the hall. He stopped at a
corner to listen to the sound of something being dragged,
the occasional buzzing of flies—and when he peeked
around the edge, he found the next stone passage
occupied by listlessly wandering human figures.

Tourists! he thought with relief. He must have landed
back at Wupatki after all. Dominic rounded the corner
and waved a hand. "Excuse me . . . ."

He stopped. In the dim light Dominic saw scraps of
cloth hanging from the slender human forms. The
nearest one approached him, and as Dominic looked up
into its face, he saw dried strands of flesh dropping from
the pale curve of bone and a wide expanse of lipless
teeth—the face of a rotted corpse.

Dominic balked in horror at the skeletal apparition.
Stringy hair hung long from bits of skin still adhered to
the bone of its skull. The figure was so decomposed that
the smells of decay had long since vanished. Only a few
dried patches of sinew and meat, neglected by the worms
of the underworld, remained. Yet the figure stood
upright and walked. It turned its hollow eye sockets on
Dominic and reached for him blindly.

The corpse spoke in a raspy, eager, female voice: "Are
you alive?"

Other figures stopped, turned sightless faces in his
direction.

Dominic hesitated. "What will happen if I say yes?"

His question went unanswered. All at once, the
scattered wretches of the underworld tunnels became a
mob, rushing at him with surprising speed. They

snatched at his clothes; bony fingers gripped his wrists. He felt himself pulled onward. Dominic uttered a helpless, desperate cry that he knew would go unanswered: *"Chad!"*

He struggled in vain against the mass of skeletal hands, was dragged down the corridor until a booming voice stopped the corpses in their tracks: "Stop! What have you got there?"

"It's a boy-child!" the corpse-woman rasped. "A live boy-child, in the land of the dead!"

"So it is. Let go; let me see him."

Dominic steadied himself, relieved to be free of those clutching skeletons. Near-panic made him want to run, but he saw that he was lost and outnumbered. He turned to the source of the commanding voice and was startled by the sight of an impossibly tall man—or perhaps a woman—of such great height that its head nearly brushed the high ceiling, and Dominic strained his already-sore neck when he looked up at it. The face contained oblong, featureless eyes, while the flesh that covered its thin body looked like polished chrome.

"What business do you have here?" the thing asked.

Dominic shuddered at the sight of the creature's wide, thin mouth and soulless eyes. "None. I fell down here by accident."

"No one falls into the underworld by accident!"

"Well, I did."

"And how did you open the portal?"

"Um . . . I didn't open a portal. I was on a mountain . . . a crack opened in the rock . . . I reached in to get something, and I fell."

"Ah. And is *this* the 'something' you reached for?" The creature extended one long, thin arm. The drumstick was clutched in its fingers.

"Yeah, that's it."

"This drumstick belongs to the underworld. It was

crafted from an underworld tree."

"I didn't know that. You can keep it. Please . . . I really don't belong here. I'm just trying to get home."

"Why?"

"Because . . . that's where I belong. I want to get back to my family. The hole I fell into is just back there. If you could give me a lift, I'll climb up again, and I'll be out of your way."

One of the corpses chuckled. Its voice came out dry and abrasive: "He doesn't belong here, he says. What do you think about us, boy? You think we belong here?"

The tall creature gazed at Dominic expressionlessly. "If you're here, then it follows that you belong here—for the time being. There's no way out but through the center. The queen of the underworld is there. Face her first, and see what fate you've conceived for yourself." It nodded at the others. "Take him."

Bony fingers sunk once again into Dominic's tender muscles, and again he was pulled roughly through the corridors. He didn't resist, but pleaded with his captors: "You don't need to drag me. I'll walk."

Instead of loosening their grip, they coiled new materials round his body, dry limbs rasping loudly as they worked. With horror Dominic saw himself constrained by ragged cloth and tough sinew—bound with scraps from the underworld's dead.

At the center of one short hall, a tall doorway stood open, and even before he reached it Dominic saw that the chamber beyond was not of the same bare substance as the rest of this stone labyrinth. Its circular walls were a deep blue, streaked with gold and lit all around, illuminating the symbols that encompassed the room. Its inhabitants were richly dressed, their attention turned to a platform upon which was centered an ornate cushioned chair. Beside the chair stood another other-worldly creature, a figure with a human body, but with a face just

as strange and startling as that of the tall creature at
Dominic's back. In place of a mouth it had a long beak,
yellow around the small nostrils and black along the
down-turned tip. In one claw-like hand it held a thick
sheet of papyrus, the bottom rolled into a heavy coil. On
the throne a woman sat: a living woman, dressed in a
simple white tunic that hung loosely over her chest and
rounded belly—and with an ornate, silvery crown upon
her jet-black hair, its thin framework set with a dozen
glittering stones.

The bird-thing stopped in mid-sentence, lifting its head
to appraise the crowd in the doorway. It moved to the
foreground; the beak opened, and the voice came high
and harsh. "Who has brought this man hither?"

The tall, blank-eyed creature stepped beside Dominic
and bowed. "He came and knocked at the gate of the
nether world."

The bird-faced person scrutinized him with round,
beady eyes.

"I didn't knock, actually," Dominic said. "I fell in by
accident."

"And what does he seek?"

"Freedom. He beseeches you to free him from his
bonds."

Dominic looked to the woman on the throne, saw her
expression changeless and calm.

"He wants to be a man again," the blank-eyed creature
said, "to live with those precious to his heart, his friends
and his family."

"Then let him be introduced."

Dominic's knees scraped the ground as his captors
pulled him close to the platform. He found himself
unable to stand, his legs twisted into haphazardly
twining cords. The crowned woman leaned forward and
studied his cowering figure from the height of her
throne. "What is it that you seek in the realm of the

dead?" she asked gently. "Do you desire the secret of eternal life, or of the portal that leads to re-birth?"

"No."

"No? Do you desire the secret of the sushumna spark, which drives from the seat of your power?"

"I . . . would just like to go back up into the hole where I fell in, so I can climb up and get back to my friend."

The woman glanced at her peers. "He wants to go back," she said, and addressed Dominic: "Why not leave your companion, and go on alone?"

"I don't want to leave him behind."

The others looked at one another, laughing discreetly, rotting hands covering rotting mouths.

"Something funny about that?" Dominic asked.

"You must be a very great friend."

He tried to shrug though his restraints. "Yeah, I'm a great friend. I hope it's a redeeming enough quality that it justifies my livelihood."

"Once in the land of the dead, the spirit can't return to its former life. You won't go back without being greatly changed—not of your own volition."

"I'm not dead," Dominic insisted. "I didn't die."

She smiled again at her companions. "He says he's not dead."

Those words filled him with dread. *It's true. I died; I'm lost in limbo; I will never see my family again. My life is over.*

"I will offer you a doorway," the woman offered, "in the form of a riddle. If you can solve it, you may return to the upper world—but you must enter it with a new name. If you try to leave as you are, you won't get far. The dead are like crabs in a bucket. They'll snare you and drag you down again." She strengthened her voice ever so slightly, and her words gained a lyrical quality:

My first, bound to the underworld, cries out as it

gives birth;
My second sits upon its base, begetting of this earth;
My third knows to absorb the water which will
quench one's thirst;
My fourth knows irrigation, all its sustenance
dispersed;
My fifth knows how to speak and scribe the others'
higher verse;
My sixth sees how to work the fourth, its fields in
dreams traversed;
My seventh, on a petaled throne, in wisdom has
unfurled;
My all compose the gates along the axis of my world.
What am I?

After the first two lines, Dominic could hardly focus. His attention dropped to the heaviness in his belly, to his bound body, his feeling of mortal dread. He wracked his brain for some meaning in those first lines and made no sense of them. "I'm really not good at word puzzles."

The woman leaned back against the stone-and-cloth chair. There seemed something ever peaceful in her movements, slight as they were. "You'll not even guess? The consequence for a wrong answer is no worse than that for none."

He considered helplessly. He felt confused even by the way she spoke. "Is it . . . a woman? . . . A pregnant woman?" Dominic paused. "Is it you?"

"I'm not pregnant," she said.

"Oh . . . sorry."

The dead laughed at him.

"Is it . . . the life cycle of a human being?"

The woman smiled with surprised satisfaction. "Closer, but not nearly precise enough."

"The birth canal?"

"No, but that's an interesting answer."

The dead laughed again, and someone murmured: "He

called it a *canal*."

"Ah . . . how many guesses do I get?"

"You don't see the answer. Then you are stuck; you must stay. Unless . . . ?" The woman looked aside questioningly.

"Can you give me a hint?" Dominic pleaded.

She ignored him, gazing at an open doorway at the rear of the chamber. "Will someone suffer the consequence for this young man?"

Dominic was shocked to see Hannah coming through the passage. She moved quietly, watching him as she approached the platform. Her red vest still hung open over the soft nightgown, and the winged helmet still rested on her head, minus the glowing stars.

She looked up at the crowned woman. "I'll suffer the consequence."

"Hannah, what are you doing?" Dominic asked, alarmed.

The woman addressed him: "You can take Hannah's passage out of the underworld."

"I don't want it," he insisted.

But Hannah came to where he knelt, and looked sadly at his bonds. She removed the winged helmet.

"Here," she said. "You can have this."

Dominic didn't know what to say, or what to think. He began to say "Hannah," but then she pushed the helmet over his head. It was too small, and it hurt his skull. It hurt a little at first, and then it hurt a lot; and then he heard a familiar, unpleasant buzzing sound, and his being filled with fear. He hoped that the buzzing sound was just another fly, but already he could feel his stomach heaving, his body changing. The dead were still gathered close, but queen waved them aside and commanded: "Make way for the *ascending dove*."

And Dominic became a dove.

Being a dove was no less strange or terrifying than

being a fish. The bonds fell away as Dominic dipped and
flailed in mid-air. He flapped madly into the corridors,
banged carelessly against the walls, and raced toward a
bit of light just ahead of him. But he wasn't trying to get
away from the underworld. He was trying to get away
from being a bird.

Up through the shaft of light he flew, back into the
Earth-like terrain above, back through the crack in the
earth and onto the mountain. He crashed there, landing
hard on the same rock where he'd spent the night; and as
he rolled his aching body aside, Dominic was filled with
relief. He didn't mind the pain of his fall. He was
already a man again, and he was just glad to be a man.

11: Leo

"I hate this place!" Dominic screamed.

His relief hadn't lasted. He was alone on the mountain, and the sun was just beginning to rise again, as though he'd been underground for a full day and night.

Dominic's hand throbbed. His body was scraped and bruised from his ordeal. He wanted to go home. He screamed at the brightening sky until someone interrupted him.

"Dom, is that you? Where the hell have you been all this time?"

Dominic turned to see a tall man standing behind him, a fair-haired man with sunglasses. He looked and sounded like Chad . . . except Chad had been clean-shaven. This man had a neatly trimmed beard and mustache, and he was wearing someone else's clothes.

"What happened to you?" Chad put his hands on his hips. "Hey, did you ever get my drum? You didn't. Well, don't worry, I lost interest in it. I've got this other thing going on."

"Why do you have a beard?"

Chad laughed. "Why do you have a head?" He rubbed his beard. "I've never really been a beard guy, but the ladies love it. It makes me stand out."

"What . . . what ladies? Are there other people here?"

"You *have* been gone a long time. Come on, come back to my place. I'll get you something to eat. You look half-dead."

"I'm not going." Dominic shook his head. "I hate this

place. I don't want to eat its food. I just want to get out."

"What, are you still afraid we're in the zodiac? Relax. We're on Earth. Come on, I'll show you. I've got a nice house in the valley."

"How long have I been gone?"

"I don't know. A year, two years maybe. I didn't keep track."

"Two *years*?"

"How long did it seem like?"

"I don't know. Half an hour."

"Seriously? See, we *are* in a time warp! Time is warped here; it's playing around with us. We're on Earth, but we're in another time. I told everyone I'm from the future."

"Another time, as in . . . not our own time? We're not home?"

"No, but this is better. Come on, I've got a logging team up here and we're about to head back. I can't wait to show you everything I've been doing."

Dominic stumbled along the mountain path. He told Chad how much it had hurt, transforming into a dove— how it had terrified him. Strangely, he felt angry at Hannah for making it happen. It bothered him so much that he nearly forgot about being saved from the realm of the dead.

"Hannah . . . you mean that whiny kid who was with us?" Chad asked. "It wasn't her, it was that witch. I've heard stories about her. She calls herself the queen of the underworld. She likes to mess with people and make them suffer. She turns people into beasts."

Dominic stopped walking. "This isn't Earth."

"It's an alternate Earth dimension. Come on, just go with it. Let me show you what's going on."

They came upon a few dozen men hauling logs down the base of the mountain. Chad introduced Dominic as his "friend from the future," and the men marveled over him, crowding close and touching the pockets of his blue jeans.

"They're pants," Dominic said. "Do you mind?"

The group descended to a vast plain surrounded by mountains. It could have been the same place that Dominic and Chad had walked across after rising from the Cancer gate—but it looked different. The shrubs had shriveled; most of the pines were gone, so that only a few junipers and pinyons stood drying in the sun; the grasses had become loose brown wisps, and the wind blew them across Dominic's feet.

"What happened to all the trees?" he asked.

"We used them," Chad replied.

For days the men hauled lumber on crude wagons. They camped out at night, and Dominic was astonished to see stars peeking from behind the clouds.

"Of course there are stars," Chad said. "I told you, we're on Earth."

When they arrived at the village, Chad showed Dominic how the trees had been put to use. He pointed to the great house, the tallest and longest of the wooden buildings, and an adjacent courtyard walled with pine. "That's my place," he said. "Wait 'til you see what it's like on the inside."

They walked through the first room of the great house, and then through a dining room, and though the other rooms which were all arranged in a row. Chad stopped to point out the decorations he'd consigned for each one; he talked about the furniture, about the superior construction of the walls, and many other things. He pointed out the stairs that lined each northern wall, leading to other rooms above. At the last room he said: "This is my bedroom. See how I arranged the shelves in this area? I was really going for an M.C. Escher type thing. And if you light these candles, they throw really cool designs across the wall. I wish I had a light so I could show you."

"You live in this place alone?"

"Well, mostly. It's mine."

"And people actually built this for you?"

"Sure. I have the knowledge, but they have the manpower. I have the contracting skills. I made some lumber contracts in the area, and we have income flowing in from my other projects, so I designed this place and paid some builders."

"You designed it?"

"Well, I designed the *inside*. Parts of it, anyway. Come and stand over here." Chad beckoned him to the middle of the room. "See how the rooms are perfectly symmetrical? If you stand here you can see through all the doorways, all the way through to the courtyard. Cool, right? Except it's not finished; I need privacy. I want to put a good quality door here, and have it hand-carved all over. The western mountains have some really great ponderosa pines, some of the biggest trees I've ever seen—but these folks won't go up there, and it's not because of the climb. They say there's some kind of beast up there, a giant mutant lion thing that preys on people."

"Nothing wrong with juniper wood," Dominic said.

"But I want the door to be one piece of solid wood, not some cheap plywood atrocity. It's all about the aesthetics. Dom, you have to help convince these guys to go up there. Seriously, we need the timber, and all this superstitious 'there are monsters up there' crap is holding us back. If there is some kind of beast up there, we can kill it and take the meat. We're short on food."

"*We* can kill it? You mean, you're going to send *them* to kill it."

"No way. I'll kill it myself. Well, I might do it with some help, but I want the credit. My man-from-the-future novelty is starting to wear off, and these guys aren't keen on the idea of carrying a solid pine slab all the way from the mountains. If I kill this monster that everyone is so afraid of, imagine what that'll do for my status. These people will *worship* me. I'll bring its head back and put it on display in the courtyard. It's probably just a mountain lion, but we'll find a way to make it look scary. We'll make it look *horrifying*."

Dominic sighed.

Late in the evening, a woman came to the dining room and served dinner. Chad and Dominic ate venison with juniper-berry sauce, and pine nuts roasted with oil and greens; and then Dominic was shown to the guest room. Through the window he saw the cloudless sky lit with stars. He went outside to get a better look.

Near the creek, men and women cooked skewered meat in a small bonfire. One of the loggers greeted Dominic: "Out for some stargazing?"

"Yeah. I never really looked at the stars before, but . . . now they seem more interesting." Dominic turned toward the profile of the western mountains. "Say, Chad was telling me that he wants to do some logging in those mountains, but people don't want to go because of a beast that lives in the woods. You know anything about that?"

"We all know about Humbaba. He's guardian of the high forest. No one dares trespass in that place."

"Oh. So, people have seen this beast?"

"A long time ago. My grandfather and his brothers saw it, and no one has gone up there since. If someone has to pass through the mountains, they prepare themselves and walk carefully. Humbaba hears even the smallest movement in that forest."

"So, what is it? Is it a mountain lion?"

The man laughed. "Humbaba is no lion. He has the body of a lion, but his face is like a coiled serpent, and his horns are like the horns of a bull. When he's angry, even his roar causes disaster. He can spit fire onto the earth, and his breath is like a whirlwind." The logger pulled a piece of spongy-looking meat from his stick and offered it to Dominic.

"Um . . . what is it?" Dominic asked.

"Tongue."

"No thanks."

The man popped the chunk of meat into his own mouth. "There's marrow and raw kidney if you want it, but the heart and liver have already been eaten, and so have the brains." He gestured to the bonfire. "Look around if you're hungry. There's lizard meat, and probably some snake and rat, and mice. People will share with you." He put another of the skewered objects in his mouth, chewed it for a while, and spat a pulp of scorched fur and crushed bones onto the ground.

Dominic's stomach turned. "Thanks, but I already ate. Excuse me—I have to get back inside."

Every day, Chad tried to convince the village that he would kill Humbaba. He began to hunt with the other men, showing off his archery skills and even butchering the meat. He walked straight and tall; he swaggered through the village with his chest puffed out.

"Try to persuade the younger, unmarried guys," he told Dominic. "The women complain if their husbands aren't around to help with the field work, and these younger men stand to benefit. They're starting their lives, they need homes and cattle. There are sheep on the mountain, and people have seen cows, really pretty ones with different colors. We can catch them and herd them back. And once we do the logging, the miners can come in. We have contracts with two different mines. We can take all that timber, and—"

"Maybe you should leave some trees," Dominic interrupted. "That's not just timber, it's animal habitat, it's part of an ecosystem."

Chad rolled his eyes. "Oh, we can't cut down the trees, the animals are using them! Well guess what, *we're* animals and *we're* using them. You think the earth can't grow more trees? The earth is powerful enough to repair any damage caused by humans. Get over yourself."

"I don't care what you do," Dominic said. "I hate this place."

"You have to come with us. I can't stand these people, Dom, they're hillbillies. I can't talk *culture* with anyone. And everyone's terrified of this beast. I need you for moral support."

"*Moral* support, huh?"

"I need your encouragement. It's probably just a mountain lion, but these guys make it sound like a dragon. I need you to knock some sense into me if I lose my nerve. Just think of how it will be, if we kill this thing. We'll be heroes. Well, *I'll* be a hero."

At last he gathered a team of fifty men. They prepared the wagons and other goods, and they set off for the western peaks—and each night, when they stopped to camp, the loggers told stories about Humbaba.

"Humbaba got my great-uncle," one man said. "He was just a young man, and he hunted in the high forest. He met a great monster with claws like an ax and a face like bloody guts. It howled and struck him with its breath; it struck him in the guts. His guts turned to water and leaked out of his backside."

Chad rolled his eyes. "You mean, he had diarrhea."

"No, Humbaba goes after your guts," another man said. "It happened to one of my family, too. He was making salves from the trees, and he decided to cut branches from Humbaba's trees. The monster struck him and blew pine needles into his guts, and tore them to shreds, and he tore out many other people's guts too."

By the time the men reached the mountain, Chad was

having nightmares about Humbaba and his own bowels.

"I don't want to say it in front of them, but I'm getting really nervous about this," Chad confided to Dominic. "I mean, maybe it isn't the monster. Maybe there's something up here that makes people sick."

"Relax. Just go with it. It's an adventure, and it's all about the experience, and you've got the knowledge, and whatever."

Chad looked sharply at him.

"I'm giving you moral support," Dominic said.

"I need *physical* support. What's with your hand?"

"It's the scorpion bite." Dominic examined the back of his hand, saw a deep red mark surrounded by swelling flesh. "It's getting inflamed. One of the women gave me some salve, but it doesn't help."

"Well, man up, because you might need to wield an ax with that hand."

The team camped overnight outside of Humbaba's forest. In the morning, the fifty loggers made ready to start cutting, while Chad and Dominic started for the center of the great woods. One of the men pointed to a wide mountain trail: "This path is where Humbaba crushed the ground as he walked. If you follow it, you'll find him easily."

Chad picked up his crossbow. He wore a quiver full of arrows on one side of his belt, and a long knife on the other side, while Dominic carried the ax. Pines stood straight and tall around the path. Occasional breezes rustled the branches, so that the entire forest seemed to whisper. Dominic saw a doe peering meekly at him from behind a tree; the sight reminded him of his own world, and his heart filled with mourning. Would he ever see that world again? And could he ever feel at home in this place? Here he had no purpose, and though he lived and talked among the villagers, every person remained a stranger.

"Doesn't this seem a little too easy?" Chad asked. "I feel like we're walking into a trap. I know a mountain lion didn't make this path."

"Don't worry. Just think of how famous you'll be. The people will . . . what did you say? Oh yeah, they'll worship you."

"You're not helping."

"They'll be astounded by your magnificent door. You can't go back without it."

"Can it already," Chad snapped. "You know, I'm doing this *for* the people. They need the resources up here. They need the food."

"Yes, I noticed that they dine on scraps while you're eating the best cuts."

"They like the scraps. They say the organs are the best parts. So what if we have different tastes? You've eaten heart and kidney before, and you didn't complain."

"I've seen people eating raw mice out by the toilets."

"Mice are pests. They get into the food supply. *Someone* needs to eat them."

The woods thickened as the men ascended. The breezes grew stronger. Chad ducked his head and cursed the pine needles that dropped around him. "Those needles better not scratch my sunglasses. I've taken such good care of these things. If—"

He was interrupted by a mighty roar, by a fierce wind tearing through the woods. The trees shook; leaves fluttered and came loose. Pine needles caught in Dominic's hair and stung his arms. He looked at Chad in horrified amazement.

When the wind died down, the men noticed a clearing just ahead, vaguely lit by the clouded sunlight. Chad slipped an arrow from the quiver. He drew it against the crossbow and advanced quietly.

Dominic crept behind him with the ax raised. He took cover behind a thick tree, at the very edge of the clearing, and slowly peeked around it.

The first thing he saw was a massive lion's paw—and above that, the head and neck of a beast. It wasn't a mountain lion. Dominic didn't know what it was, only that it looked large, and powerful, and grotesque. Its legs were that of an enormous lion, and its body was yellow with a strange, scaly texture. Two horns protruded from the head and shone like dark stone in the low light. Between them was a horrible face—its features composed of a long, coiled rope, or perhaps a snake or a length of intestine, wrapping around two dark eyes and curving into little squiggles where the teeth might have been.

Dominic choked on his own breath.

Chad stood with his back flattened against a tree, keeping the trunk between himself and the monster. "Let's run," he whispered.

Dominic glared at him. Of course, Chad was the faster runner, and the beast would catch Dominic first. He gestured toward the bow and mouthed the words: "Load the bow."

And then the monster spoke, in a booming voice that struck Dominic through with terror: *Who has attacked my trees?*

"It's talking, it's talking," Chad whispered. "No one told me it talks."

Who is felling the great pine? They'll rot like the dead; their corpses will go to the vultures; they'll be fed to the screech owl!

"Here—you shoot it." Chad offered the bow.

The wind blew again, scattered needles across Dominic's flesh and into the collar of his shirt. "I can't shoot," he whispered shakily. "You told everyone you would kill the monster. It killed the villagers, and it's going to kill us if you don't shoot it."

The monster laughed. Its breath thrashed the trees; the

ground seemed to tremble. *"Two idiots should give advice to each other! Go on and give him advice, you son of a fish who wouldn't recognize his own father! I saw you earlier, in the sea, but I didn't challenge you; I didn't hold you in my belly, as I've done with others. But you've brought this other man into my presence, and now you stand as though you're an enemy; you stand as a stranger!"* It moved, rustling the forest floor, and turned its hideous face on Chad. *"And you—why have you come here? I should wring your arrogant neck, and feed you to the scavengers!"*

Chad worked up the nerve to peer into the clearing. He gripped Dominic's arm with surprising strength. "Do you see that?" he whispered, his eyes bright with fear. "Its face keeps changing!"

Dominic took a breath. He hadn't realized that he had stopped breathing.

He looked at the beast, saw it shifting and curving in the clearing, its body heaving and retracting, its face slithering like a snake. Two eyes seemed to look out at him, but a moment later they looked like dark, featureless sockets. The creature seemed to advance without moving closer; its great paws stretched out, drawing dangerously near.

The monster roared again. Dirt stung Dominic's eyes, and he squeezed them shut. Pine needles and other debris lashed his face. He raised his hands, trying to keep the needles from blowing into his nose and mouth, into his guts.

"Shoot the damn thing before it slaughters us," Dominic said.

"I don't think shooting it will—"

"Shoot it. Injure it, and finish it off with your knife."

The beast roared again: *You will suffer for transgressing here. Your men will rot like the dead, and I will throw them to the scavengers! I would have shown you where to take a share of the juniper; that would have been more than enough. The wood for one room should have been enough, but you wanted ten rooms of three and four stories! Could you not have stayed at home, enjoying the comforts you've designed? Your food and your great rooms and your women—ask yourself why they are not enough! The men are cutting, and cutting, to make timber for the miners; they are cutting to make timber for empty rooms. I will poison their insides, and make them empty like the skins of the dead!*

Chad drew an arrow. He pulled it carefully across the bow.

Your men have felled the great tree. They will suffer like sick dogs, and—what have you? I see what you are about to do. Go away from here, and spare my life!

Chad hesitated.

"Don't listen to it." Dominic's voice trembled. He was thinking of the realm of the dead. He didn't want to go back there, not ever. "It's threatening us and begging us at the same time. Don't trust it."

"*You!*" the monster shouted. "*I hear your words. I hear even the smallest rustlings in my forest, and I heard you coming, but I let you live; I didn't go to you, though I could have carried you up and killed you! Speak wise words to this man. Tell him to spare my life!*"

But Chad turned, aimed the arrow, and shot at Humbaba. The arrow struck the monster's breast. Chad drew another arrow and aimed, but his arms shook so that he couldn't hold the weapon. The monster sank to the ground; it chest had caved in strangely, as though it was imploding.

Chad steadied himself. He aimed and shot the monster again, hitting it in the shoulder, and the shoulder caved in like a bowl, and the bowl began to fill with blood. Chad took up the long knife; he abandoned his cover behind the tree and approached Humbaba.

Idiots! Humbaba bellowed. *All the things you've gathered here—I'll blow them to dust! Do your deed together, but the two of you will never be friends again! And you, little one—I would have you carried away by the scavenger, and dragged to the realm of the dead! Only convince this one to spare my life!*

Dominic barely listened. The boom of the monster's voice pierced through him, filled him with fear. In a panic he shouted: "Finish it, Chad!"

The monster's breath blew over him. Dominic fell to the ground, eyes burning, flesh stinging with the whip of needles.

"You stupid man! May you suffer because of your words! Of the two of you, may you not live the longer. If any curse falls on you because of this, let it fall on you rather than him!"

"Chad, finish it already!" Dominic cried. "What are you doing?"

Finally, Chad moved. He leapt on the beast, and with one quick, hard stroke he slashed at its neck. The blade went in easily; it struck deep, and the neck contracted, became small and thin. Chad slashed again—and his arms shook so that he dropped the knife. The monster's blood flowed over its brutish shoulders.

"Dom, help me," he said.

Dominic brought the ax. His hand burned where the scorpion had stung him; the flesh had become swollen and raw, but he gripped the ax and brought it down hard on the creature's tiny neck. The head rolled off with one stroke.

Blood pooled over the ground, soaking pine needles, staining the bottom of Chad's shoes. He stumbled backwards and sat down hard, half dazed, near one of Humbaba's great paws.

The wind died. The forest became still and silent.

"Well . . . I hope . . . these people are impressed," Chad

said at last. "*Look* at this thing. I never expected . . . I wonder what it *is*?" He clutched his arms against his chest, trying to stop his trembling. "Look at these legs. I don't even think it has fur. It's just . . . ." Tentatively he reached out. He grasped one of the creature's toes.

The paw came off in his hand.

"What the . . . ."

Chad took off his sunglasses and knelt beside the monster. Then he pulled at the other paw. It came away easily, as though the beast was made of detachable parts.

He pulled at the monster, yanked out its insides and its outsides. Dominic, stooping and examining his swelling hand, looked up. The monster lay scattered, its body in pieces.

Chad swore, whispered curses to himself. "How was I supposed to know?"

"What's the matter?"

Chad's eyes were full of fear—not of terror, but of fear mingled with remorse. "Dom, we've done something really awful. Look . . . but don't tell anyone."

Dominic drew near. A few steps away he stopped.

Beside the paws with their long, curving claws was a section of the creature's scaly chest. Dominic reached for it. It crumpled in his hand. It was made of paper. Dominic touched a claw, and that was made of paper, too.

The yellow legs, long and wide and bent, were still somewhat intact. A human foot protruded from beneath one leg. A man's chest lay exposed above it.

Dominic looked at the severed head, at the grotesquely coiled ribbons soaked with blood.
Chad went to it first. He squatted and carefully pulled the horns away, and then he pulled off the mask. Dominic knelt beside him.

"It's a man," Chad said, "wearing a costume. I just killed a man."

The man's eyes were open. They were strange, the white of each eye just a tiny ring around the large brown iris, such a deep brown that Dominic couldn't distinguish the dark pupil at the center. Beneath the hideous mask, the eyes shone with an expression of gentleness. On the wet surface Dominic saw himself clearly reflected, along with the woods behind him, as though he knelt before a mirror. His being filled with dread. Dominic recognized those deep brown eyes, the face, the dark hair curling over the forehead.

Take care about the fabrications you read. . . . The tales that people make up to tell other people what they saw, or what they thought they saw—what they fear, what they hope for, what they believe, what they'd rather not see. . . .

He had just beheaded the man he'd encountered at the center of the Taurus labyrinth.

"Chad . . . we've done something really wrong."

"I know that, but it's too late to fix it now," Chad said. "Don't tell anyone. No one knows it was a man. At least, I don't *think* anyone knows. We'll put the mask back on." Hurriedly he covered the face, positioned the oversized mask so that the flesh was covered. He tried to fix the horns on top of the head. "We'll put it like it was, and tell people they can't touch it. We'll say . . . we'll say that it will burn their flesh and give them festering sores. The monster said so. That's our story. Does anyone know about your hand? We can say that your hand brushed against the monster's face."

Dominic barely heard him. "He wasn't even attacking us. He was standing here, and we killed him. He just wanted to protect the forest."

"Dominic, you're not going to tell anyone, right?" Chad finished replacing the horns. He removed his shirt and slashed it down one side, and carefully wrapped the head inside of it. "This is bad. I can't stand the smell of blood."

"What are you doing?"

"I'll carry it like this. We'll say we can't touch it. No one can touch it, not ever. We'll put it on display for a few days, and then we'll bury it. And these things . . . ." Chad set the bloody shirt and head on the ground. He picked up the pieces of the costume and arranged them in a pile. "Let's find a place to bury these. I'll start digging with the ax."

Dominic couldn't help bury the costume. He sat staring at the ground as if in a trance, and Chad had to bury everything himself. It didn't take long. He bunched the pieces of the costume into a ball of cloth and paper and buried it in a small hole, and then he dragged the headless body into some bushes.

"I promised meat," Chad said as they descended the mountain. "There are plenty of animals here. I can shoot an animal and butcher it, bring a few parts back and say they're pieces of Humbaba . . . ."

He strayed off the trail to investigate a small cavern, where he heard rustlings and snappings. A mountain lion crouched there; it heard Chad coming, and it growled low. He shot the lion full of arrows.

"Dom, give me the ax."

Dominic stumbled toward him and turned away, not wanting to see the animal being hacked apart. As he gazed into the cavern he noticed six small, round lights, and immediately he thought of the little stars that Taurus had held in his palm.

The lights moved. A soft cry emerged from the cavern, the cry of a kitten. Dominic moved closer. In the low light, three fuzzy little faces looked back at him—golden faces with black moustache-like markings, huddled close together, eyes full of confusion and fear.

Dominic burst into tears.

Chad fetched two loggers to collect the pieces of meat.

They found Dominic feverish and distraught. The men took pity on him and helped him down the mountain, where thick branches were piled and the carcasses of deer were laid out. The men stripped the pines to their liking. They built a pen for the cows and sheep they would catch. When no more lumber could be lashed to the wagons, and when the meat had been cured and the cattle rounded up, the team left the mountain. Dominic, weak with fever, was carried on top of the solid plank that had been cut for Chad's bedroom door.

At the river, the team split up. A third of the men hauled lumber toward the northeastern mine; a third returned to the mountain; the remaining men lashed the rest of the timber into two rafts. They fixed several oars, tied the plank on top of one raft and the cattle pen on the other, and rowed their crafts up the river.

The tributary narrowed, and the water grew shallow, so that rocks began to tear at the rafts. The men pushed at the rocks with pine branches and struggled to keep their crafts afloat. At last they reached the village, where they became stuck on the jagged stones. Dominic was lying dazed among the men; but Chad stood at the front of his raft, holding the bloody shirt, raising it like a trophy. The grotesquely coiled face peeked from the cotton fabric. All the people looked at it in awe.

Chad hung the shirt with the head inside of it in the courtyard. He nailed it high, so that people couldn't reach it, and he warned them not to touch it. It would infect them; it would give them festering, fatal sores. He told them to look at Dominic's swollen hand, where the monster's face had brushed against him; he told them to see Dominic's feverish, anguished condition as proof of the monster's venom.

As he was speaking, the stone horns fell out. They thumped on the ground at Chad's feet. "Oh," he said, "I cut those off myself. I'm going to make flasks out of them—or maybe a monument, here in the courtyard." He tried to fix the shirt so that the head wouldn't fall out, and then he stooped to pick up the horns.

The villagers gasped.

"Don't worry, these aren't poisonous—just the face is poisonous," he assured them.

No one dared touch the horrifying face that leered at them from up high. They wouldn't, even though Dominic was sitting near the stream and mumbling "It's a human head. It's not a monster. He's carrying a human head." Everyone thought Dominic was delusional with fever.

Chad went to wash the dirt and sweat from his body. As he dressed himself, a man came running into the great house.

"There's trouble outside," he said. "A woman has come to see you."

"Which one? None of these women are too much trouble for me." Chad smirked.

"It isn't one of our women. It's the queen of the underworld."

As Chad walked through the great house, the man warned him to take care. "Don't upset her, and don't go with her. Remember the stories about her. She might look harmless now, but she has power of transformation. She can grow claws like a pickaxe. She can become terrifying, like a monster of the swamp, like a great serpent with lion's claws."

"Didn't I kill the monster of the woods? I handled that, and I'll handle this woman."

Outside, the villagers were preparing the cured meat. The queen of the underworld stood nearby. She had come alone; she wore a simple white garment; her hair was gathered behind her back; no crown adorned her head. She looked unremarkable.

Dominic, still sitting near the dismantled raft, pulled

himself to his feet and stood beside Chad.

The queen addressed them both: "It's windy at the mountaintop, isn't it? People like to say it's the monster's breath, but as you now know, it's just wind."

"What do you want?" Chad asked.

"Allow me to me grant your spiritedness," the woman said softly. "Come to my house in the underworld. You mustn't avoid it any longer."

Chad scoffed. "The underworld, where you all you do is inflict pain?"

Dominic stood with tears in his eyes. He asked: "Where's Hannah?"

"She is on trial in the underworld."

"Exactly," Chad said. "See, you'd even torment a little girl. I've heard about you. You drag people into a world of corpses, and you crush them like insects. You took a warrior who lived here like a king, and you turned him into a toiling servant. Where is *his* spiritedness? You lured a shepherd and turned him into a wolf, so that his own hounds hunt him. You took a teacher into your realm, and he ended up lashed and beaten."

"I did those things," the queen replied. "But you don't see that the warrior has become a true king through his service, or that the shepherd will see the devotedness of the wolf. You don't see that your own people lashed a wise teacher for telling the truth, or that he spoke the truth despite knowing his fate—and conversely, you don't see that a corrupt teacher *must pay his due*. As for Hannah, she will become the strong lion; for her I have laid seven pits. She shall ride the seven-starred chariot and learn the wonders of the heavenly realms."

"Sure, she'll do that just like the others did. No one who has been to your realm is riding in chariots. You make people suffer, and then you glorify it to trick the rest of us."

"I haven't caused anyone's suffering."

Chad moved closer. He showed his bravery by standing face to face with the queen. "I'm not leaving," he said quietly, "and neither is anyone else. I live like a king here, and people respect me."

"In my realm there are also kings and princes. They rot like everyone else, and when you arrive, they will welcome you like a king."

Chad turned and stalked away, his face contorted with anger.

Dominic didn't watch him go. He went to the queen and looked up at her. "What about me? Can I go on trial?"

"You have already had your trial," she replied gently, "and soon you will have your justice." She turned to the crowd and raised her voice. "In the western mountains, the great forest has been devastated. The trees are being stripped; the felled trees are crushing the small trees; water vanishes through cracks into the underworld; the corpses of orphaned animals rot in the sun, feasted on by flies. This river will dry up, and the plants and animals will starve. Some of you will find sustenance beyond this land; there is clean water, and precious food, and there is grass for the animals. I will lead you there, but the man who killed Humbaba shall not accompany you."

Chad was feasting on the lion's meat. He still wore the look of rage; he shoved the skewered meat into his mouth. Suddenly he picked up a section of flesh, a piece of hindquarter that he had cured, and hurled it at the queen—but the queen fluttered, shifted, morphed into a luminescent bird. The hunk of meat sailed past her.

"Get out of here!" Chad shouted as she flew away. "See, look at that. She's nothing. She makes threats, but throw something at her and she'll scurry away like a coward. I killed this beast, and if this so-called queen ever threatens us again, I'll cut her head off too."

The crowd was quiet; but soon, someone shouted:

"Look!"

The loggers who had headed north had returned to the village. Their wagons were still loaded with wood. Chad looked at them in disbelief. He hurried toward them and shouted: "What are you doing?"

"We had to turn back," a logger replied. "The waste pond overflowed at the mine. The ground is covered in toxins."

Quickly they related what had happened. A sinkhole had formed and ruined the dam; waste spilled over, running across the land and cutting little channels in the earth, dumping arsenic and lead and other toxins into the big river, turning the water bright orange.

"Well, it's downstream from us, so it doesn't matter," Chad said. "I mean, we won't have to worry about *our* water being affected."

Dominic mumbled something in response, but he was starting to faint, and no one understood him.

He was still trying to say, "It's a human head."

For days Dominic laid in bed, overcome sometimes by chills, sometimes by intolerable heat. The servant woman brought him wet cloths to cool his fever. She rubbed salves on his swollen hand, and she encouraged him to eat and drink—but on the third day she showed up empty-handed.

"A man came today and said that another dam broke, at the uranium mine. Waste flowed into our creek and burned us when we tried to bathe." The woman touched her face, where she had splashed water from the stream. The flesh looked red and raw. Her feet were in worse shape, blistering and oozing. "He said that cracks opened in the earth and broke the foot of the dam. Our cattle died after drinking the water, and the deer and other animals are also dying. And the wells are drying up—but it looks like we're going to have rain. I'll catch some for you."

"Save it for yourself," Dominic replied. "I don't want any."

But she came back anyway, and pleaded with him to drink.

Dominic's chills returned. The clouds had drifted away and the sun shone warmly, so he heaved himself out of bed and made his way outside, leaning against the walls for support. In the courtyard he found Chad kneeling beside the pine slab with a set of carving tools.

"Oh, it's you," he greeted Dominic. "Can you believe this? I have to carve my own door because these guys think it's cursed. They think we've turned this place into a wasteland, and they won't use any more of the lumber. It's just sitting there going to waste."

Dominic lowered himself to the ground. He closed his eyes and turned his face toward the sun, waiting for the warm light to chase the chill from his bones. He asked: "Where's his head?"

"I buried it. I was going to wait a while, but these people thought it was cursing us. They're being over-dramatic. We just had rain, and there's still plenty of food. The mine owners said that no one will get sick from eating the animals as long as they don't eat the organs."

"They do eat the organs," Dominic replied. "But I suppose that doesn't matter, so long as it doesn't affect *you*."

"Why do *you* suddenly care?" Chad snapped. "You've been on this amazing adventure, and no matter what happens, you keep whining about it."

Dominic opened his eyes.

"See, that's why you're sick and I'm not. It's your attitude. You *all* have the wrong attitude. All this pollution isn't because of us—it's because of that witch! If they were smart, they'd go after *her*." Chad didn't look up as he spoke. He continued carving and sanding, carving and sanding.

Dominic pushed himself to his feet. He walked to the lumber pile and picked up the ax.

Chad paused to admire his work. "I'm getting really good at this. Maybe it's a good thing these superstitious hillbillies—"

He jumped back as Dominic heaved the ax into the pine slab. Dominic hacked and hacked while Chad screamed at him. He would have hacked the door into countless little pieces if he could, but after a few seconds he sank to his knees, trembling and panting.

"I never should have . . . looked for Hannah," Dominic wheezed. "I went to save her, and . . . she left me in this . . . this . . . ."

Chad cursed him, called him names. "Are you out of your mind? Look what you did! Do you have any idea how much work I put into this?"

"I don't give a damn about your door."

"You pathetic little twit! You should be thanking Hannah—even though she's an annoying brat. What were you doing in your old world that was so great?"

"I wasn't dying from a horrible disease!" Dominic shouted.

"I'll never be able to fix this!" Chad stared mournfully at the ruined door.

The exercise and sunlight had warmed Dominic's body. Stumbling and slightly faint, he made his way back to his room.

The servant woman continued to keep him company. At some point it occurred to Dominic to ask her name.

"I'm Marianna. And you're Dum—right?" Her smile faltered as she saw Dominic's pained expression. "Isn't that what Chad calls you?"

"Dom . . . he calls me Dom. My name is Dominic. *Dumb* is starting to seem appropriate, though." Dominic studied his swollen hand. The red area around the sting was starting to turn blue.

"The salves aren't helping," Marianna said. "Chad went to search for medicine. In the southern mountains there's a man who survived the last wasteland. He might be able to help us."

"The *last* wasteland?"

"Yes, this land was a wasteland once before, ages ago. A disaster came and wiped everything away, and everything had to grow all over again. But this man knew how to live through it. He must be three or four hundred years old now."

Dominic sat up. "I need the bathroom."

Marianna helped him walk out to the latrines. The smell of human waste reached him even before they were in sight. He was surprised to find all of the toilets in use, with people waiting in line or squatting behind the wooden outhouses. New latrines had been built with fresh lumber, but construction had stopped midway, and some of the structures didn't have doors. People sat in the open outhouses, trying to cover themselves; farther away, others tried to empty their bowels into the river.

"Everyone is sick," Marianna explained.

A man came out of an open outhouse. His legs and feet oozed with sores.

Marianna tried to help Dominic inside, but he didn't want to go. He wanted a stall with a door. Then his bowels heaved, and he hurried to the toilet. Marianna stood in the doorway, facing away, trying to offer him some privacy. She pulled at the sides of her skirt and used it as a curtain.

Dominic sat for a long time, overwhelmed by the stench and the moans of sick people. He felt as though his insides were turning to liquid. Every once in a while, villagers would pass by and peek past Marianna's arms. They would say things like "Is that the little one?" and "Is he out of his fever?" and "Still alive, is he?"

Dominic had never felt so miserable.

Back in his bed, he prayed endlessly for help—for insight, for healing, for some way to help the other sick people, anything to get past the misery. Sometimes he just wanted to vanish into a dark hole and stop existing. His thoughts tormented him through sleepless hours until exhaustion took over, and at last he slept and dreamed—or rather, he had nightmares.

"What are you screaming about? Are you coherent? I hope you're coherent; I need someone to talk to."

Dominic opened his eyes. Chad was standing beside the bed.

"It's Hannah," Dominic whispered.

"What?"

"It's . . . I was having a nightmare." Dominic was slick with sweat. He threw his blanket aside and yanked off his shirt. "Do you have any water?"

"Does anyone?" Chad pulled a chair close to the bed and sat down. "Forget water. I found something more important."

"There's no water here, and everyone has diarrhea. We're dying of thirst."

"Listen, Dom. I just walked all the way to the mountains—not the western range, but these other—"

"The southern mountains," Dominic cut in, "to look for the guy who survived the last wasteland."

"Yeah." Chad fidgeted in the chair. "You know what's strange . . . he looked like that guy who . . . you know, the one in the monster costume. This guy I found at the mountains . . . well, if I didn't know better, I'd have thought it was the same guy. Maybe it's his brother. I mean, I know that guy is dead. I buried his head before I left."

"I'm the one who cut that man's head off," Dominic said. "I'm the one who should have known better—and now I'm suffering for it. You remember Hannah, the girl who brought us here?”

“She didn’t *bring* us. I came on my own.”

“I dreamed that she came here, into my room. I looked up and saw a winged monster . . . but when I looked at its face, it had Hannah’s face. She grabbed me and dragged me back to the underworld. I could hear her voice, talking about judgment. She was taking me to the Libra constellation so that I could be weighed on the scales.”

“I don’t care about your dream. I found the plant, Dom, but I lost it.”

“What plant?”

“This guy told me to find a plant—a leafy shrub with red berries, like wolfberries. He said that this plant can get rid of every disease, make my body healthy again, whatever . . . so I looked, and looked, and I finally found one by the river. The thing was all dried up except for one small branch. So I cut the branch off and brought it back here, and I set it down, and a minute later I thought I saw it moving. Well, it wasn’t moving; a green snake had twined around it. I was looking for a stick to chase the snake away, and the damn thing swallowed the branch. What snake does that?”

“I’m surprised you didn’t use it right away.”

“I was going to let you try it first. I mean, I thought you needed it more than I did.”

“You mean you wanted to experiment on me first, in case it was poisoned like all the other river plants.”

“Why are you complaining? You’re already sick. What harm would it do? Besides, you ruined my door.”

“It was ruined when we killed Humbaba.”

“Don’t start that forest-guardian crap. That’s just hillbilly superstition. Did we make the dams leak?”

“Say what you want, but I’m starting to see this for what it is,” Dominic replied. “This whole time, I’ve felt like a tag-along on someone else’s journey. I don’t know the zodiac, I don't know enigmas. Whatever has happened, it seemed like it was all revolving around Hannah. But up there, on the mountain, I looked into that man's eyes and saw myself. I've done things . . . ."

"Good for you."

"That man we killed—I almost attacked him before, back in Taurus; but I ended up talking to him, and he reminded me to see people from another angle, to take care about the stories I hear. I . . . I have ideas about certain kinds of people. Back at the record shop, I threw someone's job application away because . . . I think that some people, because of their culture or whatever, they don't belong, or they're not trustworthy. Someone came to the shop for work, and I took one look, and I threw the application away because I decided, 'I'd rather not work with one of those people.'"

"Sometimes that's good judgment."

"Can you imagine what that would be like, going from place to place and trying to find a way to live, and having people take one look at you and decide you should be thrown away?"

"You're being dramatic."

"It's not just that. It's the reminders about preparing for ceremony, and . . . other things. This whole time, I've been walking through the zodiac with a Navajo girl. People in my family act like Hopis and Navajos are supposed to resent each another, even though we know it's a sham pushed on us by colonists."

"Oh, please. You're not even a real Hopi. What are you, a quarter Hopi?"

"My uncles remember when the dam burst at the uranium mine. Do you remember that? The animals died, Navajo people got sick, they had to have amputations. My uncles were making jokes about it— and I just sat there and didn't say anything."

"Big deal. People say cruel things all the time."

"It is a big deal. It's . . . poison." Hot tears rolled from the corners of Dominic's eyes.

Chad stood abruptly. He paced back and forth. "I need to figure out what to do with this house. There are probably places outside the mountains that have good land. I could find some healthy guys to dismantle the house and haul it somewhere else."

Dominic tried to sit up straight. He looked around for the damp cloth strips that kept him cool, but his vision blurred. "I feel like I'm burning in hell. You don't have any water?"

"I have to make this *work*, Dominic. This was my chance to get back on *top*. Speaking of the record shop, I can't go back into that nine-to-five, low-wage crap. That was supposed to be temporary. What am I going to do?"

"I feel like my brain is melting."

"I had a good thing going here. I had people coming in to build a power plant. We were going to have electricity. It could have saved lives."

Marianna slipped into the room, carrying a small cup of water.

"What if this disease gets to *me*?" Chad continued. "This whole place is poisoned. If it's getting into the food, it'll get to me eventually. How is that right? I don't even belong here." He noticed the servant woman and stopped pacing. He looked at the raw flesh of her face, at the festering sores on her feet—and he hurried out of the room.

Marianna set the cup on a bedside table, murmuring: "He doesn't belong here, he says." She leaned closer to Dominic, and his breath caught. The woman's disease-scourged face seemed to crack and peel away before his eyes, revealing patches of dry muscle and bone; her eyes seemed dark and hollow, like two gaping pits, and her voice came out in a low rasp. "What do you think about us, boy? You think we belong here?"

Dominic screamed.

12: Virgo

Descending into the netherworld had been much easier for Hannah.

The ground hadn't cracked open beneath her feet. The dead hadn't seized her.

The lion-like figure with a woman's head met her beyond the seventh gate. It stood upright, facing her, and Hannah returned its gaze for some time. The creature's eyes seemed affectionate and sad; but it smiled and said "Hello, Hannah."

"Are you Leo?" Hannah asked.

"No. I'm just a woman, like you. My name is . . . Lama-Zu."

Hannah frowned. *I'm a girl, not a woman,* she thought, but she didn't say so out loud. And she didn't like the lion-woman's name; it made her think of llamas in a foul-smelling zoo. Hannah didn't say that out loud either. "Do you have a riddle?"

"No, there's no riddle. All you have to do is walk with me to Virgo's chamber." Lama-Zu gestured to the blue dome. "But there's a condition: we have to walk hand in hand."

Hannah looked hesitantly at the woman's paw.

"Don't be afraid of my claws," Lama-Zu said. "They won't hurt you."

Taking care not to brush against the claws, Hannah slid her hand into Lama-Zu's. Together they started across the plaza.

Lama-Zu didn't say anything. She walked silently.

Finally Hannah asked: "If you're a woman, how come you have a lion's body?"

"This isn't really what I look like. The lion is a symbol of strength. You see me like that because . . . because I've learned something about strength, I suppose."

They had reached the chamber, and Lama-Zu stopped and faced her. "I wish I could tell you the answers to all of the riddles and enigmas," she said, "but I can't. I can only give you this." She gripped Hannah's hand even more firmly. "I've known what it's like to be alone, and to be afraid. Whenever you feel that way, like you don't have the courage and you need someone to hold your hand, remember how I held your hand like this. Remember that my grip was strong, and that my voice was strong, and that I knew the ways of this realm—and that my sharp claws never hurt you." She squeezed Hannah's hand and released it, and then she took both of Hannah's hands and pressed them together. "I'm giving you my grip. When you need help, hold your own hand; hold it firm, and know that you're not alone, that my strength is with you."

She ushered Hannah into Virgo's blue dome and withdrew. Inside was a hall and a door that opened to a crowded chamber. The beak-faced woman saw Hannah and said "You may enter," and Hannah entered without incident.

The trouble began later. It began after Dominic arrived.

The queen of the underworld showed Hannah around the deep blue room, which was carved all around with gold-flecked images of the heavens. To Hannah's right was the throne and the platform, and on the left side of the chamber were two tunnels that stood in stark contrast to the rest of the room. The tunnels themselves were rather small, but the ornamentation around the openings was tall and wide, intricately designed in several shades of pink, protruding some distance into the chamber.

Hannah admired the fine, symmetric detail, the soft
luminous quality of the stone. She reached out to touch
it, and drew her hand back in sudden surprise.

"They're *snakes*!"

Standing close to the right-hand tunnel, Hannah could
see that the pink stone was, in fact, the design of a wide-
open mouth—the inside of a snake's mouth. Its head of
jade stone, and its shining gold-and-black eye, were
visible just behind the gaping, toothless mouth.

"That's Hydra," the queen said.

"The constellation?"

"The very one."

"Is it dangerous?"

"That's up to you."

Hannah stepped back and gazed into the pink tunnels.
She didn't particularly like snakes, but she said, "I didn't
realize that a snake's mouth was so beautiful."

The crowd at the edge of the chamber laughed. Hannah
turned to the seven humanesque figures huddled there,
and saw that they were richly dressed, in varying
colors—but the queen beckoned her, drawing her
attention to the symbols etched into the walls. The
zodiac symbols were there, and many other images and
shapes. Because Hannah had just walked through the
gate of Cancer, the queen showed her the carving of the
crab, and the strange creature that hovered above it: a
woman with a lion's body and tail, and a pair of great
wings spread at its back.

"What are the symbols *for*?" Hannah asked. "Am I
supposed to figure out what they mean?"

"No. But tell me this, Hannah: the one called Dominic
stands over a gate to the netherworld. He has shed his
celestial garments. The dead will seize him and drag him
to me. He has been careless, and he has been unkind.
You could leave him here to become one of the dead, or
you could free him by giving him one of your garments.

What will you do?"

"I wouldn't leave Dominic here to die." Hannah paused. "But . . . I only have one celestial garment." She touched the sleeve of her nightgown.

"You're wearing a celestial crown," the queen reminded her. "Stand there, beyond the door where you entered, and wait until I call for you. Then you can decide what to do."

The bird-faced woman led Hannah just beyond the threshold. From there, Hannah saw Dominic being dragged into the chamber. Hannah listened and waited, and at the right time she put the winged helmet on his head. She watched him become a luminescent dove.

The queen went back to her tour of the chamber, but Hannah found it hard to listen. She was perturbed by the corpse-like figures that wandered the halls, concerned about Dominic's fate, perplexed by the reptilian mouths that stood gaping at the chamber's edge. She wanted to ask why Virgo was full of zombies, but it seemed a rude thing to mention.

The queen sensed her thoughts, though, and looked up as one of the corpses wandered past the chamber. "They're lost," she said quietly. "But don't worry—they won't be lost forever." She pointed to an image not far from the griffin, an eight-petaled flower etched over the letter T. "Do you recognize this?"

"It's my crown. I mean . . . it's like the crown that Taurus put on my helmet."

The tall, blank-eyed figure came to the doorway and bowed. "Excuse me."

The queen conferred there in the doorway, quietly. After a short time she returned to Hannah and spoke in a low, grave voice. "My husband has been killed in the realm of Leo."

Hannah felt mixed surprise and remorse. How could anyone get killed in Leo? It had been such a small realm—nothing more than a courtyard, with a lion-lady walking across it.

No one else in the chamber seemed shocked or saddened. Hannah, who never knew what to say when someone had died, looked up at the queen. "I'm sorry," she said, even though it seemed a strange thing to say. After all, it wasn't her fault the queen's husband had died.

"I'll go and talk to the ones who killed him, but I'll return soon. In the meantime, my seven judges will keep you company." The queen gestured to the small crowd at the rear of the chamber.

The rest of the room emptied quickly. The bird-woman and the blank-eyed man left with the queen. A corpse who had wandered into the chamber hurried away on stiff, unsteady legs.

The seven figures broke from their huddle and faced Hannah, so that she clearly saw their faces. She was disturbed by the realization that they looked a lot like her. They were about the same height, had the same thin bodies, the same round little bellies visible under their frocks and robes, the same chins and cheekbones and deep brown eyes. They could have been her sisters—or brothers.

They looked handsome, in their way. Each judge was well-groomed and dressed in neatly tailored clothes, and as they stood all in a row before her, Hannah noticed that they were dressed like the colors of a rainbow: the first judge wore red with dark-red ornaments, and the second wore shades of orange, with little fiery-looking stones hanging around its neck, and so on.

The first judge gestured to the platform. "Sit."

Hannah wasn't sure what to do. The only chair was the queen's throne, an exquisite stonework with lions carved into the foot and a dragon ascending at each arm. The queen had left her jeweled tiara on the cushioned seat.

Hannah thought it would be improper to sit there, so she perched on the edge of the platform.

"You've come a long way in a short time," said the sixth judge. "Most people don't make it this far, but you make it look easy. I bet you could figure out every enigma in the galaxy."

"Well . . . it wasn't all easy. I couldn't figure out—"

"Oh, of course, for *most* people it isn't easy, and I suppose you're like most people. But we've seen a few who come through and solve everything. They don't stumble and get stuck, and we don't have to run around trying to help them."

"Oh," Hannah said. "So . . . other people have come through here?"

"Of course. People come through here all the time, but I suppose you haven't figured that out yet."

"Everyone comes through," said the third judge, "but only a few become kings and queens of the zodiac. Our queen knows all the ways of these realms, but not many people become as powerful as she is. Of course, it is possible for anyone to develop that same power, even to surpass it—but not many people are as clever as our queen."

The fourth judge moved closer. It gathered up the skirt of its deep-green robe and sat on the floor. Hannah couldn't help admiring the silken shimmer of the material, the light trim shining at the edges, and the green stone that hung on the judge's chest. The others also sat, so that Hannah felt as though she was sitting on a stage before an attentive audience.

"Our queen is going to turn you into something," said the fourth judge. "She'll touch you, and you'll start to transform."

"What do you mean?" Hannah asked. "You mean . . . like how Dominic turned into a bird?"

"Yes, it's like that. The queen will want to change you

into some creature—just for a little while, because you'll
have a job to do—and she'll want to give you a new
name."

"You don't have to do it, though," said the first judge.
"It's uncomfortable, and you can never be quite the same
again. A lot of people just pretend to walk through
Virgo. They pick a name, and they stay the same, or they
try to transform into their own kind of thing."

Hannah remembered how Dominic had flapped around
in sheer panic. She frowned and thought: *It will be like
when I turned into a fish.* "But . . . if I don't do it, will I
still get to go home?"

"Yes, you'll go home easily. In fact, going through the
queen is often the hard way. It's not hard for everyone,
but it will be hard for you."

"But I *want* to be the same. I want to be the same when
I go home as when I came here."

"Most people do," said the first judge.

The one in the orange robe leaned forward, as if
speaking in confidence. Its brown eyes were bright with
something like excitement, or perhaps mischief. "It
could be good, though, to get what you can from the
queen, because her gifts come with power. You could
use that power to get whatever you want. When you go
home, you'll have something that other people don't
have—something that makes you special. Wouldn't that
be good, to have a privilege that other people don't
have?"

"But if you don't go through the queen," said the fifth
judge, "you can still tell Dominic that you did. You can
tell him that you learned so many secrets in Virgo, and
he missed out because he abandoned you."

At that moment, Hannah had so many thoughts running
through her head that she didn't know which one to
address first. "Well . . . Dominic didn't *abandon* me.
And I wouldn't lie about knowing secrets, if—"

"But he did. You needed his friendship, and he rejected you, because he didn't want to argue with his friend."

Hannah mulled that over. Then, a realization hit her. "You . . . you've been *listening* to us."

"We hear everything."

She was silent then, because she remembered the Capricorn's warning about an enemy. *I have an enemy who has been watching me. Maybe it's them. Or maybe . . . maybe it's the queen.* What kind of queen ruled over a realm of wandering corpses—of people unwilling to die, and unable to live? Not a good queen, probably. And her judges didn't seem kind; the things they were saying didn't sound right.

A glyph caught Hannah's eye: the flowered T, the same image that had carried the stars in her helmet. She had forgotten about the seven stars! Surely, this was the time to remember them.

She struggled to recall the ideas she had attached to each star. One, she knew, was supposed to remind her of the thank-you song—of remembering to give something back.

"Aren't you listening?"

The judges were staring hard at her.

"Sorry," Hannah said. "I was just trying to remember something."

The judges didn't ask what she was trying to remember. They kept on talking. Hannah couldn't think of what the other stars had meant to her, but she did remember that Chad had talked a lot, too, so that she hadn't been able to focus on what she was supposed to be doing. Maybe Dominic was right: she shouldn't have spent so much time arguing with Chad.

The queen was gone for a long time.

The judges wouldn't leave Hannah alone. They weren't being cruel, really, but their incessant chatter reminded her of the time she had to stay at her cousins' house for a long weekend. The three young children had behaved like beasts the entire time, as though Hannah was just something for them to pick on. Hannah's aunt and uncle served her nothing but baloney sandwiches, bruised apples, and slimy pickles for lunch and dinner. She was stuck there for three days while her cousins dumped soap in her shoes, and squirted water on her as she slept, and threw staples in her hair, and much more.

She felt like that now—like she had no place to retreat to, no place where these voices couldn't pester her.

Finally she interrupted: "Why are you telling me all these things?"

The first judge shrugged. "That's what we do."

"But what am I supposed to be doing here, and why are you called judges? Are you going to judge me?"

"Yes," the fifth judge said. "But we only judge for a moment. Mostly what we do is have conversations."

"Oh," Hannah said, because she didn't know what else to say. And then, because she felt warm and uncomfortable, she slipped off her vest. The nightgown was warm, and the chamber was stuffy. Hannah thought of how nice it would be to walk in the corridors, which were probably cooler, and might even have windows— but then another of the undead wandered past, and its one remaining eye stared unblinking and slightly drooping at her, and she decided that the corridors must not be so pleasant after all.

Tired of sitting, she stood and fidgeted. Across the room, between the two snake heads, she spotted a coat hook made of twining reeds. Hannah crossed to it and hung up her vest.

The judges tittered with laughter.

"Is this okay?" Hannah gestured to the red vest, and the judges laughed again.

"It's fine," said the seventh judge. "You can even leave it behind, if you want. You can leave Dominic here, too,

and his friend, and whatever else is weighing you
down."

Hannah leaned against the wall. She didn't want to sit
on the platform again; she didn't like being on display.
But all of the judges turned, so that they sat facing her
again.

"It's okay to leave people behind," the fifth judge said.
"Your mother would agree, wouldn't she?"

Hannah felt a small crumbling sensation in her chest.

"And your father, he would most likely agree," said the
sixth judge.

The crumbling stopped. Hannah looked from one pair
of eyes to the other and felt a rage threatening to grow
inside of her. Little strips of anger seemed to twine
around her ribs, while the marrow seemed heavy with
sorrow and dread.

Back at home—whichever place happened to be her
home at the time—Hannah could always find places to
retreat to. She needed that now: night, a warm bed, a
thick blanket. She wanted to hide in the dark and let the
grief wash out of her in countless warm tears, to cry in
private whispers, to demand of God and the universe the
things that she would have liked to scream out loud: *Why
did you take my family? You took my mom, and my dad,
and my grandma. You take everything and leave me
alone. Why did you hurt my dad? Why do you let us have
wars and so many other awful things?* People knew that
Hannah suffered, though she tried to hide it. They were
careful about the subject of her father's injury; they told
Hannah that she was strong, that she would be all right,
but Hannah didn't want to be strong. She wanted to stop
and sit down, and unleash the little-girl voice inside of
her that cried *I want my dad!* over and over again.

The judges continued their casual remarks about her
family—not cruel remarks, on the surface, though their
words struck deep wounds. At last Hannah took a breath

and responded. "You don't even know my family. You're just like the shadow-people inside of Cetus, and I'm not listening to you, because I think you're . . . you're bad people."

At that, they laughed. The first judge said: "We're not people."

"Whatever you are, you're behaving like jerks. Why would you sit there and say mean things about my life? You don't know me, and I haven't done anything to you."

"We do know you," the seventh judge said. "We know all about you. We're telling you the story about yourself."

"Well, I don't believe it. It's all lies, just like the lies I heard inside of Cetus."

"But isn't it true that your mother didn't want you?"

"She couldn't take care of me." Hannah hesitated, realizing she was being defensive. In the belly of Cetus, she had forgiven her mother; she understood why her mother was always angry. But why should she explain that to these ghouls? She added, "My mom is none of your business. Neither is my dad. You can sit there in your fancy outfits and judge me, but if you were so perfect and didn't have any problems, you'd have something better to do than pick on a kid."

The seventh judge persisted: "But isn't it true that your companions didn't want you either? Chad told you to get lost, and Dominic was silent. They let you leave; they didn't care."

Again, Hannah was taken aback. Tears stung her eyes. She became determined not to say anything more to these creatures. Nevertheless, they kept on talking.

Their casual cruelty was not the most surprising thing about them. What was truly shocking was how much they *knew*. They knew that Hannah had liked her first foster family, that she'd felt like a big sister to two little girls—and then both of the parents lost their jobs, and the family had to move to another state, and Hannah had to be transferred to another home.

They knew that Hannah's social worker tried to comfort her by saying things like "I know you'll miss your friends, but just think: now you can make even more friends" and "I know that these changes are hard, but we have to think of them as opportunities," and so on.

They knew that Hannah had lived with Clarissa, an elderly woman who tried to make her wear strange clothes and go to a strange church. Hannah didn't like the grown-ups there. She wanted to go to her own family's church, but Clarissa said no. She began to take Hannah's clothes and other belongings and throw them in the trash, claiming that Hannah's things were "bad." The judges knew that Hannah had complained to her social worker, and that she was sent to yet another home.

Et cetera.

At last the queen came quietly into the chamber. She took the tiara from her throne and replaced it on her head.

The seventh judge was still speaking, softly but cuttingly: "Dominic hasn't shown patience or loyalty. In Aries he promised to help you, but he quickly forgot his promises. Look how he abandoned you; look how he dismissed you when you were being stomped on! Why help him out of trouble, when he should learn what it's like to be neglected?"

The queen held up a hand. "Enough. Let the child be." She sat and beckoned Hannah. "Come here."

Hannah stood before the queen. She looked into the woman's warm, friendly eyes and wondered if this queen could really be her enemy. Hannah was about to complain, to say that the seven judges had said mean things, but then she remembered the queen's husband.

"Did you find out about your husband?"

"Yes. Your friends Dominic and Chad killed him."

". . . What?"

"I've spoken to them already."

"Dominic did that? Why would he kill your husband?"

"He was afraid, the same way he was afraid of Taurus—but in Leo he was more frightened, and more deceived, and he had a different companion." The queen gazed at the doorway through which Dominic had flown. "Leo is a difficult realm. Dominic has suffered there. He must walk through Virgo, and face me, but he won't find his own way. Once again, you can help him, or you can leave him there."

"Well . . . I'll help him, if . . . ." Hannah paused, remembering the judges' harsh words. "Did your husband *do* anything to Dominic?"

"No. Dominic himself will tell you that my husband committed no offense."

"How should I help him? Are you going to turn me into something?"

A faint smile touched the queen's lips. "I'll help you transform, if you'll allow me."

"What will you do?"

"No one can leave the underworld as they entered," the queen reminded her. "Anyone who leaves this place must leave with a new name."

"Does that mean I can't be Hannah anymore?"

"You'll still be yourself. But you will also have to be the strong lion. You must learn to become the lion, the vulture, the crab."

Hannah was silent. Transforming into a lion, or even a vulture, sounded all right. She didn't like the idea of being a crab.

"You can still be called Hannah," the queen continued. "Your new name is like a symbol. You can keep it a secret if you want. It's meant as a reminder, the same way your seven stars were meant as reminders."

"A reminder of what?"

"It might represent a stage in your life, or a skill that you have. Remember to think humbly about your name. It isn't a badge to wear in pride; it's a reminder of an important aspect of your life. People often want names that make them feel special and powerful. They want to be called Griffin Princess, or Star Warrior, or some such thing. But we often receive humble names. One of my first names was 'The Little One Who Laughs.' It helped me remember the importance of joy and laughter."

"What will my name be?" Hannah asked.

"Your name is Griffin Princess."

The queen took her by the shoulders and turned her toward the wall, so that Hannah faced the etching of the griffin. "The griffin has flight, it has knowledge, it has the power of transformation—and it has claws." She pointed to the symbol of the crab, resting her fingertip beneath one extended claw. "They can be used to grab or repel, to cut or hold together. Use your claws wisely. When you carry your friend, hold him tight, as though you're holding him in the grip of a crab's claw—but don't pierce his flesh."

"When I . . . when I do what?"

"You will transform into the griffin, just as you changed into Pegasus and Monoceros. You'll carry Dominic from Leo. I'll show you how."

She told Hannah where to find the great house, where to find the window of Dominic's room. "Remember your name, and remember what I say. Right now you're only a princess. Eventually, you will become a queen."

"But . . . I don't want to be a queen. I just want to go home and be normal."

The lady of the underworld laughed. "Don't worry, you won't be *that* kind of queen. You can be perfectly ordinary, and you can do whatever you like. But only when you've grown into a queen will you leave this realm—and when you go, many of the undead will go out before you. Remember to guide them to the right path, so that they might live again with new names."

The queen reached out. Her fingertips barely brushed Hannah's side, just below the hip, but it was enough: Hannah felt something move within her, felt an energy humming. And then she felt her body begin to shift.

Becoming the Monoceros had been easier, perhaps because she'd been so focused on saving Dominic. And perhaps becoming Pegasus was easier because she had done it herself, willingly, in a surge of blessed inspiration. Becoming a griffin was not easy. It hurt.

Hannah was aware of the seven judges watching as she crouched on the floor and cried out in fear. The nerves in her legs seemed to stretch tight; the muscles in her back seared. Tears ran down her face, though she wasn't really crying. She felt as though every cell in her body was humming, moving away on its own; they would all break away from one another, a trillion cells vibrating alone in the universe. Hannah struggled against the terror of not existing. *The queen is pulling me all apart, and I won't be myself anymore! She'll never be able to put me back together again!*

But the cells surged apart, and the fearful thoughts had no place anymore, no mind to form within. The cells that used to be part of Hannah floated silently in utter darkness.

And then they united again, in seemingly perfect order, and Hannah was relieved to be herself—but though her mind was the same, her body had changed. She had become a trembling, disoriented griffin, cowering on the stone floor.

Hannah pushed herself up and stood tall in the chamber, on long lion's legs. The height and the ebbing pain made her unsteady, and for a moment she felt sheer horror at the sight of her furry, strangely jointed limbs and enormous claws. And then she felt them: two great wings, extending along her arms like the wings of a bat, but feathered and soft. She felt a thrill at the thought of flying again, of soaring overhead and seeing the landscape all at once, as she'd done when she crossed from Pisces to Aries. Fear gave way to excitement: *I did it! I'm a lion-bird!*

Even without the queen's instructions, she would have known where to go, what to do. A rush of adrenaline coursed through Hannah's new form. She raced through the corridors on powerful legs, past the dead who seemed disinterested and unimpressed—as though they saw griffins running around the underworld all the time.

Up she flew on powerful wings, into the realm of Leo that Dominic knew. There was no plaza here, no lion-lady aside from herself; instead she found a dry basin surrounded by mountains, glowing pale and barren in the moonlight. The unfamiliarity of the landscape didn't impede her. She had a sense of Dominic lying far below in the great wooden house. His waning livelihood wafted up like a sour scent, and she detected Chad sleeping in the house as well—but those were the only two human beings within the realm. The villagers flickered like mere shadows; Hannah was aware of them, but she knew they weren't people. They were impressions of the realm: all part of the same intelligence, play-acting in separate roles.

Dominic, she knew, didn't have that same insight. He looked at those shadows and thought they were people. Hannah imagined him lying feverish and distraught, and she felt an appreciation of her own powerful muscles, her skilled navigation, the outcome of her journey. The judge's words floated back to her: *You'll have something that other people don't have—something that makes you special.*

Of course, she wouldn't lie to Dominic about having extra powers. Why would she need to? Being a griffin gave her more than enough. It was certainly better than being a judge in fancy clothes. Hannah decided that the seven judges didn't look so elegant after all. Their habit of dressing like a rainbow spread seemed a bit silly. Her grandmother would have called it "tacky."

The night air blew into Dominic's room in the great house. Hannah rode the current gently to the window. She perched on the sill and climbed inside to where Dominic slept open-mouthed, his breath rasping through dry lips.

Hannah whispered urgently: "Dominic!"

He looked up at her with bleary eyes. "I'm sorry," he mumbled.

"I'm taking you to Virgo." Hannah paused, feeling a twinge of disappointment that her voice still sounded like a normal eleven-year-old-girl voice. "You have to meet the queen, and probably the seven judges too—and, just to warn you, they're not very nice."

A bitter laughed sounded in his throat. "They're not very nice," he repeated. "That's great, Hannah, or whatever you are. Let's go. I'm ready."

Hannah wasn't quite as ready. She estimated the size of the window, and decided she couldn't get through it with her wings flapping and Dominic hanging from her claws.

She helped Dominic out of bed, supporting him as he stumbled weakly to the window, and sat him on the floor.

"Hold still." Hannah sat on the sill and reached her arms back into the night air. She flapped her wings and slid her talons around Dominic's shoulders.

In that way she pulled him from the house, struggling to lift him through the window and into the night air. The wooden sill scraped his back; Hannah's claws pressed too deeply into his flesh; but soon they were in the air, and Hannah could relax her grip without dropping him. She heard him groaning, and she pitied him even while admiring her own situation. Even with Dominic's added weight, she flew skillfully and powerfully. Through the opening into the underworld she lowered him without even causing a scratch, and through the corridors she carried him easily, until at last she could set him down on the floor of the queen's chamber, just beside the Hydra tunnel.

He slumped there in half death. Hannah looked on him and felt a sudden fear that he would die; but he opened his shining, feverish eyes and pushed himself up, sitting with his back against the wall and his head hanging weakly.

The queen of the underworld waited alone. She still wore the modest tiara and white tunic, but Hannah kept looking at her to see what had changed. There always seemed something slightly different about the woman— something Hannah couldn't quite identify. Her face was calm and pleasant, and yet something about it seemed ephemeral as rippling water, like a mirage always shining on the desert sands.

"By now, you know that the zodiac road isn't about word puzzles." The queen met Dominic's eyes, looking on him with compassion, and Hannah saw a look of understanding pass between the two. "Did you *want* to walk all the way to the mountains to kill Leo and cut down the forest?"

He winced. "I'm dead, aren't I?"

"I assure you that you are not dead. And neither is this girl." The queen moved toward Dominic until she caught his eye again, and added: "Never stop helping this girl until she gets home."

Hannah puzzled over those words, mystified by their familiarity, and suddenly gasped. "That's what the

Capricorn said!"

"I know what the Capricorn told you, because I am the Capricorn. You saw my face for a moment as we traveled across the sea."

Hannah looked at the queen in surprise. It seemed true enough: the queen's face did look like the face Hannah had seen upon the goat-fish's neck. Hannah remembered other things the Capricorn had said—about having to transform, about surviving in different environments. "But . . . how come you're a person now, and not a goat, or . . . ."

"The universe has rules. We wear different splendors according to its realms, but we're all part of one heart. Here in the realm of life and death, this is what I am." The queen stood close to Dominic, leaning forward and bracing her palms against her knees. "You must also transform. You'll leave the underworld a new man, with a new name."

"We're not dead?" he asked.

"No. And your new name is Dominic Masa Douglass."

Dominic leaned his head against the cool stone. "Thanks. Thank you for giving me a new name that I already had."

"Go back home and be who you are. You'll need to enter Hydra to get there."

Hannah thought back to her question: *Is it dangerous?* "But . . . ."

"The left-hand mouth would lead you back, and cast you outside the gates of Cancer. Take the right-hand mouth; it will bring you onward to Libra, and you'll be in much better shape by the time you get there. Help him, Hannah."

"In there?" From his position against the wall, Dominic didn't see a lovely pink cathedral. He saw the profile of a giant snake, its scaly green-and-black mouth gaping wide, one round eye staring directly at him.

"Don't be afraid. Hydra will help you shed your
sickness all at once, the way a serpent sheds an old skin.
When a serpent discards its skin, it isn't just revealing a
new one. It's also getting rid of mites and other parasites
that have attached to it. I know that I don't need to
explain parasitic relationships to you."

Dominic stiffened. His worn face showed exhaustion,
uncertainty, sadness; and for a moment, that same
expression of understanding passed across it again.

"A serpent will often swim in the waters first, to loosen
the skin—but you've already done that. Both of you
have."

Sure, Hannah thought, *when we turned into fish.*
"Come on, Dominic," she said softly, extending a hand.
"We'll do it together. Hero twins, remember?"

13: Libra

A memory: Dominic was in ninth grade, playing a
team-building game with his classmates. His group had
to race across the floor while carrying someone on a
blanket, and since Dominic was the smallest and lightest,
he was chosen to sit on the blanket—and his team won
the game. Other kids complained that the game wasn't
fair because no one on their teams was as lightweight as
Dominic. He saw their faces, scowling and accusatory.

Later that day, the entire school poured into the
gymnasium for "class follies." The teachers dressed up
like doctors and pretended to perform a surgery on the
principal, appearing to pull multiple objects from the
woman's torso. Since Dominic was small, the teachers
had asked him to hide in a little cabinet under the table
and pass the objects up to them.

Some of the scowling classmates followed Dominic
after the last bell rang. Outside the school, they grabbed
him and shoved him in one of the garbage cans,
backpack and all, calling him a runt and a brown-noser.

Dominic couldn't breathe. He was squashed tight
inside the bin with his chest pinning his feet. He had no
way of letting the other kids know he was suffocating.
Desperation seized him. He reached up and pushed at the
lid, but the kids were holding it down and laughing. He
banged his fists against the can. He tried to rock his body
back and forth to knock the can over, then tried to relax
and focus on drawing a breath, then squirmed about in a
useless panic.

Suddenly the kids ran off. Dominic flung open the lid, but even with a desperate surge of strength he couldn't pull himself up. A teacher—the same one who had asked him to hide under the follies table—looked in and saw his breathless, gaping mouth. He yanked Dominic out of the bin. A moment later Dominic was crumpled on the ground, breathing in loud gasps, soiled with trash.

Now, passing along the length of Hydra, he felt that same constriction, that same inability to breathe. But this time he hardly struggled against it. What was the use? This was no trash bin; this was a living monster, and perhaps this time he deserved his fate. Dominic had prepared himself for death. He had reviewed his life, counted his regrets and joys, made peace with himself.

Hydra's dark tunnel had changed beneath his touch. It grew smaller, softer, fleshier, muscular—and then Dominic was being pushed through the passage by those living walls, just as though he'd been swallowed by a giant snake. His chest heaved uselessly against the feeling of suffocation. Sensation passed from his body, and at last he lost consciousness and began to dream.

He stood before Chad's solid pine door. The wood, faded to a sickly shade of gray, bore a prominent carving: a life-sized animated figure of Chad, wearing sunglasses, waving its outlined arms. The curves of the lips also moved, but no sound came out. And in that one image Dominic saw everything he needed to see.

The blank sunglass lenses showed Chad's unwillingness to see other people. The flailing gestures spoke a desperate need to keep others' attention focused on him. The constant, incoherent chatter revealed an attempt to distract people from his true intentions. Dominic saw a man afraid of his own weaknesses, a man who pulled people down to disguise his own flaws.

But more pressingly, Dominic saw himself reflected there. He saw his own laziness, irresponsibility, and dishonesty. He remembered how he'd planned to donate money for a Soyal feast, but Chad persuaded him to spend the money on a rental car instead: *They can get food anywhere. We're paying for something better than a feast; we're going on a journey, and collecting knowledge and experience, and we'll bring that knowledge back to them. I actually know a lot about Soyal. It's all about the arrival of spring, about getting out of hibernation and going out into the world. It's not about sitting around and stuffing yourself with food. . . .*

Chad was always pestering Dominic to drink alcohol on ceremony days, though it was strictly prohibited. He would make mimosas and other cocktails at Dominic's apartment, and Dominic typically pretended to drink so that the nagging would stop. He would pour his drink into house plants, out the windows, into the sink when Chad wasn't looking—and Chad would get irritated because Dominic wasn't drunk. Sometimes Chad would offer him unmarked pills and say: *Do you really think I'd give you something that wasn't good for you? Look— I'm taking one too.* Dom would eventually pretend to take a pill, and when it had no effect, Chad would go into a rage; he would call Dominic an inept bore, or a vapid freak.

These little sabotages became more and more frequent, but Dominic had largely given up criticizing the antics. He withheld his opinions and found himself passing over his commitments to his family and friends, his own plans and dreams, the land he was raised on, while Chad spent his money and time.

Dominic knew what Chad would say if he confronted him about it now: *No one forced you to do those things. You act like you're a little weakling who lets people push you around.* He knew this because he'd heard Chad say it to other people.

And Dominic felt sorry for him.

The stone flesh broke out in dark red streaks. Then it became dark purple and black, as though bruised. The figure's eyes glowed through the lenses like white-hot fire. The lips stretched wide, the mouth gaped, and Dominic felt the inward force of the figure's breath—pulling at him, sucking. And he realized what he was seeing: a hound of the outer borders, of the chaotic edges of the universe, snapping at his soul.

And Dominic felt sorry for him, intensely sorry.

So much more became visible to Dominic in that image—about himself and his world, the significance of his experience in Leo; his habits, his laziness about choosing his friends, his slightly warped concepts of strength and love. He felt a sense of pity for Chad, and for other people who had behaved like little mites in his life. Chad pretended to be invulnerable, but Dominic had seen him crying over his lost relationships, over all of his self-induced suffering. Whenever he started to cry like that, he would slip his sunglasses on so that no one could see the grief in his eyes—and then he would get another drink. He spiraled deeper into escapism and hateful outbursts. Dominic cared. He was Chad's friend; he wanted to forgive, to be patient, to help. But he wasn't helping. He was just getting sucked in.

All these things Dominic realized in a flash, and then someone grabbed him firmly by the shoulders and turned him away from the lonely spectacle. He found himself facing a colorful world, full of people and places. In the background were the striped hues of Black Mesa and other landscapes, with vibrant groups of laughing people and a few lone figures gathered before them.

A soft voice spoke close to his ear. "Look. There's a whole world behind you."

The queen stood with her hands still on his shoulders. She gave him that knowing look again, an expression of understanding and love—and then he lurched forward, the pain of his illness surging within him. It coursed through his body, into his skin, and foamed there as though the sickness was rushing to seep out of his pores. Dominic watched his flesh become a rubbery sheath beneath the layer of foam. He writhed, though not in pain or horror; it didn't really hurt, and he remembered the queen's words about shedding a skin. The layer of flesh tore at the neck. It was a pleasant tear, like an old scab that was about to come off anyway. Dominic squirmed out as though the layer was nothing more than a full-body costume. He left it behind in a flesh-colored heap.

And then Hydra vomited him out, and he woke up.

Dominic's first instinct was to complain about falling yet again onto a hard stone floor, but the impact wasn't so jarring this time. He stood easily—and then Hannah tumbled out of the tunnel and sent him sprawling again.

"Are you all right?" Dominic helped Hannah to her feet before turning his attention to his own body. In the near absence of light he couldn't see the scorpion wound, but the swelling and pain had vanished. "I actually feel better . . . better than I've felt in a long time. It might be because I'm dead, but I'm starting to think it's possible that we'll go home after all this. What happened to you in the tunnel?"

"I felt sick, and I couldn't breathe, and I fainted."

"Me too. Did you dream anything?"

"No." Hannah sounded solemn. "I got dizzy, and then . . . I felt like the sickness became a little ball in my stomach, and it's still there."

"Well, maybe this place will get rid of it." Dominic turned to survey the room.

The chamber was dark, yet in places it was also dazzlingly bright. Holes and cracks riddled the stone ceiling so that small beams of light streamed through, accentuating and deepening the surrounding blackness.

The topmost lengths of the walls were illuminated enough to show that the chamber was enclosed in a perfect cube. The largest beam shone down like a spotlight; it centered on a small square-cut pedestal, and upon the pedestal was a fine wooden chest, its edges banded with gold.

Also perfectly highlighted was the gold-hued glyph that stretched across the floor, comprised of simple, connected lines. It looked like three sides of a rectangle, with the shortest side forming the base of a triangle. While the longest lines were revealed by narrow strips of light, a larger shaft of light illuminated the whole area of the triangle.

"It's the Libra symbol," Hannah said.

At the moment, Dominic didn't care about the symbol. The ceiling, the beams that streamed through it—those were sunbeams. How could any grown human being, having lived and thrived by the sun for all the years of its life, mistake true sunlight for anything else? Dominic went to the nearest strip of light and passed his fingers through it, comforting himself with the idea that his own world was close by. All he needed was to exit the chamber, and he would be home.

He turned away from the bright beams and tried to re-adjust his vision to the shadows. An image began to take shape there in the dark: to his left was a structure that resembled a store front, bordered with embellishments. Dominic moved closer and found streamers hanging limply from the frame, tangled with strings and ribbons. On either side of the doorway were two wide plastic windows, and behind them Dominic could see what looked like merchandise on display. He recognized the dark outlines of mannequins in dresses and wide hats on one side, and unrecognizable shapes on the other, along with something that looked like a floor lamp. A small sign behind the window read "Exit through the gift shop."

Dominic stepped back and squinted at the unlit neon sign above the doorway. It bore three words in scrawling cursive: "Shop of Illusions."

"I hope they're not trying to tell me that nice clothes are bad," Dominic said. "I mean, I'd rather not look like a slob when I . . . Hannah?"

He caught sight of her as she opened the lid of the small wooden chest. She stood on her toes and looked inside. "It's full of gold coins."

"Don't take any."

She closed the lid and beckoned him. "Fine, but look over here. I think this is our enigma."

Dominic followed her to the center of the triangle. The stone floor bore a few lines of writing, etched in gold. He got on his knees to examine the passage and read aloud:

One path to a true treasure leads,
though one may pay in labored time;
the other is the quickest price,
inadequate and less sublime.

Dominic stood up. He turned around and looked at the two golden lines that trailed away from the base of the triangle. The right-hand line seemed to lead into a tunnel, obscured by darkness. The left-hand path led past the treasure chest and ended at the storefront.

"I'm disappointed," he said. "It's like they're not even trying anymore. You can't get much more obvious than 'Shop of Illusions.' Actually, I'm kind of insulted."

Hannah peered at him. "You must feel a lot better."

"Well, don't get me wrong. I'm still not in love with this place." Dominic met her gaze and asked, "Are you still mad at me?"

"I wasn't mad. I was . . . disappointed."

He ducked his head. "I'm sorry."

"You didn't mean what you said back in Aries, about helping me find my clan. You acted like you cared, but you forgot about it right away."

"I meant everything I said. You're smart, you're conscientious, and you have brothers and sisters in Navajo land, and we'll round them up and bring them to shake hands with your dad."

"He's in Phoenix. No one will do that. Anyway, you'll forget."

"No, I won't. I promised."

Hannah gave him a suspicious look. After a moment, she removed the deer pendant from around her neck. "Here." She started to place the leather loop over Dominic's head.

He drew away. "What are you doing?"

"You can use this to find my clan. Otherwise, it'll just remind you of the promise you broke."

"You shouldn't give me this."

"You can give it back after you keep your promise." She dropped the loop around his neck.

"Fine." Dominic nodded toward the tunnel. "Let's go this way."

"So where are the scales?" a voice asked behind them. "I was expecting to find Lady Justice, or that Egyptian deity, whatever her name is."

Dominic froze.

Chad stood behind them, at the point of the triangle. He wore his sunglasses despite the low light. His face looked freshly shaved.

Hannah, who had never seen him looking any other way, was nevertheless astounded to see him. "How did *you* get here?"

"Easy. I followed the stars. I walked toward the Libra constellation all night, and at sunrise I came to this cave. So I went into it, and *voilà*, here I am in Libra."

"How did you get in?" Dominic peered into the dark corners. "I mean, just now, how did you get into this room?"

"Back here. There's an opening . . . somewhere."

"You were supposed to go through Virgo," Hannah said. "She has to give you a new name."

"What for? Wait—you mean that witch from the underworld? No thanks. Anyway, I already have a new name. I have Navajo buddies, and every once in a while they get new names at a ceremony or something. My friend Bill gave me a Navajo name right before we went out to Wupatki."

"What is it?"

"Chąą' Yázhí. It means 'Star Warrior.'" Chad moved past Hannah and Dominic, studying the riddle with his hands on his hips. Suddenly he looked at Dominic. "Hey, that's what I *am* right now. It's the role I'm playing. We're in the zodiac, in the stars, and I'm the *Chąą' Yázhí*. See how it all fits together? I can't wait to go home and tell people about this incredible adventure I've been on."

"That's not the same," Hannah protested. "Virgo has to give you a name."

"Well, apparently she doesn't, because I made it to Libra without her. And I figured out something about this journey. I was up at that mountain, talking to that guy about the plant—and his name was Utan-pishtim, or Utna-pishtim, or something. I've been trying to figure out where I've heard that name, and I finally realized: It's Gilgamesh."

Dominic and Hannah stared at him.

"The Epic of Gilgamesh," Chad said. "It's an ancient Sumerian story. King Gilgamesh kills the mountain beast, he goes on a quest to find a plant that grants eternal life, and he gets it from this Uta-pishtim guy . . . or whatever. I'll have to look it up when I get home. But

I realized, *I'm* Gilgamesh. I killed the beast, I rejected the underworld witch, I found the plant. Gilgamesh was, like, the king of Babylon. I got to come here and play out his role."

"Did he turn Babylon into a poisonous wasteland?" Dominic asked.

Chad glared at him. "That's not the point. Gilgamesh was a half god, I think. And I'm realizing that's what I am, and that's what we all are, only some of us don't know it. We're human, but somewhere inside of us, we have the power of gods. We just have to learn how to unlock our power. And that's what I'm doing here: I'm opening up this shared cosmic experience. I'm being initiated into something ancient, something powerful— something that's written in the stars." He turned toward the pathways. "There's even a connection between my being in Libra and having a Hopi name. See, if you look at the symbol from here, it looks just like the symbol for the Hopi Life Plan."

"You said you had a Navajo name," Dominic said.

"Same difference. Anyway, one of these lines represents the false path, and the other is the true path. And I can already see which one is mine. I *know* this place. This looks just like the neighborhood I grew up in. My house would be right here, and on that block we had a little gift shop. I used to go hunting for pennies, and then I'd walk to the store to buy penny candy."

"Don't go that way!" Hannah called.

Chad was already on the path, walking rapidly toward the treasure chest.

The chest's gold edges gleamed, and its wood was of rich quality, glowing a deep reddish-brown in the spotlight. Chad stopped and flipped open the lid. "See?" he called, holding up a few gleaming coins. "All that crap in Leo was all just a bunch of theatrics, to test my level of fear."

"Chad, it's a trick!"

Chad waved the palm of his hand at Hannah. "I'm following what I know. You guys are making this way too difficult." He paused, studying the store front. "Check this out: 'Exit through the gift shop.'" He laughed. "Not what I expected to find in Libra, but whatever. See, that's how our store was set up; you would walk in on one side, and walk out on the other, so you'd have to walk past all the new merchandise." He turned briefly, watching Hannah and Dominic through the dark lenses of his glasses. "See, what you still don't get about this place is that people get what's coming to them. You probably went through some unpleasant crap in Virgo because you expected to suffer, Dom got sick because he didn't have enough confidence, but I came to the stars and created an *empire*—well, a mini empire, or the beginning of one. I was King of Babylon. It's all about unveiling the best within yourself."

"If the best within yourself means turning a perfectly nice valley into a stink hole of death," Dominic said.

Chad cast him a sharp look.

The store lights flicked on. They blazed so brightly that Hannah and Dominic shielded their eyes.

A short, bearded man came to the front of the store, carrying a straw broom and grinning. "Ah—a customer! Glad to have you—heh heh!" He waved his broom, gesturing for Chad to come inside.

Chad looked like a child walking into a giant toy store. His mouth hung open in awe. Through the windows, Hannah could see very little. Trails of lights and tinsel obscured the way, hanging like fancy spider webs or the decorations of a gaudy holiday store. From where she stood, she had only a view of what stood just beyond the entrance: cardboard cut-outs of cars, houses, and people.

"Pick anything you like." The shopkeeper grinned as he swept small heaps of litter from the floor. "Anything

you want can be yours, for a mere token or two. If you
don't see what you want, I can have it custom made—
heh heh!" He paused to straighten his hat, a small and
pointed thing that slid backward every time he looked
up. "Heh heh," he chuckled again, as if the act of fixing
his hat amused him.

"I don't get it," Chad replied. "What is all this?"

"All this can be yours. Find something you like, buy it,
and it'll be yours when you leave this place. This is a
shop of splendors—heh heh!"

Dominic winced at the sound of the laughter. It
sounded blatantly sneaky. The shopkeeper kept grinning
at Chad as he whisked the broom back and forth,
sweeping up dust that never seemed to diminish.
Dominic saw, then, that bits of cardboard were falling
from the structures that lined the walls of the shop. They
were crumbling, and the shopkeeper couldn't sweep fast
enough to clear the floor of the dust of their decay.

"Chad, that's just garbage," Hannah yelled. "It isn't
going to make you happy. Come with us."

"Oh, what rubbish!" the shopkeeper exclaimed. He
managed to scowl at her with his eyes, without losing his
cheerful grin. "*Some*thing has to make you happy. What
else would do it? *No* thing?"

"Not *those* things," Hannah replied haughtily. "They're
illusions."

"But you can see for yourself that they're real. Eh?" He
nudged one of the cardboard cars, as if touching it would
prove his point.

"They're fake. Besides, the sign above the door says
'Shop of Illusions.'"

The shopkeeper hesitated. "What sign?"

"Right there." Hannah pointed.

The shopkeeper lifted his broom, covering a small
portion of the neon sign. "It doesn't say 'illusions.' It
says 'illustrations,' because these are all illustrations of

things."

Dominic placed a hand on her arm. "Let him go, Hannah."

"Here, what's this?" Chad picked up a cardboard cut-out of a young woman in a blue skirt and shoulder-length hair.

"Ah, yes. We sell people for a good price. Those are your friends—the new friends you'll have when you go back out into the world."

"No way," Chad murmured. "So, I'll actually meet these people when I get out of here?"

"Of course! You can pick any of them."

"I'll definitely take this one." He handed the cardboard woman to the shopkeeper.

"Very good! I'll put it in your pile."

"See, it's like the law of attraction," Chad said to no one in particular. "You envision these things for yourself, you believe, and you start to receive."

But Hannah's look, as she watched Chad stacking cardboard on the counter, was one of disbelief. "You don't even know what those people are like—and you're not a good friend, so they'll turn to garbage anyway."

Chad whirled around sharply. "You know, I don't need to listen to this crap from a ten-year-old," he snapped. "I've lived four times as long as you, Hannah, and I've been out in the world—so why don't you go stick your nose in one of your fantasy books, instead of lecturing me about my choices in life." He picked out a cut-out of a man in a tailored suit and sunglasses. "What the hell, I'll take this one too. He looks like he's got a lot going for him."

Dominic slipped his hand into Hannah's. "Let's go."

Together they walked down the right-hand path. They entered the dark tunnel, and Hannah tightened her grip. Tiny flashes appeared, just ahead in the dark: pairs of eyes reflecting the light that filtered into the tunnel.

Dominic heard sounds like dozens of soft whispers.

"Something's wrong," Hannah said.

"Don't worry, we're almost there."

"No. Something's wrong . . . with me."

Dominic stopped. At that moment, a small hand slid around his arm.

He jerked away in surprise, but the unseen figure grasped him again, more firmly this time. Two little hands held his arm, their fingers soft like a child's fingers.

Another hand touched the small of his back, nudging him onward.

Dominic strained to see in the darkness. "Who is that?"

"Someone is grabbing me," Hannah said.

No one else answered, but Dominic heard other movements all around, close and quiet. Another hand pressed into his back. People were pushing him, pulling him. Dominic tensed as they approached the light at the end of the tunnel.

The light turned out to be a large white room. Rather, the tunnel opened into a plaza; it was plain and nearly featureless, and its expanse of white flooring was surrounded on three sides by several stories of open halls. Countless people wandered on nearly every level, or stood looking down at the newcomers—people with blue-tinted flesh, a deep hue that stood out against their identical off-white frocks and the vast white background.

Dominic was struck by the brightness of the place. He looked down at the face beside him, the face belonging to the child who clung to his arm. The child's flesh was faint shade of aquamarine, a strange luminescent color that gave the child a ghostly quality. But what Dominic found even more haunting were the eyes: pitch-black retinas, or perhaps just two large black pupils, looking up at him expressionlessly.

Unsettled, Dominic looked up at the halls. He saw that

each level looked much the same, but some of them
appeared at first to be moving. Dominic had a quick
view of a white platform rising past the levels, all the
way to the top, where several people disembarked—and
then more hands grabbed him, and he was pulled sharply
to the left. Dominic saw that the tunnel they'd emerged
from was not the sole entrance to this place. The nearest
wall was made of rock, streaked with grey and red and
other colors, and its face was riddled with cracks and
larger openings, much like the tunnels he remembered
from Wupatki. He felt a small surge of hope at seeing a
familiar place, at the idea that he'd soon be home.

The plaza, being nearly featureless, had one interesting
adornment along the rock wall: a large mural of a
crocodile head, with rough green flesh and large black
eyes. An opening in the rock served as the beast's wide-
open mouth, rimmed with metal. Long silver teeth
protruded from the top and connected with the floor—
evenly spaced teeth that made the opening look like a
frightening little prison.

Dominic was standing in front of the teeth-gate when
the ghost-like children pulled it open. He tried to pull
away, but they crowded close and shoved him through
the opening. Hannah tumbled into him. The metal jaws
slammed shut.

14: Tagua

Hannah and Dominic weren't alone. A man sat in a rear corner—a small, stout man with dark circles under his pale blue eyes. At the arrival of the new prisoners he began to stand, leaning against the wall as he rose.

"They're just children," he said, and then he looked at Dominic and corrected himself. "The girl you've taken—she's just a child."

The phantom-like children stared silently through the bars.

"What's going on?" Dominic asked.

The man gestured to Hannah. "Tagua wants this girl. He wants her to solve a riddle."

"Who's Tagua?"

"He's a demon. Well, he says he's a man. He used to be a man, I suppose, a long time ago."

Dominic made a sound of disbelief. "Great. Maybe we should've exited through the gift shop after all."

Hannah scrutinized the other prisoner. Despite a pale-blue tinge to his flesh, he didn't look like the others; his blue eyes were tired-looking, but quite ordinary. He wore gray pants and shoes under his long off-white tunic.

"Are you a person, like us?" she asked.

"Yes. Maybe. I've been here a long time. I guess I'm not sure what I am, now; but I was a man when I fell in. My name is Wibben. I lived in Frankfurt." He walked to the bars and looked out at the upper levels. "Tagua has been watching you, to see how well you've done on the zodiac road—how well you've solved the riddles."

"What riddle does he want me to solve?"

He shrugged. "It doesn't matter. Don't solve it. It would have been better if you'd never been caught, and I'm sorry I couldn't warn you. He locked me in here so I wouldn't interfere."

A commotion started among the ghostly onlookers. The bars opened. Wibben was grabbed and yanked from the cage, and the door slammed shut again. Hannah watched as he was swallowed up into the growing crowd.

Dominic slid down against a side wall and sat on the floor.

"If he just wants me," Hannah said, "maybe he'll let you go."

Dominic stared at the ceiling.

"I *could* stay longer," she mused. "No one would miss me that much."

"Hannah, that's not true. Your dad will miss you, whether he knows it or not, and your foster parents are terrified of losing you, and . . . the world would miss out on you."

Hannah rolled her eyes.

"We'll figure something out. You don't belong here. You shouldn't be with these things." Dominic gestured to the creatures that shifted anxiously nearby. "They're . . . they're not good. I think they're possibly evil." As he watched, one of the phantom-children grabbed the arm of another and, very rapidly, bit into it over and over again. The injured one shrieked and pulled away, and fled at lightning speed while the others chortled with laughter.

"Forget that I said 'possibly,'" Dominic said. "They're evil."

The gate opened again, just an inch. One of the creatures hissed: "Tagua wants to see you."

Dominic stood, but he wasn't fast enough. Two ghostly figures hurried inside and grabbed Hannah's arms. She was out of the cage before Dominic could reach her.

"Hannah!" he called, but all he could see were countless blue faces staring back at him. "Hannah . . . don't do anything he says."

Tagua looked like a man. He wore a deep purple robe over white pants, which made him easily recognizable; and though his pale flesh was tinged with blue, his eyes granted him a certain uniqueness. Hannah could vaguely distinguish the dark retinas around black pupils, and his eyes bore a more striking difference: while the other ghost-figures stood gazing listlessly about, Tagua looked at Hannah with intensity and intelligence.

The strange children had taken her on one of the platforms, up to a third level, where Tagua waited. Nothing existed here but a bare white floor, with an expanse of wall and a narrow hallway some distance away. Tagua clasped his hands together and regarded Hannah warmly. "Hello, Hannah. So you're the girl who's been learning the ways of the starry realms, and solving the mysteries of the zodiac road. You've had an exciting time, I know—but I also understand you're eager to go home."

Hannah didn't respond, so he continued: "There is a portal here that can take us all back to your world. It would take us to the places we fell in, without any further obstacles—but the doorway is locked with a riddle . . . a puzzle, of a sort, like the ones you've been solving along the zodiac road. And if you were to solve this one . . . ." His voice trembled. "Well . . . perhaps you would like to see it."

Hannah considered, and said "All right."

She followed Tagua along the divider. It opened into a short hall with passages on either side—passages to small white cubicles, featureless and empty. Farther in, the hall came to an end, and Hannah finally saw a bit of color as she entered a large square room with a black-and-white tiled floor. In the center were two identical wooden chairs, painted blue and red and gold, looking lonely in the barren room. Hannah raised her eyes to the only other decoration: a round disc on the far wall.

The golden disc stood even taller than Hannah, positioned with its base at the floor. Jagged bits of metal protruded from behind its circumference, like stylized sun rays. Hannah knew immediately that this must be the portal entrance. Its face was etched with thin lines, dividing the disc into twelve sections, like a clock face. In the center of the grid was another golden disc whose circumference was surrounded with small round symbols: jugs, faces, towers, other objects. And in the center of that smaller disc, a few verses were etched:

Living creatures show the map by which they grow and thrive,
patterned on the bud and limb, seen by the learned eye.
Form and color may abate as all reduce to basic state.
Dextral mapping leads halfway to loosening the beast;
young relative steps widdershins, and he shall be released.
A map within a map unlocks the door and marks an end,
and starts the world where this will happen time and time again.

Tagua explained that the disc was a dial—that it served as a lock, and that the symbols must be rearranged to unlock the portal. Hannah studied the symbols and counted nine in all. There were forty stylized images of mask-like faces with wide-open mouths, nine images of reddish-brown jugs on a yellow background, five black towers on white backgrounds, and varying numbers of six other symbols.

Tagua slid one of the symbols across the surface of the disc. "They're magnets. You have to slide them into their proper places on the doorway, but no one has figured out how to position them."

Hannah didn't have the faintest idea how to begin. None of the symbols on the dial seemed to "fit" with the riddle. She supposed that the circular arrangement meant that the pattern happened "over and over again," like a spinning wheel—but that was her sole idea, and it was hardly helpful.

"I don't know it," she said softly.

"No one does. Not at first. But careful study could lead you to the answer, and we can share what we already know. There are one hundred and eight pieces that must be moved. That number has geometrical significance, in the arrangement of the cosmos and of everything within it. It's a number of completion, of harmony and order. Our universe is created around one hundred eight and its multiples."

"I'm bad at math."

"It doesn't matter. You're good at puzzles, and you have a studiousness about you—and the zodiac realm seems to favor you. *That* is important. And Hannah, you will learn great things in this realm. You must know now that there is a meaning to the order of the stars, a meaning that is not immediately apparent. The universe moves and organizes itself in a delicate balance. I can teach you how to understand and use that balance to your advantage. You will learn many mysteries of the cosmos, great mysteries that you can take back to your world . . . eventually."

Hannah examined the disc again, hoping for a flash of insight. "How long have you been trying to solve this?"

Tagua took his time in answering. Hannah glanced up

and saw that his warm eyes had dulled. He looked away, toward the chairs at the center of the room. "Let's sit. We should discuss these things where we're comfortable." He reached out to take Hannah's hand, but she stepped back.

"Very well." He smiled patiently. "Follow me."

Tagua waited for her to sit, and seated himself across from her. "There are no thrones here," he said. "You and I are equals." Hannah didn't reply, so he continued: "Hannah, you'll have to forgive my extreme measures—my insistence on keeping you here. But as you can see, I have an entire village of people to think about."

"Do those other people want to leave?" Hannah asked.

"Of course. We're all trapped. We don't belong here."

"You don't belong in our world either."

"Oh, but we do. We belong there just as much as you do, if not more. Our race is older than yours. We lived in your dimension for a long time before being imprisoned here."

Hannah paused, thinking this over. "But you weren't human?"

"Yes, we were human—a very ancient race of humans. We knew things about the origins of the world that younger races have forgotten. We could read the map of the night sky; we knew how to draw magic from the movements of the planets, and we knew how to make medicines and talismans from the plants that filled our land. But there were others who wanted our lands and our magic, and, just like your own people, we eventually went to war. The wizard Askha-Quyllur and her army attacked us and caught us unprepared. We had to escape by hiding in another dimension. We thought we would be safe here, but Askha trapped us with the magic of the sun gate, so that we couldn't return. We have lived here like ghosts for thousands of years, in limbo—not alive or dead, but drifting aimlessly until the day we can become human again, until we can finish our lives in our own world. We're like you, Hannah. We just want to go home."

Hannah looked at him intently, trying not to let him see her own doubt. He didn't have eyes quite like a human being. It was hard to look into them and see if he was telling the truth—but she found something else about his words incredibly disheartening.

"So . . . you've been trying to solve this riddle for . . . thousands of years?"

"Don't let that discourage you, Hannah. Your world has great libraries, instant connections between peoples and nations, shared research. We had none of those things."

"Can't you just try all the combinations until you find one that works?"

"We've tried that," he snapped. Tagua's eyes gleamed with sudden anger—but after a moment his face softened, and he lowered his gaze. "We have trouble keeping track of what we've tried. It has frustrated everyone. But you, Hannah, can pursue this riddle in the proper way—and to do so, you will need to travel between this realm and your own world. You can collect clues, study patterns, and bring your ideas back with you. As you see, there's not much here in the way of research. We've tried keeping records, but they fade quickly. They fade from sight; they fade from mind. Everything does." A vague note of grief sounded in his voice.

"You mean, you'll let me go home?"

"Not completely. You may return to your world on occasion, and only for a short while; but there is something you'll need to do first. You have to put on the holding crown."

"What's that?"

"Come, I'll show you." Tagua beckoned to her, and as

Hannah stood, he moved to put a hand on her shoulder; but she backed away, staying well out of his reach.

They retreated past the dividing wall, where they had a view of the plaza and its rising and falling platforms, its community of wandering ghost-children. Tagua leaned down slightly so that he matched Hannah's height. He pointed to the left-hand wall. "Do you see that object over there?"

She looked up, to the highest level, where there was no floor to walk onto. That place was just an expanse of bare wall, and at its center Hannah saw a single ornament. It did resemble a crown, one made from mismatched metal scraps that jutted upward into shining points.

"The crown is made from pieces of the sun gate," Tagua explained. "When my people became trapped here, we tried to force the gate open. Pieces broke off, but we quickly realized that the gate isn't one that can be opened physically. It must be done energetically. We used the broken fragments of the gate to make the holding crown. It carries the same energy as the sun gate. When you put it on, you become bound to this dimension."

Hannah felt a pang of alarm. "You mean . . . it will trap me here, like it did to you?"

Tagua paused. "Eventually," he replied quietly. "You'll be able to travel between dimensions for a while, and only for short periods, as I said. But once you open the sun gate, the crown's power will be destroyed. It won't be able to hold you anymore."

"But what if I can't open the gate? *You* couldn't open it, and you've had thousands of years to figure it out."

"And that's why I need you," he replied. "The crown's power is much weaker than that of the gate. It takes time to create a full effect. So, for some time, you will travel; you'll have access to books, to libraries, to history. We don't have that same advantage. Our connection to the Earth dimension is very remote. We can see you only a little, through tiny magic windows, and from far away. We learn nothing new, except from visitors like you."

"But . . . ." Hannah paused, frowning. "But I don't *need* the crown to be in this dimension. I got here without it."

"That's true."

"Then why would I have to use the crown?"

"Because I am demanding it of you," he said calmly. "It's my guarantee that you'll come back and try to open the gate. Because once you've put it on, you can't ever remain home again, unless you figure out that riddle."

"But . . . that's not fair," Hannah protested. "It's not *my* fault that you're stuck here."

"No, indeed. But I'm afraid I've grown rather desperate. We're tired of being ghosts, Hannah. We can't live, and we can't die. We're stuck here for eternity because of that gate. I don't think you can imagine what we suffer. If I need to kidnap you in order to free my people, I do it without any guilt. Now it's up to you to decide if you want to live here as a prisoner in a cage, or if you want to live here as someone who can free all of us."

Hannah stared at him in silence.

"I know how it sounds," he said. "It's true, it isn't fair to you—but you're looking at it with a fearful heart. Think instead of how things could turn out to your advantage. This may seem like a strange new place, but it will likely become your life's greatest adventure. That's how you must think of it. You have opportunities and magic here that you won't find anywhere else. All you have to do is discover them."

She looked away, gazing for some time toward the haphazard crown. *Another home, another adventure . . . .*

"How does that sound?" Tagua prodded her.

"It sounds like something my social worker would say," she replied dryly. "You know . . . I'm not a grown-up. I'm only eleven."

"I realize that. But sometimes, with age, we accumulate ideas that obscure our vision. A young person like you may be just what we need. After all, you've figured out more about the zodiac than people two or three times your age."

"What else will happen to me? I mean, if I *choose* to stay, and if I use your crown? Will it change me?"

"The crown will realign your body. When you put it on, you'll start to become . . . closer to this place."

"What do you mean?" Hannah's gaze moved over the plaza, over the perturbed creatures lingering below.

"I mean that the crown will change your energetic being. Your old dimension will slowly become poisonous to you. You can go back for a day, a half day, a few hours; you'll know when your time is up. If you stay too long, you'll get sick. If you persist, you could die."

"But if I stay here, will I become . . . ." Hannah gestured to the plaza. "Like them?"

He chuckled dryly. "Not unless you've been trapped here for hundreds of years."

Hannah lowered her eyes, feeling helpless. "And if I figure out how to open the gate . . . ."

"Then all we have to do is pass through it. It will change our energy systems so that we can live in our former dimension. We will become human beings again."

"But . . . how else will I change, if I put on the crown? Will I look like you?"

"No, not quite. Oh, I suppose that your coloring will change a little, but nothing too drastic—and you'll only appear different in this realm. You'll appear like yourself in your own dimension; and once the gate is open, all signs of this realm will vanish from you."

Hannah shuddered. "I suppose it doesn't matter. But . . . will I start to *act* like . . . like them? I mean, will I become different on the inside?"

"You will be yourself," he assured her. "Of course, when your energetic body changes, it may have some small effect on the way you think and feel—but that is nothing new. It's the same in your own dimension: your environment always has some effect on your feelings."

Hannah felt a mournful weight in her chest. She knew that the crown might change who she was. *I might forget about Dominic. I might turn into someone bad. . . .*

"It's nothing to worry about, really," Tagua continued. "The changes will be slight, and you'll be treated well here. A solver of riddles is of the greatest use to us, and you will enjoy a high status. You will be our Princess Hannah."

"I don't want to be your princess."

"Very well. You can simply be Hannah—the solver of enigmas."

Hannah frowned. She wanted to say: *I don't want to be a solver of enigmas*, but she was quiet for some time. She thought of Dominic, of his plans and his yearning to see his family—the people who missed him, who would be heartbroken if he never came back. "If I promise to stay and open the gate, will you let my friend go back to his own world?"

"I could arrange it . . . if you were to put the crown on first."

"I could put it on," Hannah said hesitantly, "but I won't help you with anything until Dominic is back at Wupatki. He would have to get there safely before I would do anything else."

Tagua nodded and smiled. "Of course. We could bring him back to the Scorpio gate. He'll have no problem returning to his own dimension."

Hannah lowered her eyes once again, staring at the
blank white floor as she considered her fate. The
underworld queen had said that Hannah would do
something important. Perhaps this was it.

"Why don't you take some time to think it over?"
Tagua asked gently. "You can relax in the portal room
while you decide what you'd like to do. I can make it
comfortable for you."

But Hannah shook her head. "No," she said. "I don't
need to think about it. I'll stay. I can go and put the
crown on now." And to show that she meant it, she held
her hand out to him.

Tagua smiled.

Dominic was not quite alone. Wibben had crept back
to the cage. He stood close, speaking through the bars in
low tones while a small crowd of ghost-children lingered
nearby.

"I fell in, like you did." Wibben's pale-blue eyes were
tired, yet intense. "Tagua captured me and commanded
me to open the sun gate, and I . . . haven't been able to
do it."

"How long have you been here?"

"I don't know. Time is a tricky thing here. It exists; it
has a linear feel to it, but . . . ." Wibben shook his head.
"I don't remember how long ago I fell in, but I'm
resigned to my fate here. I've been able to do one good
thing, and that thing is preventing Tagua from opening
the gate." He sat down with one shoulder leaning against
the bars, his face still close to Dominic. "Some of these
people are still coherent. They've told me things about
him. They all lived in a village together . . . I don't know
where. Somewhere on Earth. Tagua was the ruler of this
place, and someone supposedly put a hex on him—or he
was poisoned, or something. He started to die, and he
demanded that the whole village be sacrificed with him.

They all went into some sort of burial chamber, and somehow, it became this place." He gestured widely toward the plaza. "I don't understand all of the details, but there are things I've picked up on. Tagua was a wizard, and he was in the practice of stealing the life force of other people. He drains them, slowly, like a vampire. He did it on Earth, he does it here, and that's why all these people look and act like zombies—and that's why he wants Hannah. He wants her to solve the riddle, but he's also looking for another life to drain, to buy himself some time."

"Has he tried to do that to you?"

"He *is* doing it. I fight it at every moment, but it takes a toll."

"You'll have to tell me and Hannah how to fight him off."

Wibben looked gravely at Dominic. "I'll talk to Hannah, but I doubt he'll keep you here. It's easier for him to manipulate one person—a young, naïve person— than two people who support each other. He has ways of dividing people, but the easiest way is to keep Hannah and send you home. He's done that before. The last people to get caught here were two young brothers from Spain. Tagua kept one and released the other."

"He kept him? He's still here?"

"He's out there somewhere." Wibben gestured to the ghost-children. "He's not distinguishable from the others anymore. I've seen people fade quickly here. Things start to vanish—memories, ideas, beliefs. Over and over, I have to tell myself: My name is Bernhard Wibben. I lived in Frankfurt. I have a sister, Inge, and I had two little brothers who died." He paused. "I used to recite their names, but now I can't remember them."

"I don't get it," Dominic said. "We've met people here . . . we met a queen, and other people, who have power. They know everything that goes on here. What are these people? I've never been interested in mythology, or astrology, but Hannah and the other guy who was with us—they can make sense of all this. They recognize these people as mythological characters, or as zodiac symbols."

"What kinds of mythological characters?"

"I'm not sure. Hannah knew some of the characters from Greek mythology, and . . . ."

"Then she's been exposed to Greek mythology. This place takes the stories you're familiar with, and it alters them a little, to give you a message. Everyone sees it differently."

"But I saw them, too—the same people Hannah and Chad saw."

"You're playing off their imaginations. You said you're not interested in star tales; you don't have the stories to build on, so their stories dominated. But you still got the message you needed. Don't you feel that this place was trying to tell you something important?"

"Yes."

"It's the same with me. When I came here . . . I wasn't doing a good thing. This place has forced me to look in the mirror. It has forced me to do a good deed."

"Okay, but now that you've done your good deed, why don't these other people intervene? Is this guy Tagua just another of them, or . . . ."

"Tagua isn't one of them." Wibben smiled—a forced gesture, without any humor or pleasure. "And I think it's right that they haven't intervened for me. I don't think I deserved any help."

Dominic looked out at the plaza, where the crowd of drooping, dull-eyed ghosts was beginning to stir. "And what about Hannah, or the boy who Tagua captured? Hannah is an eleven-year-old girl. I can't imagine she's done anything to deserve being trapped here."

"Maybe it isn't something she's *done*," Wibben

began—and then an excitement rose among the crowd. Both men looked to the opposite side of the plaza, to the platform that was descending to the ground.

Hannah stood upon it, accompanied by a few of Tagua's phantom-like minions. It took Dominic a few seconds to recognize her. She wore an oversized, off-white tunic over her clothes, so that a bit of red and brown stood out above the low collar. She left the platform and walked to the right-hand wall.

"What is she doing?" Dominic asked uneasily.

Hannah carefully stepped onto the next platform. She looked up expectantly.

"Ah," Wibben said, and sighed. "It looks like she's letting them take her."

"Take her where?"

"She going to put on the holding crown. It's made from pieces of the sun gate, and it will hold her in this dimension. She won't be able to leave unless she can unlock the gate."

"Can't you do something?"

"If I try to interfere, Tagua will kill me. And if I'm dead, I won't be able to . . . ." Wibben trailed off. He gazed upward in silence.

The platform began to rise, with Hannah still in the midst of her captors. Dominic crossed the cage and pressed his face against the bars, yelling: *"Hannah! Hannah!"*

But Hannah didn't look his way. She let the strange children take her hands. They pressed tightly around her, as if to prevent her from making a sudden escape. Up they went, until they reached the sculpture that hung alone on the topmost wall. Hannah didn't show the slightest awareness of Dominic's cries, and perhaps his voice was drowned out by the murmuring of the crowd. The sounds became excited whispers as Hannah reached out and took the jagged crown from its place, and those whispers echoing against the walls sounded to Dominic like the scuttling of thousands of creeping insects.

Hannah hesitated just a moment. She lowered the crown onto her head.

It seemed an unremarkable action, at first. The crowd hushed, and Hannah stared frightened and unfocused into the crowd of onlookers. The platform began to descend.

The crown suddenly sparked and flashed. Hannah's eyes squeezed shut; she grimaced and her mouth fell open, as if in pain, and all at once her skin blazed with a dark blue light. Streaks of red and purple streamed around her, and spots of white light floated before her, as though a firework had exploded.

The light faded, but Hannah's skin remained a deep, luminescent shade of blue. She opened her eyes then, tried to focus, searched the lower level until she met Dominic's gaze. She stared down at him with sadness in her eyes, and then she raised one hand and waved at him—and he understood that she was waving good-bye.

"*Hannah!*" he cried, grasping the bars. "*Take it off! Take it—*"

A band of deep-blue creatures opened the cage. They grabbed Dominic and pulled him away, so roughly that he fell back and lost sight of Hannah. He twisted madly in their grasp. He kicked and screamed, even tried to bite, as they dragged him from the chamber and into the rocky tunnels. Dominic was hurled at a dizzying speed through the rough, narrow spaces; he bumped his head, banged his jaw, felt his flesh scraped and bruised. The tunnels seemed to become smaller and darker. He could barely fit through. The violent phantoms were no longer visible to him, though at least two of them was still pulling him by the feet. He kicked as hard as he could, trying to free himself; but their grasp was strong, and their speed never faltered.

At last he plunged into a small chamber. Dominic fell
face forward, his chin knocking hard against the
limestone floor. He hardly noticed the pain. Scrambling
to his feet, he turned around, trying to see his way back
to Hannah; but the crevices around him were too small
to fit into.

"Hannah!" he cried wildly. "Hannah!"

Above him was light. Dominic crawled toward it,
seeing that it was the only way out—probably the only
way back to Hannah.

But he came into a familiar cavern, empty except for a
lone figure who was descending through the blowhole. It
was a woman, small and thin, a harness around her torso
and a flashlight strapped to her forehead. She saw
Dominic just as her feet touched the stone floor.

She let go of the rope and leaned over him. The
headlamp shone in Dominic's eyes, so that he could only
see the dark outline of her figure.

"Sir," she asked gently, "are you all right?"

15: Strange Dreams

"Are you all right?"

Surina stood near the counter at the record shop, looking at Dominic with concern.

She had come to drop off copies of her cartoons. Some of the local artists—cartoonists, writers, illustrators—brought samples of their work and stuck them in a rack near the cash register, on the "Local Zines" shelf. Surina's zine was called *Snapshots from the Dreamworld.* It was full of cartoons, mostly of her own dreams, sometimes other people's dreams.

Dominic was staring at the cover. It showed a toilet in the middle of a crowded dining room; a waiter was gesturing to it and smiling, while an illustrated version of Surina covered her face in frustration. Normally, Dominic would have opened the booklet and read the whole cartoon, which was titled "I Am Unable to Find a Suitable Toilet," and he would have laughed; but the image reminded him of the open latrine in Leo, where he'd sat in full view of the villagers. It reminded him of Humbaba, and of Hannah.

In the days since leaving Wupatki, he had not stopped thinking of her.

Chad was sorting records nearby. He waved a hand dismissively in Dominic's direction. "He's traumatized because a little girl fell into a hole when we were at the Wupatki ruins. You should have seen this guy. People are standing around this blowhole and shouting, and it turns out this little girl has fallen in—and then this old lady starts insisting that Dominic crawl down and look for her."

"I read about that," Surina said. "You were there?"

"Yeah. Dominic was *really* there. This idiot actually crawls down to look for this girl, and he falls and hits his head. He's lying down there with a head injury, and he gets hit with a dose of scorpion venom, and there are probably fumes coming up through the rocks, and he starts hallucinating. We finally pull him up, and he starts yelling about how he found this girl and she was abducted by an underground demon." Chad began to laugh; but when he saw the perturbed look on Surina's face, he immediately checked himself. "It's sad, really. She probably crawled away into the cracks or fell farther down. The tunnels go on for such a long distance, there's probably no way anyone will find her—and they're so narrow, it's hard for people to look. They're using heat-sensitive instruments to look for her, but if she's dead . . . ." He shrugged.

Surina's eyes were full of sorrow. "I'm sorry. That's awful."

Dominic wasn't listening. He was still frowning at the booklet. "Let me ask you something," he said. "How do you remember your dreams? Most people can't. I've heard that people have techniques that they use to try to improve their . . . dream memory, or whatever you would call it."

"Well . . . I just remember them," she replied. "I guess I used to use techniques, back when I was a kid. I bought a book about lucid dreaming, and I used that for a while, and it helped." She paused. "I can bring it by, if you're interested."

"Sure. Thanks."

She hesitated, as if she wanted to say something else; then she finished stacking her zines on the shelf and left.

One copy was on the counter in front of Dominic. She always left a copy there, because she knew he liked to read it.

Chad approached the counter and sighed. "Forget it, Dominic. The whole thing was a hallucination."

Dominic didn't reply.

"I hope your Wupatki experience didn't kill your enthusiasm about Mexico. This temple complex I want to go to, it has underground tunnels that are off-limits, but they might let us in if we pay extra. No one has photos of those tunnels except the archaeologist."

"I'm not going to Mexico."

"What? You mean, you don't want to spend your savings. Don't worry, we'll—"

"I mean I'm not going to Mexico or anywhere else with you."

Chad stared at him. "What's with you?"

Dominic looked steadily at him. "You know what it is. I won't be the first person to say it to you. Your other friends, and your girlfriends, have said it."

Chad's eyes flashed with sudden outrage. "What the hell is that supposed to mean?"

"You want me to elaborate?"

"Is this about Wupatki?"

"Look . . . do you remember when you came to my sister's graduation party? My cousin Sarah was there, and you asked if I was embarrassed around her because she's disabled. You didn't just ask; you went on and on about it, all night, and made jokes where other people could—"

"You're mad because of something I said about your cousin?"

"The point is, I'm embarrassed around *you*. You're a liar and you don't give a damn about anyone but yourself. And whenever I talk to you about it, you just get defensive and act like more of a jerk, the same way you do with every person who confronts you. I don't like the way people look at me with pity in their eyes, like 'Why is he hanging around with that jerk,' whenever—"

"I'm sorry, *you're* embarrassed about *me*?" Chad snapped. "What makes *you* so great? You think I look good standing next to you?"

"I'm always making excuses for you, saying things like 'He has some good qualities' and 'That's just how he is,' because you constantly insist on acting pompous, and spiteful, and manipulative, and . . . et cetera."

Chad glared at him, but Dominic saw a flash of hurt in his eyes. "Fine. You think I can't find someone more stimulating to hang out with?"

"I'm sure you can, easily."

Chad gave a little shrug of his shoulders. "Yeah, I can. Have fun wallowing in your victim mentality." He gave another small, spasm-like shrug. "It's not like you take an interest in anything anyway. I take you on these amazing journeys, and you just follow me around like a dummy." He looked up as the little bell sounded above the front door. A young woman in a white blouse and blue skirt walked in. Black hair brushed her shoulders as she flashed a quick smile at the men; then she disappeared behind racks of records and CDs.

Chad smirked and murmured: "I can, easily. Don't forget to put your stepstool away." He stalked across the store, and Dominic heard him talking: "Hi. We're actually about to close, but maybe I can help you find what you need. . . ."

Dominic pushed the stool under the counter and headed for the door, leaving Chad to close up—but on second thought he turned around, grabbed Surina's booklet, and shoved it in his backpack.

At his apartment, he turned off all the lights and stood alone on the balcony. He watched the stars appearing one by one in the darkening sky.

How could he ever look at those stars again, and not think of his journey? Always, there was some symbol in the night sky that told the story. He could not see Orion facing Taurus without remembering Hannah in her ridiculous suit of armor; he could not see Sirius, the dog star, without remembering how Hannah had saved him from the savage-looking hounds.

Dominic reached beneath his collar and pulled out a small object, grasping it firmly as he gazed at the night sky.

He was holding Hannah's deer pendant. It still hung around his neck, where she had placed it. He hadn't realized he was still wearing it until he was undressing at night, after the rescue from the Wupatki blowhole and his short trip to the hospital. He wore it every day as a reminder that his journey was more than "just a hallucination."

No one believed his initial pleas about having to save Hannah from a "demon," but people knew that he had found her somewhere in the underground maze. How else could he have learned so many things about her? Hannah's father was, in fact, Navajo, and lived in a care home in Phoenix; her mother lived in Costa Rica; Hannah had gone home early from Girl Scout camp, and she did love Greek mythology and word puzzles. The police concluded that Dominic had climbed through a tunnel into another chamber and found Hannah there, that the two had talked as they waited for help—and that Dominic began hallucinating.

Dominic outwardly agreed: Yes, you're probably right; the conversation was real, but my panic over Hannah being kidnapped by an underground demon was the result of cave fumes, a lack of oxygen, scorpion venom, stress, et cetera.

Chad remembered nothing. He had passed out near the blowhole and woke up "a minute later," according to the other bystanders.

At last Dominic climbed into bed. He made sure he had a pen and notebook on the bedside table. He paged through his new copy of *Norton's Star Atlas*, and then he looked through Surina's cartoons, which had titles like "Spiders in Your Ear" and "It's Just Like Wearing a Swimsuit."

Dominic had been dreaming of Hannah. She came to him with urgent pleas, showed him images he couldn't remember. At first he passed his dreams off as expressions of his own helplessness and grief, but Hannah's pleas were persistent, demanding. She kept creeping into his ordinary dreams. He dreamed of being in high school and saw Hannah waving urgently at him from a classroom, marking the whiteboard with stellar graffiti. He dreamed of playing childhood games with his sister and saw Hannah reaching from behind the curtains, arranging the game pieces in the symbol of a labyrinth. Over and over again she showed him the same symbols, until he began to recall the simplest details: A labyrinth. An ornate pillar. A decorated wheel, a puzzle that she needed help solving.

Immediately upon waking, Dominic would write and sketch every detail he remembered. He meant to keep his promise: he would not abandon Hannah, would not stop helping her until she was home. He researched the constellations, studied mythology and did everything he could think of—but mostly he depended on Hannah to point him in the right direction. Every night he laid down and invited lucid dreams.

Dominic switched off the light. He settled his head into the pillow, closed his eyes, and waited.